What others are saying…

"I'm always on the lookout for books for teen readers and Bradley Caffee's novels do not disappoint! Scavenger is a coming-of-age story set in an apocalyptic world where three teens just want to survive. Caffee captures the nuances of friendship and survival while thrusting his characters into situations that demand they either rise or fall. Combine that with a grim world and forgotten science, and you have a stellar read."

— Morgan L. Busse, Award-winning author of the *Skyworld* series and *The Nordic Wars*

"In a post-apocalyptic world, doing the right thing always lands three young scavengers in danger. How can they protect each other? I couldn't put down this powerful story of friendship and faith."

— Sophia Hansen, Award-winning author of *Water's Break*

"Gripped me from the first page. Caffee adds another great dystopian to his collection and I am HERE for it. A high-stakes dystopian for both parents and their teens to enjoy!"

— K. D. Shade, Award-winning author of *Dreamteller*

SCAVENGER

SCAVENGER
A Sci-fi Dystopian

By
Bradley Caffee

To my wife, children, friends, therapists, and all those who helped me scavenge for the scraps of hope after I burned out of the pastorate, thank you for being there to help me survive my own personal apocalypse. This book is for you.

But God demonstrates his own love for us in this: While we were still sinners, Christ died for us. Romans 5:8

Chapter One

"Come on. There's got to be something worth finding in this place." Jimmy Hunter stared at the screen on his controller. The oversaturated night vision of the drone's camera display on his screen cast a green glow on his face. It was the only light in the room, but that was on purpose. He didn't want to miss a detail that a glare on his screen might obscure. Whenever he scavenged a new building, he'd enclose himself in this windowless room. This one was at the edge of the drone's range, and he hoped it would bring results.

"Bro, how many floors have you searched in that building?"

Jimmy jumped at the sound of Wyatt's voice. He'd forgotten his friend was sitting in the darkness with him, watching over his shoulder.

"This is the seventh. Place is picked clean." Jimmy's hands were cramping up from the fine adjustments the drone's flight path constantly required. He allowed the craft to hover for a moment so he could flex his fingers. Tired knuckles popped with each movement. "If I don't find anything here, I'm giving up. Battery isn't going to last much longer, and I'll need enough to fly it home."

He swiped at a bead of sweat that trickled down his forehead. The July heat made their hideout stuffy like an oven, yet they didn't dare reveal their whereabouts by opening a window, even at times when they didn't need total darkness. Elena, the third in their group, had nearly murdered Wyatt when he blew their cover the last time by turning on a light after dark. Invaders had come not an hour later to loot their place, and the three of them had moved from place to place for a month before finding their new digs. He'd put up with the heat if only to stay off Elena's bad list.

The drone's image revealed a door, cracked mere inches. Jimmy paused to assess. Scavengers like himself had cleaned out most buildings. Usually, they were in a hurry and didn't typically close doors as they left. A door that was only slightly ajar could mean a room that hadn't been searched. Or it could mean nothing.

It was the one disadvantage of scavenging with a drone. A simple door could stop his progress. Still, it was the right way to search. The drone was safer and kept him, Wyatt, and Elena off the streets as much as possible, which was wise since gangs and various other dangerous groups controlled the ruined city since the pandemic wiped out ninety percent of the world's population. Ironically, he indirectly worked for the more organized of those dangerous groups as useful items could be traded for food. The drone allowed him to search places that were out of reach and get into building entrances that were otherwise unreachable.

He eased the drone forward, bumping the door as much as he was willing with his precious tech. No movement. That was a good sign. The lightweight drone could nudge doors that swung freely, but that also meant a simple breeze through an open window could be the reason it was nearly closed. An immovable door had a higher chance of having something behind it.

He backed the drone up and peered at the gap on the screen.

"Don't do it." Wyatt sighed. "You remember the last time you tried that?"

Jimmy bit his lip. "That was smaller than this gap."

"You can't really know that. Seriously, it's not worth it."

Jimmy stared at the black line on the screen between the door and the frame. True, the last time he'd attempted a stunt to get through a door like this, he'd misjudged the size. The result had been a wrecked drone that took two days to retrieve and another week to repair.

"Dude, move on. There's probably nothing in there anyway." Wyatt's nasally voice grated against his nerves. "You crash that thing, and I'm not going out there after it. You're on your own. If you ask me, it's too risky."

That's what makes me a good scavenger. I'm willing to take risks. Still, he didn't want to think about the look Elena would give him if he had to admit he crashed the drone again.

Dismissing the thought, he jammed the control stick forward. The door loomed larger on the screen. At the last possible moment, he rammed the control sticks in opposite directions and clicked the stunt button that caused the drone to perform a flip. The drone should pass vertically through the few inches the door allowed if he'd timed the maneuver correctly. He gritted his teeth, expecting the screen to flicker, a telltale sign the drone had crashed. For a moment, the screen was a blur of green doorway, and then it went black.

Slowly, the greenish hue of the fixtures in the room began to take shape as the camera adjusted. It was a custodial storage closet. In the corner, a mop and wheeled bucket lay ready for use. A mop sink protruded from the wall, with several dry rags draped over its edge. Several shelves were perched above the sink. Most contained supplies of extra rags, plastic trash bags, and a few overturned boxes. Someone had gone through this room. Any chemicals or tools seemed long gone.

He turned the drone a few times, making its camera scan the room to be certain it was empty. The smallness of the closet was going to make repeating his flip maneuver difficult when he attempted to leave the closet. If he crashed and had to retrieve the drone, he wanted it to at least be worth it.

Shelf after shelf passed across the screen as the drone flew upward. Empty cans. A box that had once contained tubes of caulk. A worn copy of *Sports Illustrated*. Nothing of use.

Jimmy sighed in resignation as the last and highest shelf came into view. It was empty, probably unused. He stopped the drone's rotation. A small cardboard box rested in the corner, pushed all the way back from the edge.

Jimmy eased the drone closer, and the box grew larger on the screen. His breath caught.

The tiny box sat covered in a layer of dust, apparently forgotten in time since before the pandemic. There were several readable words printed across the side in black lettering, but only one interested him.

Batteries.

"I don't care what you found, it's too late to go out there." Elena stood with her arms crossed, glaring at Jimmy with her dark-brown eyes. She wore a pair of jeans and a black, fitted short-sleeved shirt. Her ebony hair was pulled back in a sensible ponytail.

"You're cute when you're mad." Jimmy couldn't help but chuckle as he spoke.

"And you're an idiot if you think it's a good time to be wandering around the city. The sun is going down. I may not be seeing any movement out there, but you and I both know this area is going to be crawling with creepers." Elena glanced out the window, then took a step deeper into the shadows so as not to be seen from the outside. She gestured with a thumb. Creepers were the name they'd given to the kind of people who lurked in the city at night—dangerous and usually in packs. "Wyatt, help me here."

Wyatt knelt over a backpack, checking it for supplies. He looked up at the two of them, his eyes shifting back and forth. "Well, you know I usually agree with you, Elena, but it's a pack of batteries. Do you have any idea what we could get for that? We could eat for a week."

Wyatt was right. It had been three years since the pandemic had run its course, and Jimmy knew things like batteries with any life left in them were in short supply. Traders would pay handsomely for a box of them.

"The batteries will still be there tomorrow."

Jimmy stepped forward. "We don't know that. Besides, I don't want to risk leaving the drone out in the open overnight." He lowered his voice to avoid sounding like he was whining. "We don't want to go back to searching buildings on our own."

"You should have thought of that before sending the drone out this late in the day." Elena rested her forehead in her hand. She took a long, deep breath, as if trying to calm herself. Then she placed a hand on his arm. Her hardened expression softened. "I don't want anything to happen to you. Either of you."

"I'll be fine." Jimmy turned to Wyatt. "I'm going alone."

"What? Bro, come on." Wyatt stood, knocking over his backpack in the process. He scowled at Jimmy.

"No, not alone. And not tonight." Elena waved a hand in the air.

"Yes." Jimmy walked over and grabbed the backpack. "I'm less visible by myself, and I can move faster."

"I'll try not to be offended by that," Wyatt muttered.

"Just the facts, man." Jimmy laughed and slapped Wyatt's shoulder. "Elena, I promise I'll be careful. It has to be tonight. I parked the drone in the closet. It's giving off its encrypted GPS signal, so I can follow that directly to it. I'll be in and out in no time. Back here in less than an hour with the drone and a pack of batteries to trade. If I wait until tomorrow, the drone will run out of power, and it'll take me a lot longer without an exact position."

Elena sighed, her features hardening again. She pointed a finger at him. "Back in one hour. No exceptions. If you're not back, we'll come looking for you."

Jimmy clicked his heels and saluted her, producing a chuckle from Wyatt. "That's why you're the brains of the operation."

Elena allowed a tiny smile. "Don't you forget it."

Jimmy stepped outside the back entrance of the former real estate office. The building had become the perfect hideout for their little crew as the spartan office had not been much of a target for looters. Food, tools, and medical supplies were in the highest demand. An office housing contracts and computers with no internet service were of little use to anyone in this ruined world. He pulled his drone controller out of the backpack and flipped the switch to GPS mode. The drone's location appeared as a blinking dot on the basic map. One thing the pandemic hadn't touched was the satellites circling the earth.

Tiny droplets of sweat clung to his upper lip within a minute of entering the sweltering summer humidity. It was hard to imagine that only a few years ago he'd have stepped from an air-conditioned building into an air-conditioned car, the oppressive heat only a momentary inconvenience. Now, nature dictated life. The world had been thrown more than a hundred years backward in time. Only crumbling reminders of what used to be remained.

Down the street was the Italian restaurant his family used to frequent. One more block was his mother's favorite coffee shop, where she and her friends had met on a regular basis to catch up on each other's lives. Both were now burned-out husks that bore little semblance to his happy memories.

The thought of his mother made him pause before leaving the protective shadow of the building. He fingered the ring hanging on a chain around his neck. The ring had belonged to his late father. His mother gave the ring to Jimmy when he turned thirteen. He could feel the tiny ridges of the engraving inside.

Greater love has no one than this…

The inscription was burned in his memory. Though the full saying did not have to do with marriage specifically, his mother had explained that she'd had it inscribed on the wedding band because it was the way his father lived—sacrificially for others. It was how she had lived for him when his father had died when Jimmy was a child.

Then the pandemic took her. Now he lived the life of a scavenger, where theft and taking care of himself was primary. He loved his parents, but their way of life didn't seem to fit into this new world. His family was gone. Wyatt and Elena were all he had.

Wyatt had been his best friend since middle school. He'd latched on to Jimmy from the first day they met, and the two of them had been through everything from preteen awkwardness to the despair of seeing the world die around them. In many ways, he'd always taken care of Wyatt, whether it was dealing with bullies or helping him study for tests or finding food in this new world. Wyatt would be lost without Jimmy's help. He was grateful to have Wyatt with him, but on important excursions like this one, he preferred not to have his bumbling friend along.

Elena. She was special. They'd met in the hospital three years ago when the virus was only beginning its deadly spread. Each of them had a parent in the ICU, some of the earliest victims. The days and weeks as they waited for someone somewhere to come up with a solution to the disease created a bond between them. Both of them would become orphans.

The pair were friends bonded by tragedy. They would die for each other. Beyond that, he had to admit he was a little unsure about their relationship.

Jimmy took a long breath and carefully began padding down the sidewalk, hugging the edge of the building. To Elena, his behavior appeared reckless. Going out this late was risky, but he knew that rare items like working batteries could demand a high price at the trading floor. He couldn't risk someone else finding them. There was no telling who might have spotted his drone entering the building.

The shadows grew uncomfortably long as the day neared its end, and he rounded the corner of the block. His next move would be the most dangerous as he would need to cross the street, completely exposing himself to view. Once he crossed, he could use the alleyway to hike the remainder of the way to the building he'd explored.

Jimmy scanned in all directions but saw no signs of life. He crossed the street in several stealthy leaps that he thought would impress a cat and flung himself into the shadows of the alley. He stopped and listened. Somewhere, two raccoons fought for whatever scrap they'd found. Elsewhere, a gunshot rang out, but it was too distant to be dangerous to him.

Nothing unusual.

The best he could tell, he'd gone unnoticed. He checked his bearings on his screen one more time. Until he heard it—the distinct scrape of a shoe across the cement. So short-lived, he thought he'd imagined it. He held his breath, willing the noise to repeat itself and confirm someone was there.

Nothing.

The presence of another person did not necessarily mean danger. They might perceive him as the danger and be equally frozen in place, listening for his retreat. But there was no sound. Gazing at the sky, the dwindling light filled him with urgency.

Carefully placing his steps, he began to traverse the alley in silence. With each step, he allowed himself to breathe more deeply.

They must have gone the other way.

Minutes passed in tense travel until he found himself on the backside of his destination. The building had been a multi-use office complex, housing different businesses on each floor. Turning his gaze upward, he stared at the second-floor window that was busted out. Conveniently, it was only a few feet from the exterior fire escape.

This was it. Somewhere inside, his drone lay next to a pack of batteries. He'd promised Elena he would be back within an hour.

Time to get moving.

Chapter Two

Jimmy winced as the fire escape ladder creaked loudly enough to wake up the neighborhood. He lowered it to the ground and began his climb. Once he cleared the second-floor railing, he pulled a folded rag from his pocket and wrapped it around his free hand, then punched out several pointed shards of glass jutting from the broken window. Each landed inside with a sharp clatter as they broke on the floor.

Grabbing the window frame, he extended his leg and balanced his weight between the window and the fire escape. He took a deep breath and allowed himself a silent three count before pushing away from the railing. With a yank of his arm, he shifted his weight to the window and snaked his body in through the open hole.

Bits of glass crunched under his sneakers as he stood in the dark office. The light of his phone cast a green glow over the vacant cubicles. Dust coated every surface. The place looked like it had gone untouched for months. Making his way across the room, he headed for the stairway on the other side of the elevator lobby.

His breaths echoed off the concrete walls of the stairwell as he climbed the five flights to where he'd left his drone. Stepping out in the lobby of this floor, a sign stood in the middle of the room.

Welcome to Monroe Wealth Management. We make your dreams a reality. The open doorway at the end of a lobby revealed a rounded reception desk, behind which stretched a long hallway containing offices and conference rooms. The maintenance closet he'd found was at the end around the corner.

Passing the desk, he peaked in the window of the one closed office door. The words *Walter Monroe, CEO, Founder* were frosted in block lettering on the glass. A large mahogany desk and two expensive leather chairs faced the window. There was a third, larger executive chair opposite the others, turned toward the door.

It was still occupied.

Jimmy's breath caught. The desiccated remains of Walter Monroe, still dressed in a suit and tie, leaned awkwardly to one side. A bourbon glass sat on the desk adjacent to a small glass vial. Jimmy could only guess what kind of poison the vial had contained. A picture of a couple lay next to the glass, presumably Walter and his wife.

The darkest days of the pandemic had led many to lose hope. The loss of loved ones combined with the degradation of society as so many perished had pushed some to accept death on their own terms. It was not the first body Jimmy had discovered in his search, but finding one always unnerved him. He felt as though he were robbing a grave.

His stomach flipped. He turned from the window. Any thought of breaking into Walter's office to search was gone. Best to stay on mission and grab what he knew was here.

His target was at the end of the hallway. Jimmy pushed the door open, giving his eyes a moment to adjust to what little illumination the waning light provided to the closet. He spotted the corner of his drone poking out from the edge of the shelf he'd landed it on.

A stepladder stood in one corner. Jimmy grabbed it and climbed to the top step. He strained to reach over the edge of the highest shelf. *Where was it?*

His fingers finally brushed the small cardboard box. Jimmy smiled. He rose onto his toes, and he caught the edge of the box. A flick tipped the box, making it land close enough for him to grab it. His smile broadened as he lifted the container and felt its weight.

Definitely not empty.

He held his breath as he opened the lid. The shiny surface of the plastic container reflected his silhouette. He exhaled in relief. Sixteen AA batteries lined the unopened container. The expiration date indicated these would still have life in them.

Jimmy couldn't believe the discovery. With the price the batteries would bring, he hoped the trading floor would have something better than canned vegetables this time. He shoved the pack of batteries into his pocket and turned to reach for his drone.

Crash.

Jimmy started at the noise and nearly slipped off the step ladder. Someone else was in the office. He thought back to the footsteps he'd heard on the street. Had he been followed? He held his breath and strained to hear any sound.

Angry whispers came from the lobby. "Dude, are you kidding me? You didn't see the sign in the middle of the room?"

"Sorry, man. Wasn't looking." The second voice sounded pained like he'd hurt himself knocking over the sign. "Doesn't matter anyway. He's cornered in here."

Jimmy's mind raced. He was indeed cornered in this closet. Any attempt to make a run for the fire escape would require crossing the hall in full view of these two men entering from the lobby, assuming there were only two. He didn't want them to get these batteries, but he *couldn't* let them get his drone equipment. Slipping his phone from his pocket, he placed it on the upper shelf, shoving it out of sight. He grabbed the drone off the middle shelf and did the same with it. Stepping down to the floor, he searched the edge of the upper shelf for any sign of the drone. It was out of sight.

"Hey, check this out. Old man must've offed himself." The second voice chuckled as he spoke. They were passing Walter's office, which meant Jimmy had seconds.

He had one shot to do this right, and it wasn't going to be fun. Bursting from the closet, he bolted around the corner and into the last office. He knew there was no escape, but he needed them to believe whatever was worth having in the closet was on him.

"There's the guy!" The first man growled.

Jimmy darted across the office and ran his fingers across the top of the window. Flipping the lock, he forced it upward to reveal the fire escape. Hands grabbed his shoulders from behind. With a violent jerk, he was ripped backward and thrown. The desk caught his right hip, and he flipped backward over the surface. Crashing to the floor, he barely got in a breath before hands were pulling him upward. The face that met him was grizzled and dirty. Dark shadows hung underneath the man's eyes and greasy black hair hung in stringy waves down to his collar.

The man grit his yellow teeth and drove his fist into Jimmy's stomach. All the air involuntarily expelled from his lungs, and he collapsed to the floor. He felt as though his insides were attempting to become his outsides, and he was sure he'd vomit if he could only get a breath.

He was yanked upward again and shoved against the wall. The greasy man pulled him forward before slamming him against the wall again. Jimmy saw a flash in his vision as his head smacked the drywall. The room spun, and now he was sure he'd vomit.

"Think you're going to run from us, rat?" The raspy voice identified this as the first man he'd heard. His white T-shirt was stained, and his jeans were splotched with paint and sported a hole in one knee. His breath smelled of cigarettes and decay. Had this man ever brushed his teeth?

"Yeah, find something you want to share?" The second man walked around the desk, apparently the one who'd thrown him over it. He wore a mechanic's coveralls. He was much larger than his partner, but the vacant expression on his face made it obvious why he was not the one in charge.

"I-I—" Jimmy made a show of eyeing the window before glancing back at the man. "I don't have anything." He was rewarded by a second slam into the wall. If these guys wanted him to talk, making him woozy might not be the best plan.

"Don't lie to me." Greasy man flicked a knife open and held it up for Jimmy to see. "No one runs like that unless they scrounged up something." His eyes scanned him up and down. His lips spread into a smirk when his gaze landed on the obvious bulge in Jimmy's pocket. "What have we here?" The man's grip on Jimmy tightened as he flicked his eyes at his friend.

Coveralls stepped forward and jammed a meaty hand into Jimmy's pocket. Ripping the batteries out, his eyes widened. "Whoa, Dirk. Check this out."

Dirk swiped the pack of batteries from Coveralls and examined them more closely. "I see why you made a run for it. Pretty good score. Could have traded this for some serious grub. Looks like we're eating well tonight, Tommy-boy." He tossed the batteries back to Tommy, who eagerly examined them in his huge hands.

Jimmy's heart sank as the men absconded with the batteries. Even though it was the plan to keep their eye off the real prize in the closet, he still couldn't believe his rotten luck. Still, he had to be convincing before they wondered how he'd found them so quickly. "P-please. I need those. I haven't eaten in—"

"You think we care?" Dirk squinted. "We rule this neighborhood, you hear me? We saw you crossing into our turf. No one searches these buildings except us. Got it?"

Jimmy nodded in presumed agreement.

"Good. Because I'd cut you if I thought you felt differently, but since you've provided us with such a sweet score, I'm feeling merciful."

"Dirk?" Tommy sounded concerned.

"What is it, moron?"

Tommy nodded twice to the window. Outside, the light had faded to purple. Dark would come soon, and that meant the real dangers would be lurking. Even these two creepers didn't seem the type to wander in the open at night.

For an instant, fear filled Dirk's eyes. He turned to Jimmy, flipping his knife closed in one hand. "Guess we'll be taking our leave. Good luck getting home after dark." He reared his fist back.

Stars filled Jimmy's vision as Dirk's fist connected with the left side of his jaw. The world blurred as Jimmy slid down the wall in a heap. Then, blackness overcame him.

"Jimmy? Jimmy?" The voice sounded far off like a phone call from inside a tunnel. "Jimmy, wake up. You okay?"

His awareness sharpened, and he could feel someone shaking him. He opened his eyes to two dark figures looming over him. He jerked into a defensive position, remembering the last two people who stood over him.

"Jimmy, it's me, Elena. What happened to you?"

"Yeah, bro, you look awful." Wyatt's lack of compassion confirmed his identity, despite the brightness of the phone screen he shone in his face.

"W-what time is it?" His voice creaked as he spoke. Sitting up, he felt like his head would split open. He fell back to the floor, both hands on his forehead.

Elena sat backward onto her feet, apparently satisfied that he wasn't in danger. Even in the dark, he could see her posture morph from concern to anger as she crossed her arms. "It's a lot later than the one hour you promised you'd be back, that's what."

This time, he took sitting up more slowly. The headache was still brutal, but at least he avoided any sharp pangs. "Look, I'm sorry. I—"

"Got jumped." Her raised voice hurt his head. "You're lucky that's all that happened. You could have been killed."

"I know. I know. Save me the 'I told you so' speech. Trust me, I feel every bit of the bad choice I made." He rubbed at his temples.

Elena stood, retreating from him. "I'm not here to tell you that, Jimmy. I told you we'd come looking for you if you didn't return. I've been sick to my stomach." Her voice cracked, and he could tell he'd hurt her. "I'm mad at you, Jimmy Hunter, but I'm mostly glad you're okay." Without another word, she stormed from the room.

"Dude, I couldn't keep her at the hideout. I mean, I tried." Wyatt held out a hand to him. Jimmy grasped it and grunted as Wyatt pulled him to his feet. "You know how she gets. There's no stopping her."

"You should have tried harder." Wyatt winced at the anger in Jimmy's tone. He took a breath. "But thanks for coming with her. You're right, there's no stopping her when she's set on something." Jimmy took a deep breath to assess his body. As he feared, everything hurt. Being tossed over a table, punched in the gut, and knocked out will do that to anyone. He turned to Wyatt. "I had them, man. Sixteen fresh batteries."

Wyatt put a hand on his shoulder. "I get it. I'd have done the same thing if you'd let me. Guess I should have come after all. You need someone to watch your back."

"No. These guys would have taken us both. We'd both be on the floor, and Elena would be out searching for us on her own. I don't like the thought of that."

"Come on, man. The days when you have to defend me are ancient history. I'm better in a fight than you think." Wyatt grinned at his own remark, but it quickly faded to a frown. "I guess they got the drone, too."

The drone!

Without a word, Jimmy shoved Wyatt aside and sprinted to the closet, ignoring what the sudden movement did to his headache. Entering the closet, he took the stepladder two steps at a time. Reaching out, he found his phone.

That's one thing they didn't score.

Illuminating the screen, he turned to the other section of the upper shelf. The shiny plastic chassis of the drone reflected the light from his phone. Relief flooded his body. They would live to scavenge another day.

Emerging from the closet, he held up the drone for Wyatt to see. "At least they didn't get this. Guess they were dumb enough not to look if there was anything I missed."

Wyatt agreed with a chuckle.

"Yeah," Elena said reemerging from the darkness of the hallway swiping at a tear, "but they were smart enough to get to whatever hole they live in before dark. *We* still have to get home."

Everything felt amplified at night. Traversing the path back to their hideout was filled with sounds that gave them pause more than once. The three of them kept their heads on a swivel. Here and there, they could detect distant commotion. Shouting. Screams in the darkness. Gunshots. The night was alive with terror.

To their relief, they made it undetected to their hideout, circling a couple times to ensure they were not being followed or watched as they entered. Ducking into the alley behind the building, Wyatt made quick work of the combination padlock they used anytime all three of them were gone. Upon entering, he used the same lock to latch the door from the inside.

One of the reasons the office space was the perfect hideout was the stairs to their place were actually inside an unassuming closet. No one entering the place would immediately see that there was a second-floor access. And, they'd reinforced the door as another layer of security.

Elena took care of securing this doorway as they walked upstairs. Jimmy set the drone on the table and plugged in the charging cord to the solar charger mounted in the window. The rest of the window, as with all the others, was blacked out. From the same charger he unplugged the battery-powered lamp and turned it on, taking care to point the light downward to the floor. The extra time on the closet shelf had drained the battery much lower than Jimmy normally allowed, and it would need a good charge before he could conduct another search. Wyatt flopped on the mattress in his corner, and it was only minutes before they could hear the steady breathing of his sleep.

The former studio apartment provided only the most basic accommodations. Three corners had a mattress on the floor surrounded by blankets over cords to provide some privacy. The fourth corner contained a kitchenette and small table with chairs. A wall across from the entrance had two doors—a restroom and the walk-in closet he used to pilot the drone in darkness.

Jimmy eyed his bed. Everything in him wanted to lay down and sleep off his headache. He might even have a concussion. All he knew was he was exhausted, and nothing sounded better than laying low for a day to recoup. When Elena sat down at the table instead of heading to her corner, he knew sleep would have to wait. He walked over to her.

"Power working tonight? If so, I'll heat some water for tea." Whether or not the sporadic power was on was a daily conversation for them, and he longed to have a normal conversation. Elena's silence on the walk home had been more than a necessary precaution for their safety. Her expression told the story. She was hurt, and he needed to make it right.

"No power since yesterday. Coming less and less now." Her voice was flat, communicating the topic was unengaging to her.

Okay, Jimmy. No small talk.

"Look, Elena, I promise you. I'm sorry for going out there. I really mean—" She held up a hand, cutting off his words. Her eyes glistened in the LED glow, and he could see she was on the verge of succumbing to her hurt again. He shut his mouth and waited.

Elena let out a long, slow breath. "Jimmy, what you did today was reckless. More than reckless. It was stupid." He winced at the word but knew better than to question it for now. "No set of batteries are worth going out at night. They would have been there tomorrow, too."

"But the drone—I couldn't have just left it."

She didn't let him finish. "Yes, you could have. Those guys must have followed you to the building. It's likely no one would have known the drone was there. Or even better, you could not have sent out the drone so late in the day. Or brought it back before the battery was so low."

"Elena, I get it, but—"

"No, you don't, Jimmy." Her voice rose, and this time a single tear escaped her eyelid. "There were half a dozen other choices you could have made."

"I was only thinking of—"

"—of what *you* wanted to do. Do not fool yourself or even think of trying to fool me into believing this was purely out of concern for Wyatt and me." She lowered her gaze to the table. "I know you'd do anything for me, Jimmy, but today was about you."

He leaned forward, pleading with her. "You know I would. I'm so sorry. I promise."

She nodded, and a wave of relief spread over his body that she believed him. "Still, I need you to understand that I'm not interested in losing you to this world. We promised to help each other survive, and that will sometimes mean *not* doing something. Make sense?"

A warm flutter in his chest caught him off guard. Once again, his mind waded the muddled thoughts of whether he meant more to her than simply a survival companion—or whether he felt the same in return. He nodded to let her know he'd heard her.

She smiled and grabbed his hand. "Good. Then I'll finally say that I'm glad you're okay. It scared me finding you like that, and I don't want to ever feel that frightened again." She squeezed and let go of his hand. Pointing at the drone, she smirked. "If we get some sunshine in the morning, let's send that thing out by noon. I have an idea of a place we can look."

He smiled back at her. It felt good to be talking about sending out the drone again. Food stores were running low, and they needed something to trade soon. If she wanted him to send the drone out again so soon, then she hadn't completely lost her trust in him.

He promised himself that he would find something tradable by the afternoon to make up for what he'd done today. Lying down on his mattress, he imagined finding an apartment building that had miraculously gone undiscovered, filled with cabinets of food. The thought made him smile, and he found himself praying he'd wake up to a sunny morning.

Chapter Three

"Do you really think he should be flying the drone again today?" Wyatt's whispers invaded Jimmy's consciousness as he lie half asleep. The air of the apartment already felt like it was warming, and he hoped that meant the day had brought plenty of sunshine. He took a long deep breath to rouse himself awake, though he continued to remain still. "After yesterday, I don't know if he's in the right place to fly today."

"Wyatt, it's sweet that you care about him so much, but Jimmy is going to be fine." Elena's whispers were softer, but he could sense a note of exasperation in her tone. This conversation had been going on for a while, and she'd tired of it. Somehow, Wyatt missed her thinning patience.

"It's not that—not him. I…er…what I mean is he nearly cost us everything yesterday. He could have lost the drone permanently…or gotten hurt worse…or you. You shouldn't have to go out after him like that. It's too big a risk."

"Last I checked that was my decision, not yours." Jimmy cracked an eyelid to see her standing with her hands on her hips. Wyatt had questioned her independence, and if he wasn't careful, she would knock him out. "Besides, we need more supplies."

Wyatt ran his hands through his hair. "I-I know. What I mean—" He shook his head in frustration. "Ugh. I'm not doing a good job explaining myself, am I?"

"Not really. What *are* you suggesting, Wyatt?"

"Let *me* fly the drone." Wyatt held a hand up when Elena started to turn away. "Seriously, I know how to do it, and I won't take the risks Jimmy does. Tell him that you want me to fly it for a while, and I'll prove it to you."

Elena clicked her tongue. Wyatt had overstepped, and Jimmy could see it all over her face. This would be fun to watch. "First of all, that's not happening. We both know he's the better pilot. Last time you took it for a spin, you crashed the thing, and we spent a week drumming up new parts. Secondly, Jimmy did what he did *for* us. It may have been stupid, but he was trying to help us. You can't blame the guy for that."

"But, Elena—"

"No." Her voice rose with a firmness that said the conversation was over. "We're not discussing this anymore." She turned and walked away from him into the bathroom, not quite slamming the door.

Wyatt stared at the door longingly. "I can take care of you, too." The words came as the tiniest whisper, almost inaudible. He hung his head in defeat and turned to retreat to his corner. Throwing his sheet closed, Jimmy heard him flop down on his mattress to sulk.

Jimmy stayed in bed for a few more seconds, amused. Sunny or not, this day was off to an exciting start. Motivation to find something big started building in his gut. He could not have Wyatt casting doubt on who should be flying the drone. Elena had not gone for it, but that didn't mean it was the last time Wyatt would bring it up. Jimmy had seen it before. Wyatt had rotten luck when it came to girls, and he always seemed to fall for the ones who had zero interest. It was no secret to Jimmy that Wyatt had feelings for Elena, and it wasn't the first time he'd brushed Jimmy aside to try to prove himself to a girl. Time and again, Wyatt managed to get his heart broken, but the two of them had remained friends through it all. This would be no different. He only needed to give it time.

As for the drone, daylight was precious. Time to get to work.

"So where did you have in mind?" Jimmy smiled at Elena as he unplugged the drone. The battery was fully charged, and he was eager to put any doubts to rest that may be lingering in her mind after Wyatt's failed play to become the pilot that morning.

Elena sighed like she was about to share bad news. "I want to check out an apartment complex farther out of town. The one across Highway 4."

"An apartment building? Don't you think that'd be picked over by now?" Wyatt stood nearby working at a piece of his lunch that'd become stuck in his teeth. "Every one that we've checked has been empty of anything worth finding."

"Except that this complex was under construction when the virus hit. The first tenants had only started moving into the completed section, and the rest was still a construction zone." Elena offered a slight shrug. "There's a chance it has gone unnoticed since it appears so unfinished."

Wyatt pointed to the drone. "Isn't that out of range for the drone?"

Elena nodded. "Yes, but we can climb to the roof of the Chambers building a half mile from here to cut that distance and get the extra range on the controller that we need."

Wyatt smiled and hit Jimmy's shoulder with the back of his hand. "Sounds like she has a plan, bro. Good call, Elena."

Jimmy held up a hand. "Except the range of the drone is not why she sounds less than excited, Wyatt." He stepped closer to Elena and spoke as if sharing a secret. "That's near the dark sector."

The dark sector was a section of the city everyone knew to avoid. The name had been dubbed when it became the first area of town that lost power permanently. Anyone who knew anything about surviving in this version of the world knew to avoid the zone. It was as dangerous during the daytime as the rest of the city was at night. It was controlled by the Brotherhood. They'd agreed to never even get close, and now Elena was suggesting they do exactly that.

"Yes, it is." She looked down. "Which is why there's a chance no one else has tried looking. I'm only suggesting we fly the drone to see what's there."

"If we find something? What do we do then? At some point, we'd have to go ourselves."

"I'm saying we look and make a decision once we know what we find. If it's not worth the risk, we don't do it."

Jimmy had to admit that the idea had merits. Proximity to the dark sector meant that any finished apartments could potentially be a treasure trove of undiscovered goods. With supplies dwindling, they needed a quick score. Not to mention this was a chance to shore up Elena's trust in him.

Wyatt stepped up next to Elena. "I think we go for it."

Jimmy pursed his lips together. He'd been ready to agree to the plan, but now he was going to look like he was capitulating to the pressure of the team. He nodded his agreement anyway. "Let's get moving then. We've got a half mile walk and a whole lot of stairs to climb."

Jimmy's quads burned as they climbed the last flight of the Chambers building. Twenty floors of switchback stairs were no joke. The drone wasn't heavy, but between it and the controller, he had no hands to grip the railing, making the effort that much more strenuous. The three of them panted heavily as they reached the top landing.

Forcing open the roof access, sunlight flooded his vision. Jimmy squinted in the brightness, searching for the appropriate corner of the building from which to launch. From the top of the Chambers building, they had a 360-degree view of the area. To the north, the jagged remains of the downtown high rises jutted into the skyline like jagged teeth. An unfinished skyscraper had collapsed a year earlier creating a domino effect damaging most of the buildings in the area to some degree. He was no engineer, but he guessed that most of the buildings in downtown were no longer structurally sound.

To the west, the bulk of a suburban town lay in the distance.

The east was mostly undeveloped land, though he could see the scars created by overzealous developers who had at one time been eager to put up as many overpriced homes as possible. It was the south that drew his attention. An older part of the city, the once rundown area had become a popular spot for revitalization. Trendy neighborhoods, breweries, and local shops had started to move into the historic buildings and homes. When the power services became sporadic, the older infrastructure couldn't handle the constant surges each time the power returned. The zone went dark and never came back on.

Between the dark sector and their building, he could see the top of the unfinished apartment complex they were targeting. A developer's gamble to build on cheap land he'd hoped would one day be worth a fortune, the exposed steel beams stood in contrast to the trees surrounding the area. On the left side, he could see the finished section of the building.

"Think it'll reach?" Wyatt asked. "That's still pretty far off, bro."

Jimmy eyed the distance one more time. "It'll reach." He placed his phone on the controller and hit the button to link the devices. A second later, an image of his feet standing on the rubber roof material appeared on the screen. "Ready to launch."

Elena nodded, and Jimmy pushed the joystick under his left thumb forward. The blades of the drone whirred to life, and the device lifted off the roof. His screen showed the camera pan up his leg and side until his face came into view. He waved at the camera.

"Did you just wave at yourself?" Elena asked, her expression somewhere between amused and confused.

He cocked an eyebrow and gave her a smirk. With his other thumb, he jammed the other controller forward, and the drone shot off the roof and into the distance. The screen showed the tops of trees skirting by, and he reminded himself not to fly too low. He'd fished the drone out of a tree once before and had no desire to repeat the adventure.

After a couple minutes of flying, the trees disappeared, and the apartment building came into view. He circled the unfinished section, avoiding the flapping plastic sheeting on the side of the building. Slowing the drone, he panned along the side of the finished apartments. Wyatt and Elena drew close to his side, the three of them searching the screen for a sign of entry.

"Over there," Elena shouted. "No, back to the right!"

Jimmy turned the drone and zoomed the camera. The welcome sight of an open window filled the frame. With the adeptness that came from years of practice, he guided the drone on a smooth path that kept the window in frame. He breathed a sigh of relief as it became clear there was no screen covering the window. Either it had not been installed, or the tenant had taken it down for the winter.

"Think it'll fit? That's a pretty narrow gap." Wyatt's brow scrunched in concern.

Elena turned to him. "Jimmy? What do you think?"

Jimmy grinned. "It's tight, but I got this." He guided the drone to line up in front of the opening. *There'll be no doubting me after today. Here goes nothing.* Slowly, he approached the window. He held his breath.

Crack!

The window shattered on the screen followed by the reverberating sound of the gunshot in the distance. He backed off the drone and whirled the camera in every direction. A man stood on the balcony jutting out from one of the apartments. He wore a pair of loose overalls and no shirt. Silent words shouted from his lips on the screen. Jimmy didn't care to try to read his lips. He only cared that the man pointed a rifle directly at the camera. Jimmy jammed the controller to the right.

Crack!

"He's shooting at the drone!" Elena screeched. "Get out of there."

Before he could relocate the man on screen, Jimmy throttled the drone into motion at top speed. With a flick of his thumb, he jerked the drone back and forth, keeping it from becoming an easy target. He prayed the man, whoever he was, was not an expert trap shooter.

Crack!

One more shot rang in the distance. To his relief, the image on the screen remained, and he continued to put as much distance as possible between the apartment complex and the drone. Trees and streets whizzed by on camera, but he gave no mind to where he was going.

"Oh my. Oh my. Oh my." Elena was pacing back and forth, her hands on her forehead. "That was too close."

"Who was that guy?" Wyatt asked.

"Obviously someone who has taken up residence in the *forgotten* building that didn't take kindly to our poking around."

Jimmy reminded himself to breathe. Elena was right. That was too close. He placed the drone into hover and turned to his friends. "I think we're okay. If he was still shooting, we'd hear it."

Stepping toward them, he pulled Elena and Wyatt into a group hug. Elena's breath shuddered like she was preventing herself from becoming too upset. Wyatt stood deathly silent.

"I-I'm sorry. This was my idea." Elena pulled away and swiped at the sweat beading on her forehead. She blinked heavily a couple times and took a long slow breath. "We never should have flirted with the dark sector."

Jimmy sighed. "It was a good idea, El. Really, it was."

"Yeah." Wyatt agreed. "Who could have predicted the crazy hillbilly living there?"

The three of them chuckled, the moment bringing some needed relief. Remembering the controller in his hands, Jimmy lifted it to glance at the screen.

"Where is the drone, anyway?" Wyatt peered over his shoulder. "Can we get it back?"

"Getting it back is not a problem as long as it's in range." Jimmy pointed to a button on the top of the controller. "This will make it head straight back to our location. All it would need is enough altitude to make sure it doesn't run into anything."

"Then, let's get it back and be done with this." Elena sounded exhausted by the stress they were all under.

"Just a second. Wherever it is doesn't look familiar. We should at least look around."

The three of them huddled together again. Jimmy slowly

turned the camera in different directions. Thick trees filled the frame. Moving a little farther, a road came into view. It was a single lane each way without even painted lines. Wherever it was, it was out of the way.

"Just a small country road leading out of town." Wyatt sounded disappointed. Jimmy guided the drone along the path of the road. "Dude, you're going to get it out of range and get stuck."

Jimmy rolled his eyes and continued moving. The road was bracketed by forest with deep ditches to either side. No homes. No buildings of any kind. How far had he flown? And in what direction? Wyatt's warning suddenly sounded like reason, and he paused. Best to bring it home before they lost it. Putting it back into hover, he gave the camera one last 360 degrees whirl.

"Wait. What's that?" Elena pointed at the screen. Something at the edge of the trees.

Jimmy dared to inch the drone farther down the road, while at the same time zooming in on the spot Elena was referring to. Something dark protruded from the tall grass in the ditch.

"It's probably nothing. Get the drone home before you lose it." Wyatt was sounding annoyed. He was probably right, but Jimmy couldn't help but be curious. Plus, he wanted to give Elena a win after her failed apartment idea.

The dark shape expanded in the camera image. He paused the drone and allowed the camera to focus. In and out of blur, the camera adjusted. The three of them collectively gasped. The unmistakable sight of a tire sticking above the grass filled the frame.

Jimmy guided the drone lower and nearer to the tree line. The underside of a car became visible between the vines that had grown overtop it. Hidden in the overgrown grass on the side of a road no one would bother traveling, an undiscovered car wreck lay untouched.

A wreck meant a driver.

A driver headed somewhere meant they would have whatever supplies they needed.

Supplies meant tradable goods.

It was the discovery for which they'd all hoped.

Chapter Four

"It's a stupid idea, and you know it." Elena stood over Jimmy, who sat staring at the blinking map location. He'd marked the GPS coordinates before recalling the drone. As soon as they returned to their hideout, he presented the idea of looting the overturned car.

"That car could be full of who knows what. Food. Tech. Who knows?" Jimmy made his case.

"That's the point. You'd spend hours traveling out to some God forsaken road that—by the way—takes you right by the dark sector to find a car wreck that may have nothing."

"Or it may have everything." He whispered the words as though talking to himself.

Elena crossed her arms. "I can't believe I'm hearing this. We just rescued you from one foolish mission, and now you want to take on another. You really must be concussed if you can't see how blind you are."

Wyatt chuckled repeating the ironic words to himself. "*See how* *blind* *you are.*"

"Shut up, Wyatt." She glared daggers at him.

Wyatt's expression melted into seriousness, and he dropped his gaze.

Jimmy stood and searched Elena's face for some ounce of grace. He found none at that moment. "Elena, I know it sounds crazy. But this time it's different. The drone isn't in danger. It's here. I'll go by myself, and—"

Elena opened her mouth to interrupt. He held out a hand.

"Let me finish. I'll go by myself. I've written down the coordinates. If I don't return in the time I say I will, you don't have to come looking for me. Send the drone. You can find out what happened to me without ever endangering yourselves." He glanced at Wyatt for confirmation that he understood the plan. He didn't want his friend letting Elena venture out again to rescue him.

Wyatt nodded. "I'll stay here with you, Elena. You know I can pilot the drone well enough to find his sorry backside on the side of the road."

The memory of Wyatt's hushed conversation with Elena from that morning bit at Jimmy, and he didn't want Wyatt anywhere near the drone trying to prove himself to Elena. Still, it was the only plan he could conceive of that she might agree to.

"Please, Elena. We have to know. If it's nothing, I'll come right back. But what if it's not?"

Elena's eyes met his and softened. "What if you get caught in the dark sector? What if, loaded down with your treasures, you get seen? You won't get robbed, Jimmy. You'll get killed. On the spot and without warning. People who enter there don't come out."

Jimmy grabbed her hand in both of his. Out of the corner of his eye, he could see Wyatt watching them intently. "I'll return. I promise. And it will be worth it."

The night air was cool on his skin. The humidity had broken into an afternoon rain, and the result was a pleasant night for traveling on foot. He breathed deeply as he stood outside their hideout, allowing his eyes to adjust to the darkness. Keeping his ears tuned in to the slightest sounds, he began lurking down the sidewalk, hugging the shadows of the buildings created by the almost full moon.

The smell of damp asphalt filled the air, and he wondered if life would ever return to a time when he could simply take a stroll at this hour. Before the virus, he imagined he and Wyatt would be hitting the streets on a night like this. Catching a movie or meeting their friends at the local coffee house to complain about the approaching school year would have been the normal activity for a summer night. Instead, a deadly virus that killed almost everyone and three years of decaying society meant that being out at this hour bordered on suicidal. Still, without the virus, he'd never have met Elena.

He wouldn't wish this life on anyone, but he had to admit meeting Elena was the best part of the whole ordeal. The thought filled him with resolve to make it to the car wreck. He needed to show them he wasn't being reckless.

The danger of the night was a blessing and a curse. The everyday creeper didn't dare come out at this hour, which was good for him. Fewer eyes to see him moving about. The downside was they were not out because the few who came out at this hour were the worst of the bunch. With luck, he could traverse their section of the city unseen.

Thirty minutes later, he crouched at the corner of a building. Across the street, a park stretched between the city blocks. Going around would be the safer option but would take a lot longer. He'd made a promise to be back by sunrise, and he couldn't waste any time. Crossing the park would save precious minutes. Besides, he was as likely to run into shady characters along the buildings at the edge of the park as he was in the park. At least on the open lawn, he could see them coming. But…that meant he was just as exposed.

He chewed at his lip, trying to make up his mind. Scanning the street right and left, he saw no movement. The only sounds carrying through the night air sounded distant. Making up his mind, he launched himself from the ground and strode half-crouched across the street.

Ducking behind the first tree, he allowed himself a moment to calm his pounding heart. The scent of damp earth rose through the overgrown grass. To his left, the remains of rusty playground equipment caught his eye as the old swings swayed slightly in the breeze. His target was to his right, a street that headed straight for the dark sector.

The darkness of the city, which was without power on this night, made the moonlight and starscape seem all the brighter. Without the light pollution from the city, the sky was brilliant with stars and swirling bits of the Milky Way. Now that he was in the park, the illuminated open stretches of grass appeared like they were under spotlights.

Do it, Jimmy. Get it over with.

Before he could give it another thought, he began a slow jog across the park. Tall grass made a swishing sound as it brushed his legs, depositing their dampness on his jeans, which began to feel cold as the water soaked in.

Halfway across the park, he let out a sigh of relief. No sounds aside from his own. No characters stepping from the shadows. He'd made it across the park and saved time.

"Going somewhere, kid?" The voice halted Jimmy in place. Instinctively, his hands rose to defend himself. Scanning the moonlit park, he could see no one. A thump to his right drew his gaze. A man stood at the base of a tree, shrouded in shadow. Two more figures dropped from the branches on either side.

They were in the trees. They must've been watching me this whole time.

He cursed under his breath for being so stupid. He rose to his full height to face the shadowy figure. Stepping into the light, the man appeared to be in his thirties. Wiry whiskers made a patchwork beard across his chin. Aggressive tattoos covered his arms and face, sporting images he could only guess at in the near darkness. In one hand, he held a machete lazily at his side as though he didn't want to be bothered to use it. His friends, if that's what they could be called, produced blades of their own. Even as silhouettes under the tree, he could tell they were more than capable of using them.

"P-please. I'm just passing. I have nothing on me." Jimmy held his hands out to show he wasn't carrying anything. He pulled his backpack off and yanked the zipper open. "See? Empty. I'm not looking for trouble." He became acutely aware of the lump his phone made in his pocket.

The tattooed man stepped forward and raised the machete. "Should have thought of that before you entered our park." He waved the machete. "Get over here, kid." The two other men began slinking to either side to cut off Jimmy's flank.

These men had no interest in robbery. While others might insist on taking his shoes or his jacket, Jimmy knew none of that would interest these men. They wanted violence for no other reason than it was their way at this hour. Unless he did something, he'd be dead on the side of the road, only to be robbed by some other opportunistic person lurking around after dawn.

"I said get over here, kid."

Jimmy's body tensed. The nerves in his legs twitched, ready to fire at his command. He breathed a prayer of thanks that he'd worn his tennis shoes and not his boots.

Machete man took another step forward, and it was all the cue Jimmy needed. He lunged in the one direction the men had not cut off. Adrenaline flooded his veins as his legs began pumping. Behind, he heard the man curse followed by three heavy sets of footfalls.

He'd hoped getting a jump start would convince the men that he wasn't worth the chase. Apparently, they were in the mood to hurt someone. Their shouts and curses were not far behind.

A rock hidden in the grass caught his toe, and he stumbled, the ground rising to meet him. Tucking his shoulder, he transitioned his fall into a roll. A tree root jabbed into his back mid-roll, and he grunted as he used his momentum to get his feet back under him. Pushing up from the ground, he forced the pain of the fall from his mind and pumped his legs all the harder.

The voices were closer.

Jimmy was not unathletic, but he'd not eaten well in days.

His body felt sluggish without sufficient carbohydrates. He could only hope the other men were in the same condition.

The edge of the park drew near, and he darted across the street. Daring a glance over his shoulder, the three men crossed a second after him. Building after building passed on his right and left as he raced down the middle of the vacant street. He considered trying to enter one of them, but a single locked door would stop him long enough for the men to catch up.

Buzz. Buzz. Buzz.

Streetlights glowed into brilliance as the unpredictable power snapped on. Jimmy cried out in frustration over his rotten luck. Normally, some light would be a blessing, but darkness was his friend in eluding these men.

His lungs burned. A stitch began forming in his side. He couldn't keep up the footrace much longer, and if his hearing was correct, they were gaining on him.

The end of the block opened to an intersection with now blinking traffic lights. Without thinking of his whereabouts, he turned left down the road, scanning for a hiding spot. The streetlights made everything seem visible. That was when he saw the wall of blackness ahead of him.

The dark sector.

One does not simply run full speed into the dark sector without a care as to what lay ahead, but the knowledge that certain death was right behind pushed logic aside. He sprinted straight into the darkness of the next block, relieved to once again feel shrouded in shadow.

The relief was momentary. Some part of him had hoped the

men would stop at the edge of the light, unwilling to enter the dark sector. He'd been wrong.

"You can't hide in there, runt." Machete man's voice sounded frighteningly composed. Had he been a track runner in his former life? He didn't sound winded at all.

He was going to lose this footrace. His legs grew heavier with each step.

Boom!

Jimmy fell to the ground at the sound of the gunshot. Sharp bits of roadway tore into the flesh of his hands as he broke his fall. His feet scraped along the asphalt, trying to find purchase. His left toe gripped the road, and he pushed forward. Diving behind a dumpster, his breath came in heaves as he pressed his back into the metal container.

The only sound was the strained voice of machete man.

Peering around the corner of the dumpster, Jimmy gazed backward. In the darkness, he could only see a lump writhing on the ground. The grunted curses confirmed it was his pursuer, apparently the recipient of the gunshot. On either side, he could barely make out the two friends whirling about, unsure which way to run.

Before they could take off in the way they'd come, a Jeep roared to life and pulled out into the roadway, bathing the men in the beam of its headlights. The passenger door of the vehicle opened, and a man stepped into the light. He wore dark clothing, and the pistol in his hand kept the two remaining pursuers from moving.

"Ugh. Come on, man. Why'd you have to shoot me?"

Machete man continued his squirming on the ground, clutching his stomach.

The man with the pistol inhaled on a cigar which glowed in the darkness. "You men are trespassing. State your intent."

"That's none of your business, you—" The goon hurled a few choice curses at the man.

Boom!

The muzzle of the pistol flashed. Machete man lay still.

The other two men fell instinctively to their knees, placing their hands up in surrender. "Please, man, don't kill us," one of them cried.

Removing the cigar from the side of his mouth, the man pulled a radio from his belt. "Two for processing." A second truck roared around the corner and pulled up next to the group. Two men leaped from the truck. In seconds, they had the park creepers bound with zip ties and began loading them in the truck.

The driver of the Jeep stood in his seat, peering over the top of the roofless vehicle. "What about the one they were chasing?"

The cigar glowed again. "Probably long gone. Alert the perimeter guard that we still have one unaccounted for. Bring him in for questioning." Without another word, he slid back into the passenger seat of the Jeep. Both vehicles turned and rumbled down the street before turning several blocks away.

Jimmy had heard stories about the dark sector and The Brotherhood.

But he hadn't expected anything like that.

They were organized. And equipped. And unquestionably dangerous.

Chapter Five

Jimmy lay on the ground next to the dumpster for several minutes, his heart thunderous in his rib cage. Those men executed the thug from the park without a thought and had taken the other two. He considered his options.

Staying in the dark sector felt insane. Cutting through wouldn't be faster. He knew it would be suicide after what he'd seen. The car wreck required getting close to the dark sector, but he could go around, staying clear of the border.

He emerged from the dumpster and began making his way back the direction he'd come. Guards were on alert for him, but for now he knew the street he'd used was clear as the guards took their prisoners away. Tiptoeing up the sidewalk, he tried hard not to glance at the body of the slain man. Would they leave him there?

In a strange way, this hazardous turf had saved his life, but he wanted out. Minutes later, the streetlights filled him with a sense of warmth. He was safer here, despite the dangers. He'd take on a dozen men like machete man before he'd ever step foot in the dark sector again. He considered heading home, but he could still make the trip and return on schedule.

This car had better be worth it.

Taking his time, he spent the next hour ducking from shadow to shadow. It was slow going, but he wouldn't risk exposing himself again. Turning the block, the road broke out from the rows of buildings and disappeared into the trees.

The edge of town.

There was nothing out here. The city transitioned to country quickly with only an occasional gravel drive jutting off into the forest to indicate a residence buried in the trees. Based on his estimates, the car wreck was approximately a forty-five-minute walk in the darkness.

He hiked along the edge of the roadway, keeping his footsteps as quiet as possible. He'd had enough action for one night, and though the likelihood of someone being out here was remote, he wasn't taking any chances.

His body trembled in the cool darkness as he considered what he'd been through. Elena would kill him if she knew what he'd seen, and he debated whether to tell her or not. He supposed it depended upon what he found in the car. If he came home empty-handed, she'd never again let him out of her sight after what he'd risked.

The roadway banked to the right in front of him, and he stopped to close his eyes. Picturing the overhead view he'd seen from the drone, he imagined where he was on the map. The car had been located up the road from a sharp bend. He glanced at his phone.

Forty minutes.

He was close. The car had to be nearby.

He allowed himself to speed up to a slow jog to traverse the bend in the road. Nighttime sounds of crickets and small animals moving in the undergrowth filled his ears between the muted tap of his sneakers hitting pavement.

The road straightened, and he slowed. Turning on the flashlight on his phone, he began to scan the edge of the roadway for signs of the vehicle. Nothing but tall grass. His mind raced to confirm his location. Could he have messed up the location?

With each step, his anxiety that he might be in the wrong place grew. He really didn't want to have to go down into the ditch to search through the grass unless he knew he was close. If his calculations were off, he could waste hours hunting along the side of the road.

Minutes ticked by. No car.

He stopped and took a deep breath. He had to find it soon, or it would be time to return to the hideout. The thought of going back without finding the car ate at him. He shook his head in frustration. Perhaps this had been a fool's errand.

He wiped his face with one hand and gazed down the roadway. In the moonlight, he noticed a dark patch on the road, about ten yards ahead. Taking a few steps, he approached the spot and shone his flashlight on the asphalt.

The mark was worn from years of weather, but the pattern was clear enough. A tire had locked up and skidded in this place. The skid stretched in a straight line before taking a wild serpentine trajectory. A car had tried to stop quickly here and lost control.

He turned the flashlight to the edge of the road. Two stripes of dirt were exposed in the gravel. He walked over to where the stripes disappeared in the grass. Sweeping the tree line with his flashlight, a glint of reflected light caught his eye. He moved the beam of light backward until he found the spot. Something in the blades of glass was shining its light back at him.

He took a cautious step into the grass. He couldn't see anything, but the grass was waist high where he stood. Slowly, he made his way down into the ditch, following the reflected light. At the bottom of the slope, a heap of weeds and vines sat in front of him.

Panning the light from his phone upward, muted black rubber with the word Michelin protruded from the weeds. It was the tire he'd seen on the drone. Stepping forward, he grabbed a bundle of grassy vines and yanked. The plants tore free, and a rusting muffler lay exposed.

He'd found the car.

It took him twenty minutes to pull the weeds away from one side of the car. His back ached from the exertion, and his hands felt raw from ripping at the plants. He whispered a quick prayer that none of them were poison ivy. Both windows on the side of the car were shattered.

He got on his hands and knees to peer first in the driver's window. His breath caught at the body in advance decay suddenly illuminated by his light. The driver still wore a suit and tie. He could only guess what injuries had caused the driver's death but given that he was still belted into an upside-down vehicle, his death must have been quick.

Across from the driver, a briefcase dangled. It had been

curiously belted into the passenger seat, so that it now hung in midair. Who would buckle a briefcase in? And why? Reaching across the car, careful not to disturb the body, he clicked the buckle of the belt. The case fell to the ground, and Jimmy snatched it up. Pulling out of the car, he sighed at the combination lock on the side. Whatever it contained, it wouldn't be much. He set it down to go through the rest of the car. The briefcase might be tradable, more so with the lock intact. He'd have to crack the combination later.

Scooting down the car, he scanned the back seat. Hopeful to find boxes of supplies, such as food or tools, he was amazed that there was nothing. Whoever this man was, he had been traveling somewhere outside the city after the pandemic with almost nothing. Anyone bent on survival would have brought everything they had. Where was he going?

Jimmy cursed under his breath. This trip was starting to look more costly than the reward he was gaining. He would hear it from Elena when he returned. He thought for a moment and then returned to the front of the car. Reaching in, he found the trunk latch and popped it open. A single duffle bag fell to the ground.

Bingo. That was more like it.

Scrambling to the back of the vehicle, he threw the zipper on the bag open. The man's personal effects were inside—clothing, shoes, and a copy of *The Hobbit*. At least the guy had good taste in books. In the side pocket, he found a mostly full tube of toothpaste, a razor, and a pair of reading glasses. It wasn't much, but the contents of the bag were definitely tradable. They would be able to restock their food stores for a few days at least. He breathed a sigh of relief. He wasn't going home empty-handed. It was a long way to come for a few items, but they were in better condition than most of the goods found at trade.

He rezipped the bag, promising himself to get top dollar for each item to help his crew. Though, he might keep the book for himself. Most survivors of the virus weren't interested in reading anymore. He'd welcome the distraction.

Looking back to the side of the car, he considered the briefcase. Whatever was inside, it was important enough to the man to ensure it remained safely connected to the seat.

Throwing the duffle strap across his shoulder, he scooped up the briefcase. Stooping to glance one more time in the trunk of the car, he noticed a tire iron strapped to the side wall. He grabbed it. At the least, it would give him a weapon for his return, though he had already planned a much different route in his head to avoid both the dark sector and the park.

He strode back up to street level and turned one more time to gaze at the vehicle. From this vantage point, he was not surprised it had never been discovered. The grass was so overgrown that the rare person travelling this road could easily miss the tire sticking out of the weeds.

He whispered a quiet prayer of thanks for the man. Whoever he was, he had met an unexpected end and died alone on the side of the road. Not how Jimmy wanted to go. His death would provide them a few days of food at least, and for that he was grateful.

He extinguished the light on his phone and pocketed it. The surrounding darkness adjusted in his vision to a surprisingly visible spectrum under the moonlight. Like some sort of lost businessman, he began walking the dark roadway, briefcase in hand. He had barely enough time to return home before Wyatt would insist on flying the drone to look for him.

The hideout never looked better as he approached. The sky had transitioned from starlit black to a soft hue of purple. He was relieved to be back, but he also knew what awaited him. He'd have a lot of explaining to do as he was certain Elena would want every detail about his brush with death in the dark sector. No matter how hard he tried, he couldn't bring himself to lie to her. She would know everything by the end of the conversation, and she wouldn't be happy. He only hoped his small prize from the car would soften the blow. With most of the buildings in the surrounding blocks picked over, it was more than they'd found in a long time.

He rapped in code on the door and waited. A minute later, he could hear the interior latch being thrown, and the door cracked open. Wyatt's smirk met him in the dim light.

"You're lucky, man." He laughed as Jimmy stepped inside. "Five more minutes, and she was going to send the drone out looking for you."

Jimmy sighed then turned to snap the lock in place. "It's not like I'm late. I promised to be back before dawn, and the sun's not even up yet."

"Still, you know Elena. If you're not early—"

"—you're late. I know."

The two of them trudged up the stairs to the second floor. The moment he stepped into the room, he was smothered in all five foot four of Elena's hug.

"Thank God," she whispered. "I was starting to get nervous."

"Nervous? Aww. So glad you care."

She pulled away, rolling her eyes. "Shut up. I'm just glad you're back in one piece."

He smiled at her. "When have I ever not come back in one piece?"

She glared at him with a look that said *not funny*, and he elected to drop the humor. He shrugged and turned his palms up. Her eyes locked on his forearm. He was immediately conscious of the scrapes on his arm from his fall in the park.

Elena's expression darkened. "What happened?"

"Oh, that?" he said, trying to sound nonchalant. "That's nothing."

She stepped forward and grabbed his wrist, twisting his arm uncomfortably to examine the wound. "It doesn't look like nothing. It looks like you fell and tore up your arm in the proccss. Tell me what happened."

"Look, Elena. I'm fine. I had a little problem in the park with some guys who thought they could rob me. I took off running and that was that."

"That was that? You just…outran the guys?"

Jimmy knew that his expression was betraying him. Why couldn't he lie better to this girl? As she crossed her arms and waited for his answer, he knew that she would demand the entirety of the story. Worse, she'd know if he left anything out.

Better get it over with.

"Wait." Wyatt stepped in between them. He turned to Elena

while keeping Jimmy in his peripheral vision. "Before Jimmy shares what I'm sure is a *riveting* story, are we going to ignore the fact that he has two bags with him?" He turned to Jimmy. "Dude, what's the take?"

Jimmy chuckled and slid the duffle off his shoulder, handing it to Wyatt, who was doing his best to avoid Elena's glare. "Have at it, man."

Wyatt clutched the duffle as he retreated to the table to unpack its contents. He pointed a finger at the briefcase. "What's that?"

Jimmy patted the outside of the case. "A little puzzle for me to figure out." He paused. "And, yes, I call dibs."

Elena walked to the table and pulled out a chair. She gestured for him to sit. "Not before you tell me what happened."

An hour later, Elena fumed at the table, unable to meet Jimmy's eyes. The more she heard about the men in the park and the experience in the dark sector, the angrier she appeared. Jimmy tried to reach for her hand, but she pulled away.

"Elena, I know it sounds like I took too big a risk, but I really wasn't in as much danger as it sounds." She gave him a doubtful glance at these words, and he had to admit he wasn't sure he believed them himself. "Besides, it's not like the batteries. I actually returned with something this time."

"Honestly, this stash isn't too bad." Wyatt was still going over each item from the bag, looking for any imperfection or mark that could be used against them in negotiating their trade. "Whoever this guy was, he had nice stuff. The trade boss is going to have to give us more than the usual rate for clothes in this condition. I mean, I haven't seen a pair of socks this white in a couple years."

Elena harumphed and adjusted in her chair. She was not convinced, and Jimmy didn't fully blame her. In many ways, she was the heart of the group—the one who felt everyone's emotions and carried everyone's stress. While he may not crumble under the strain of what he'd just experienced, it would only be amplified in her. It's how she cared about them, and he couldn't get frustrated at her for that.

"I'm sorry. I don't know what else to say." Jimmy sat quietly waiting to see if she'd answer.

After a long moment, Elena turned her gaze toward his, which was so hard that even Wyatt stopped his rummaging. The tears gathered at the corner of her eyes, and she blinked them back before they could fall. "Two days ago, I thought we'd lost you when you didn't come back." She held up a hand to silence Jimmy's immediate protest. "I know. I know. You were fine. We found you, and it turned out okay. But it could have easily gone the other way. Those men could have killed you. Or we could have gotten hurt on the way to find you."

Elena stopped to gather herself. "Then, our drone got shot at. It was one hundred percent my fault."

"Elena, please."

"No, it was. I suggested that spot. That led to you going on this crazy mission to a car in the middle of nowhere. If something had happened to you—" She stopped to swipe at a tear that threatened to escape the corner of her eye. "If those men had found you, I couldn't live with—" This time, she couldn't contain the emotion. Her head fell to her hands and the sobs came. "I—I just can't handle it sometimes…this world we live in."

Jimmy's eyes fell to the floor. She was right. This was not a world in which they should take too many risks. Survival *required* being smarter than this. This time, when he reached his hand out for her, she didn't deny him. He grabbed it with both hands as she finally allowed the bottled-up emotions to flow.

Wyatt scooted his chair over and grabbed Elena's other hand. Minutes passed as the three of them sat in silence.

Without warning, Elena's head found Jimmy's shoulder, and she slid into his arm. She allowed a long sigh as the tearful flow came to a stop. He pulled her in tightly. Wyatt straightened and slowly pulled his hand from Elena's, keeping his eyes on both of them.

"We will do better." Jimmy winced at his own words, but he could not think of anything else to say. "We will trade this stuff and be more careful moving forward. Okay?"

"Okay." Elena's voice was a raspy whisper.

"Okay," Wyatt parroted. "Speaking of goods to trade, you want me to take a crack at that briefcase?"

After a long moment of silence, Elena sniffed and raised her head. She grinned. "I believe dibs were called, and dibs will be upheld. Do not question the authority of dibs."

Wyatt held both hands up in surrender as his mouth contorted trying to contain his laughter. Jimmy bit his lip, attempting to control his own rising chuckle that threatened to escape his gut. It didn't feel appropriate to laugh after so many tears, but Elena was the one who cracked the joke after all.

Then, Elena snorted a laugh.

Wyatt spat as his laugh raspberried from his lips. Elena's hands shot up to cover her mouth as a chortle escaped her throat. Jimmy, still trying to control himself, began to shake with silent laughter until it forced its way from his mouth in a giant guffaw.

That only encouraged the other two to chuckle harder, and before long the three of them were doubled over with their arms across their stomachs like the amusement would burst from their bellies if they didn't contain it.

Tears of despair morphed into a fit of hilarity. As if on some sort of silent cue, the three of them let out a long, high-pitched sigh to calm their aching abdomens.

Jimmy pounded the top of the briefcase in frustration. The process of opening the briefcase was painstaking, and his fingers were growing numb from turning the tiny combination dials. Without any guesses as to what the proper combination would be, he'd had to start at zero, zero, zero and work his way through every possible combination. The latch on the right side of the briefcase had taken an hour before it clicked open. Now, the left side was proving to take just as long.

"I swear, if we don't trade this briefcase for something good—" Jimmy clicked to the next number and muttered a curse as the latch again refused to budge. "If I wasn't trying to keep it in such good condition, I could have pried it open with a screwdriver an hour ago." He rolled the dial to the next number…547.

Click.

The sound of the opening latch took the breath out of the

room. Jimmy tilted the briefcase and set it gently on its side. Elena and Wyatt both approached the table silently as if the sound of their footsteps would undo their sudden fortune.

"Here goes nothing." Jimmy whispered, shooting a glance to his friends.

He gripped the supple leather of the once expensive briefcase and opened the lid. The interior contained several papers, many of which were partially crumpled as though hastily shoved in the case. Pens and pencils stood in a row in their holders inside the lid. In the pocket at the top, a red file folder peeked out from the silky interior with the words, *Project Lifeboat*, on a white label stuck to the folder's tab. It was the other object in the briefcase that drew their attention.

On top of the crumbled papers was a tablet. An actual, likely working, piece of technology that appeared in pristine condition as though the previous three years of pandemic and chaos had never happened. When the death toll had effectively shut down the government, most tech stores were looted in the ensuing chaos. The majority of surviving technology was battered and well used, if not already beyond repair. This item didn't even bear a scratch.

A find like this could feed them for weeks, maybe months with the right offer. Jimmy imagined the traders in a bidding war over this rare item. Not that it was an item critical for survival, but a tangible reminder of the world that once existed had incredible power over people. Traders would overpay to simply hold an item like this.

And it was all theirs.

He turned his gaze away from the tablet to face his friends.

Elena's mouth stood agape, her eyes wide like saucers as they glanced from the tablet to Jimmy and back. Wyatt was breathing quickly. His eyes darted left and right as though already counting the goods they could get in return for this. He stopped and smirked at Jimmy.

Giving a slight elbow to Elena, Wyatt joked, "Was the trip worth it now?"

"Shut up, Wyatt." Elena's whisper held no anger in it. More than anything, it communicated that the moment wasn't to be ruined.

Jimmy held his breath as he gripped the tablet with both hands. The smoothness of the glass screen under his thumbs took him back to days when he took things like this for granted. The weight of the robust tablet surprised him for a moment as he lifted it carefully from the briefcase. Old muscle memory kicked in as his finger slid up the side of the device to the power button in the top corner. He pressed it.

Nothing.

He pressed it again.

No response.

"It doesn't work?" Elena asked, her voice laced with concern. She was right to worry. The value of the item would plummet if they couldn't prove it operated.

Jimmy sighed. "I guess we should have anticipated that it wouldn't turn on. Who knows how long it's been out there. Battery was sure to have died a long time ago."

"Let's just hope it's not so long that it's gone bad and won't charge." Wyatt said what they were all thinking.

Jimmy turned the tablet over and examined the charging port.

He pointed to it. "Got a charger that matches this, Elena?"

She bit her lip as she took a closer look. Without a word, she turned and crossed the room in three urgent strides. Grabbing a shoebox off the shelf, she popped the top open and began to rummage around the rat's nest of scavenged cords inside. Twice she pulled an end out to examine it, only to shove it back in the box with an expression of exasperation. The third was the charm as she found the connection she was looking for. The box and its contents dropped to the floor, and with a few firm shakes, the cord wiggled free of the tangled mess that had come with it.

Elena returned to the table. She tilted the tablet upward with one hand. With the other, she fit the cord into the charging port. It slid into place with a satisfying snap. Taking the tablet from Jimmy's hands with a gentle grip, she walked the prize over to the window. Unplugging the charging drone from the solar panel in the window, she plugged in the tablet.

For a moment, nothing happened.

Then, a battery appeared on the screen, blinking red.

It was charging. They only needed to wait.

Chapter Six

Jimmy's eyes cracked open. It had taken quite a while to quiet all the imaginative thoughts racing through his mind about the tablet, but eventually his all-night excursion caught up to him. He'd slept for hours according to the clock on his phone.

"I'm not sure what we're waiting for," Wyatt complained in hushed tones. "The traders are open, I think we should go and off-load this thing as soon as possible."

"Off-load what thing?" Jimmy voice croaked with sleep, and he stopped to moisten the inside of his mouth.

"You're up? Finally." Elena stood across from Wyatt. Her arms were crossed, and she was obviously not happy with him. "You slept like the dead."

"That's what traveling all night and running for your life will do to you."

"Not funny." Now she was glaring at Jimmy.

He smirked. "Wasn't trying to be, but I get the confusion." He sat up and rubbed his eyes. "So, what's the debate this time."

"Nothing, bro." Wyatt stammered. "Just didn't know when you'd wake up and thought we should hit the traders right away. The battery is charging, so we know the device works. I think we should get what it's worth before we accidentally do something to it."

"I thought we should wait to discuss it as a group." Elena scolded Wyatt. "We do things together, remember?"

"I know. I know." Wyatt placed both hands on his stomach. "Just getting a little hungry, and I can't help but imagine how we'll eat when we trade this thing."

"That's Wyatt." Jimmy laughed as he stood and stretched. "Always thinking with his stomach."

Elena's expression transformed from annoyance to concern. She gazed at Jimmy, shaking her head slightly.

"What is it?" Jimmy asked.

Elena pointed to the briefcase. Several papers had been removed, smoothed and stacked. On top of them all was the red folder. "I've been spending time during your nap to take a look at the paperwork in that thing."

"A waste of time if you ask me." Wyatt huffed. "We aren't going to get a thing for a bunch of paper."

Jimmy approached the table. Flipping open the red folder, the word *classified* caught his gaze. Whatever Project Lifeboat was, it wasn't meant for them to see. Skimming the pages, he could hardly make sense of the lists of names and occupations—doctors, scientists, construction engineers, hydroponic farmers, water purification specialists. What did it all mean?

More pages of data followed, mostly having to do with the spread of the pandemic. At least, that was the best he could tell from the headings. Occasionally there were hand scrawled notes in the margins. The most ominous of these were the scribbled words that came on the final page of data. At the bottom was a date about seven years in the future with the title *Re-entry Date*. Next to the date, the notetaker had hastily scribbled '*Too Late.*'

He was about to tell Elena that there was no way to make any sense of this information until he looked at the one remaining item in the folder. He pulled the thick glossy image from under the rest of the papers. A full-color satellite image displayed a forested area. At the center of the woods, a clearing was cut near the bottom of a hill. A concrete structure had been built onto the hill, and even from the steep angle of the photo, Jimmy could see the large doorway. In the lower corner, coordinates in latitude and longitude had been redacted.

People with specific occupations.

A hidden door into a hill in the middle of a forest.

A *re-entry* date.

"Do you think—?" Jimmy's words cut off. The idea seemed so unbelievable to him. "I mean, there's no way this could lead to—" Again, he couldn't finish the thought.

Elena walked over to the tablet and quietly unplugged the cord. Pressing the power button, the screen illuminated with the startup screen. Returning to the table, she held the tablet out to Jimmy. "There's only one way to find out. You're better with something like this than either of us. See if there's anything on it."

Jimmy took the tablet and sat down. He started with the email application. Scanning the inbox told him that all of these messages were dated prior to the pandemic. Not helpful. The file storage held more scanned documents of data like the one in the folder, which remained meaningless to him. He sighed. Maybe this was only the personal tablet of the driver and didn't have much.

He sighed as he flipped the screen image to the right and left examining the various options. Social media apps. A fantasy football app. Even a video streaming service. Nothing that would provide anything now that the internet no longer existed. He was ready to give up when the icon in the upper corner caught his eye.

He touched the picture app.

The screen expanded to an open photo of a man in his middle forties with sandy brown hair. He was dressed in a buttoned shirt and tie with khaki pants. Next to him, a woman about the same age with blonde hair and a kind smile stood with her hands on two children—a barely teenage boy and a girl that looked upper elementary school age. The driver and his family. It must have been the last thing he looked at before he packed up the suitcase to protect its contents, perhaps even in his dying moments. That's why the photo was still open in the application.

The image of the corpse in the car flashed into his vision. He'd been the only occupant. There was no wife or children in the car. Either they'd not been there or had survived to escape. But wouldn't they have taken the briefcase and bag? Of course they would. In this world, every little thing had some value. Jimmy concluded they must not have been with the man when he died.

He closed the photo and scrolled to the most recent entries. He was surprised to find several video files. The last one had a thumbnail image of a flushed-faced man with a wound on his head. Jimmy recognized him as the man in the family photo.

He pressed the video file and held his breath as it opened. The man's face filled the screen. His hair was mussed, and his features seemed odd. Then it occurred to Jimmy. He was upside down, still strapped into the car. His voice was shaky and weak.

My name is Doctor Harold Sheppard. I was on my way to the Lifeboat when a deer struck my car. I-I've been in an accident. My car flipped, and I'm stuck in here. S-something must have struck me as the car rolled. As best I can tell, the object...maybe a log or large rock...came through the window as the car rolled over it. My head is bleeding, but I th-think the real injury is inside. Something jabbed me in the back. I-I can't see it, but there's blood soaking into the seat.

I'm not s-sure h-how long I have before—before—.

The man's voice cut off for a moment as several sobs overwhelmed him. He swallowed hard to regain his composure.

No one really travels this road anymore, so I'm not sure if I'll get found. I don't even know if the car is visible from the road anyway.

Who-whoever finds this, p-please do this for me. Please review the video f-files. There is a bunker where people w-went to escape the virus. My wife and children are there. The videos explain everything. P-please go there. Open the bunker.

Open the bunker? Was that what the man was doing?

Cyndi, I love you. I'm sorry I didn't make it. Matthias, I am so proud of the man you are becoming. There is still a world left to live for. Vanessa, you are dad's angel. Keep being the amazing young woman you are. I love—.

The video cut off, possibly the point at which the battery died. Jimmy placed the tablet on the table and reminded himself to breathe. He turned to Wyatt and Elena. "What do we do?"

Wyatt shook his head. "We sell the thing. The guy is dead

anyway. It doesn't matter. We need to eat."

Though a little insensitive, the idea made sense. There seemed little they could do about some bunker in the woods God-knows-where. He glanced at Elena, whose eyes were glassy with tears. "Elena?"

"I don't know about any bunker, but the man's dying wish was that we watch the other videos. Before we do anything with this tablet, I think we can at least do that."

"What does it matter?" Wyatt scoffed. "The traders are going to close in an hour. If we hurry, we can still make it and be eating again by tonight."

Both of them stared at Jimmy, pleading their case with their gazes. Jimmy's stomach rumbled its agreement with Wyatt's logic, but he could not take his eyes off Elena's pained expression.

"We watch the videos. Then, we will decide what to do."

Elena nodded. Wyatt threw his hands up in resignation.

"And let's open the last two cans of tuna," Jimmy offered, receiving a look of hope from Wyatt. "Wyatt is correct. We need to eat something. No matter what, we will trade the contents of the duffle tomorrow, so we can spare the last of our supplies tonight."

Wyatt rushed off to grab the cans from their storage in the other room. Elena slid into the seat next to him.

"You sure you want to watch this? Could be hard to view if it's more like that one."

Elena sighed deeply. "Yes. I want to watch. You shouldn't have to do this alone, and I'm not sure Wyatt really cares."

Jimmy reached over and squeezed her hand. It was the

boldest move he'd ever made with Elena, and he wasn't sure what he meant by it. He only knew it felt like the right thing to do…and then she squeezed his hand back with both of hers. His gaze met hers, and they allowed their eyes to lock for a long silent moment.

In the other room, the sound of a can being opened caught their attention. The smell of tuna fish quickly wafted throughout the apartment. On cue, his stomach gurgled a long, low growl. Food would taste good. Between his trip to the car and back and his unexpected nap, it occurred to him that he hadn't eaten a bite in almost a day.

He propped the tablet up against a stack of books on the table and swiped to the earliest of the video files. It made sense to watch them in order. The paused image was that of a woman sitting in a chair. The window behind her looked out onto a street with homes lining the road. Her pale skin color, cracked lips, and bloodshot eyes were an all too familiar sight. She was a victim of the virus that killed most of the world. This was not going to be fun to watch.

He pressed play.

Chapter Seven

My name is Victoria Clarke, and these will be my last recorded words on this earth. After a year and a half of this dreadful virus, we are seeing the first signs that this pandemic might soon reach its zenith. The toll here has been as terrible as it has been everywhere. I am sending this video to you, the other keepers of the six Lifeboats worldwide, over a secure channel. I don't even know if you will receive this. We were sworn to silence lest the world open the Lifeboats too soon, but I am afraid I will be derelict in my duties.

As you can plainly see, the virus has found its way to me, despite my efforts to separate myself from the infected. I am not long for this world, but I would be remiss to not tell you what I know as I have dedicated myself to studying this deadly plague.

The woman in the video lifted a shaky hand to brush a tear off her face. Next to him, Jimmy could sense that Elena was crying already. They'd seen others die of the disease. It was never easy.

The truth is that the virus is relatively easy to figure out. You have heard that aphids were the cause. They are the number one destroyer of crops in the world, and the search for a genetically modified crop that could fight off aphid attacks ended with the discovery made by Ravi Gupta. Hailed as a victory, the new strain of wheat was quickly implemented, followed by similar crops for all major food sources. No one anticipated the aggressive nature of the new crops, which quickly crossbred with others nearby. Before long, much of the world's food was at least a crossbreed of the altered source plants, many of which produced terminator seeds, which are sterile and useless. Hope for the end of crop shortages led the scientific community to drop their guard so to speak. Predictions of the effects on the aphids came too late. The need for survival led to the mutation of super aphids, resistant to the new modifications. What caught the scientific community by surprise was the plant's ability to then fight back—and the virus was born. In another time, the world health community would have been fascinated by the first ever virus to cross from Kingdom Plantae to Kingdom Animalia, but it's spread was so—so—fast. Transmission between humans was frighteningly simple. So many died. So quickly. Scientists like me could not stop to wonder at this creation, but rather our efforts had to focus on survival.

Since I was chosen to remain above ground to watch over the British Lifeboat, I resolved to have answers when we opened the gates of it to reintroduce the people below to the world. I have spent countless hours in my lab, isolated from the dying world. And I have learned this—the virus, though deadlier than any other known to humankind, has a weakness. It lives in the bloodstream of the host, but it cannot thrive in all blood. Specifically, it cannot survive in type B blood. Essentially, that means that ten percent of the world is immune to this killer. I imagine that will be all that is left of the world in another year or so.

She stopped to swallow hard. Licking her cracked lips, she grabbed a glass of water from the table next to her and took a tentative sip.

Ironically, I made this discovery only days before contracting the virus myself. I have type O blood. I will not survive long enough to see the virus' rage pass over humanity and burn itself out. I will not be able to open the Lifeboat here.

I tell you, the other Lifeboat keepers, because if my findings are correct, the virus will kill faster than we can imagine, but it will also die off or mutate into a less deadly form sooner than we thought. The world will become a shell of itself, and the hope that is in each Lifeboat will be essential to the survival of our species. At least one Lifeboat must be opened to save humanity. We cannot wait the ten years until they open on their own. The heirloom crops they contain are the only hope for the world. Any genetically modified crops that have not already been burned must be destroyed, though I imagine most have died through neglect.

My friends, stay hidden. Stay alive. At the current death rate, I believe you may open your Lifeboats in February of next year. God help us all.

Jimmy's body shook as the video ended. The realization that there were people hidden underground around the world with the crops to save the human race seemed unreal, like something out of a book or film. It couldn't be true, could it? And yet, they sat here with a tablet from a man who also claimed knowledge of the Lifeboats.

The next few videos were short, mostly introductions as the Lifeboat keepers broke their silence and introduced themselves. The other four seemed grateful to share their burden with each other, and they celebrated as Victoria's date neared.

That's when the videos took a dark turn.

During one, an Australian man was sharing photos of his family and talking about seeing them again, when an earthquake hit. The ceiling of his home collapsed burying him alive on camera before the video feed cut off.

A week later, an Indian man named Rajesh, contracted the virus. Jimmy and Elena could hardly finish the video as he shared images of the horrors of the virus in a country as densely populated as India. Piles of rotting corpses lined the streets with no one to dispose of them. Rajesh prayed a blessing over the other keepers through cracked and bleeding lips before signing off. It was his last message.

Jimmy shut off the video of the Brazilian man who spent several minutes despairing over the state of the world and insisting that there would be nothing left to save. When he'd brought the gun to his chin, Jimmy had swiped to the next video.

Elena sobbed in the seat next to him. "I don't know if I can watch anymore, Jimmy. Maybe Wyatt is right, and it's not worth watching."

"There's only two videos left. February was six months ago. Maybe one of the Lifeboats has been opened. We've come this far. I think we should find out." He sniffed through glassy eyes as he gazed at Elena. She nodded her agreement.

The next video showed the terrified face of a Chinese woman burning documents in a bucket.

I've been discovered. The local mafia that controls my city intercepted our last couple communications. They are coming for any information I can give them. I am erasing all evidence of the Lifeboat in China, and I will smash this tablet as soon as I push send. They'll kill me for this.

She stopped and picked up the tablet to gaze directly into the camera.

Dr. Sheppard...Harold...you are the last of us. Stay hidden, please. Protect yourself. You can open the North American Lifeboat in just three weeks. Promise me you will stay safe. Promise me you will tell what is left of the world what we all did to protect this secret.

A loud pounding came from the door behind her, and she raked the remaining papers into the bucket.

Bye, Harold.

The camera showed the room of her apartment rock back and forth as she raised the tablet and brought it down to smash it. Then, the video cut off.

One final swipe brought the familiar face of Dr. Harold Sheppard to the screen. Surprisingly, he appeared pleasant on the screen. Jimmy tentatively pushed play.

Today is February 1st, and I, Dr. Harold Sheppard, am privileged to see the day in which the first of the worldwide Lifeboats can be opened. Contained inside are the leaders, scientists, and experts to restart the world's crops and organize the chaos around us. While it will take time to get to the other Lifeboats, I'm certain the remaining military forces will be able to see to their opening.

Mostly, I'm excited. I get to see Cyndi, Matthias, and Vanessa.

With a smile, tears escaped Dr. Sheppard's eyes. He didn't even try to swipe them away.

I get to see them...tonight. I can't believe I'm even saying that. When the other keepers died, I didn't think I'd make it to this day. But now I'm only a short drive out of town to see my family again. It's been a long three years. The cost has been high, but I believe that Victoria's calculations were correct. And by God's grace, I and my family all have type B blood.

This time, he brushed away a tear.

Anyway, I'm making one last video here for posterity, I guess. I want to honor my colleagues around the world who gave their lives keeping the secret of the Lifeboats to prevent their discovery before the proper time. Now, the time has come. Tonight, I will be opening the doorway to the North American Lifeboat and can rest knowing that my part is finished.

God bless the human race. See you on the other side of this momentous day.

Jimmy placed the tablet on the table. "He never made it. The last person who knew about the Lifeboats was killed by a deer leaping out in front of his car." The gravity of it all hit Jimmy in the chest, and he found it hard to breathe.

"He was so alive in that video." Elena smiled softly, her brow creasing in sorrow. "He thought he would see his family in a matter of hours."

The two of them sat silently at the table for several minutes. Wyatt entered from the other room, still savoring the last bites of his can of tuna. "You guys done with that mess yet? I'm up for a game of cards before we turn in. I want to hit the traders first thing to get the best deals."

As if Wyatt hadn't even spoken, Elena turned to Jimmy. "All the keepers are dead. What do we do?"

"What's a *keeper*?" Wyatt asked while snacking on a bite of tuna.

Jimmy took a long look at Elena, studying her face. Tear lines streaked her face, and he squeezed her hands. He glanced at Wyatt, who watched them intently. He held out a single hand in a half-shrug, awaiting an answer to his question.

Fingering the ring hanging around his neck, he asked himself what his mother or father would do in his shoes. He thought of what Dr. Sheppard and the other keepers had sacrificed. *Greater love has no one than this.*

Jimmy took a breath, considering his next words. "We're keepers. Not all the keepers of the Lifeboats are dead, Elena." He held up the tablet in one hand. "Dr. Sheppard saw to that."

Chapter Eight

Morning took forever to arrive as Jimmy spent most of the night wide awake, his mind racing through all he'd learned from Dr. Sheppard's tablet. They'd spent the remainder of the evening trying to feel normal despite Wyatt's repeated questions about what Lifeboats were and how they were supposed to be keepers now. He'd been unwilling to watch the videos, and their emotional exhaustion had finally led to an exasperated promise to explain it more in the morning.

He rolled out of bed and stretched as he stood. The duffle bag sat by the door, packed and ready to head to the traders. Wyatt had seen to that at least. Perhaps it would be good to do something relatively normal after what they'd learned from the tablet yesterday. They needed time to process and decide what to do.

Jimmy, though, knew they needed to do something. Wyatt's calloused opinion that they should sell the tablet and be done with it felt misinformed. All of the keepers were dead, having given everything to keep the information from getting into the hands of those who would only see the Lifeboats as a target to raid. Elena had suggested recording everything from the tablet on paper and wiping its memory. Jimmy dismissed this since the complicated information was too much to write down, and the tablet would likely be their best ticket inside the Lifeboat—if they ever found it.

The knowledge that the world might have been saved six months ago weighed heavily on Jimmy. The reality that if he did nothing, the world may never be rescued pressed in on his soul even more so. But what were they supposed to do? Travel aimlessly until they found the redacted location on the tablet and simply knock on the door to the Lifeboat? That didn't seem feasible. They needed help.

For now, they would go to the traders and get supplies. Full stomachs would help them think clearly. As if on cue, Wyatt groaned in the corner about his stomach churning. Elena emerged from behind her curtain, dressed and ready to head out. She gave him a knowing glance. She apparently hadn't slept either.

Wyatt extended his arms into the air with an enormous yawn. "You guys ready to go? I'm starving, and I'm not letting you waste another day watching that stupid tablet. If you ask me, I still think we should sell it and be done. We'd be the talk of the trading floor if we showed up with that thing."

"Which is exactly why we're not going to show up with it." Elena crossed her arms. "You know we like to keep a low profile when we're there. Remember the Wilson twins?"

"Yeah, yeah. I know. They showed up with a working laptop, and they were mugged on the way home when they couldn't get what they wanted for it."

"Killed, Wyatt. Not just mugged." Elena pointed a finger at him. "And I don't want any of us ending up like that, so it stays here."

Wyatt rolled his eyes. "Yes, ma'am. Can we go already?" He muttered under his breath something about how they'd be fine.

Jimmy picked up the duffle bag and slung it over one shoulder. With a nod toward the door, he threw the lock and opened it. It was time to head to the trading floor.

The trading floor was too formal a name for the rundown school gymnasium. Inside, the wood floor that once held local basketball games was stained with mold as the broken doors and ceiling allowed the elements to have their way with the indoors. Most vendors set out their tradable goods on blankets spread across the floor. Some hocked scrap pieces of salvaged electronics, while others attempted to sell clothing that were obviously stolen from less than desirable places, usually graves. Still others tried to appeal to nostalgia, trying to make a penny on items like toys or books, which had little to do with surviving the state of the world. All of it was junk. Aside from the beggars, which were everywhere accosting those with tradable goods, most everyone visited a single corner of the gym. Two folding tables sat side by side in front of the doors labeled 'locker rooms.'

The table was run by a minor boss who controlled their section of the city. Every neighborhood had some boss that had set himself up as the kingpin in the area, taking control of what little was left to be found in the city. Above each of these were greater bosses, though no one really knew who was at the top. Below them, every leader had their group of thugs. Jimmy never ceased to be amazed at how quickly the city had descended into this kind of street rule as though they were living in some kind of apocalyptic movie. He joked they'd have to fight in the Thunderdome at some point.

Sure enough, two of the thugs sat at the table. Actually, sat was too proper a term. On the right, a large-bellied man with a grizzled face and wiry beard reclined with his leather boots resting on the table. Tattoos covered both arms, and a cigarette hung from his lips. To the left, a woman dressed in a men's red checkered flannel, jeans, and sneakers sat on the edge of the table with one foot pulled up next to her. She yelled at the person at the front of the line. Her massive nest of dreadlocks was tied together in back and moved back and forth in unison as she shook her head. Jimmy had hoped Ruby would not be in today.

"You think we want your junk? It reeks of the dumpster you crawled out from. Get out of here, you…" Ruby's raspy voice continued as she wove a tapestry of offensive descriptions of the woman who'd attempted to trade a holey winter coat that sported a still-dripping stain of goo on one side.

"P-please, I h-haven't eaten in days," The woman begged, extending the coat toward dreadlock woman.

"Ugh. You disgusting piece of filth." Ruby leapt off the table and grabbed the terrified trader by her collar. "I said get out of here." She yanked the woman, who stumbled, the coat falling from her hand. She dragged her across the filthy floor out one of the exits. Jimmy couldn't be sure, but it sounded like she'd delivered a kick or two before reentering the building.

"Great," Wyatt whispered. "Ruby is in a mood today."

"Quiet, Wyatt." Elena held a finger up to her lips. "She'll hear you. Let's just hope we get Big T today."

No one knew Big T's real name, but he was without a doubt the more reasonable trader of the two at the table. Currently, he was negotiating with a man who held out a flashlight. A minute later, Big T handed the man two boxes of macaroni and cheese. The man clutched his new prize and made a quick retreat from the gym.

"Next." Big T's voice was as deep as his gut was big. "Now what we got here?" Seeing the duffle bag on Jimmy's shoulder, he pulled his feet back under himself and actually sat up. "That thing looks cleaner than anything I've seen today."

The threesome stepped forward. Jimmy took a deep breath and prepared to pitch his goods. He'd discovered his ability to be a bit of salesman, usually driving up the price of goods high enough to get full value without overshooting and spoiling the negotiations.

"Big T, how are you, man? Long time no see. It's not the bag that you'll be interested in, but what's inside." Jimmy smiled, receiving a disbelieving huff from Big T. It was too much show. Jimmy silently scolded himself to back off a bit.

"Let's see the goods, boy." Big T reached for the duffle.

Jimmy surrendered the bag to Big T's grip and watched as the man yanked the zipper open. "I think you'll find the condition of the goods inside to be of rare quality." Was that 'backing off?' Jimmy bit his tongue before he said too much.

Big T took a long drag on his cigarette and allowed the smoke to exhale in puffs as he spoke. "Fancy stuff here. Come take a look, Ruby."

Please don't involve Ruby.

Ruby slammed a can of anchovies on the table, ripping a pair of shoes out of an elderly man's hands. "That's all you get, grandpa. Choke on 'em, and do us all a favor." She sauntered over the Big T. "Whatcha got, big stuff?"

The only thing grosser than Ruby's hatred of everyone in line was her flirtation with Big T. Jimmy swallowed to avoid vomiting in his mouth.

Big T handed her a pair of slacks, which she held up to her nose. "Smells like some pretty boy owned these." She eyed Jimmy through squinted eyes. "You didn't off anyone I know to get these, did you?"

Jimmy shook his head. He could feel Elena and Wyatt retreat a half-step behind him as if to avoid Ruby's glare.

"Premium stuff here." Big T let out a long sigh. "Can't say the boss is looking for anything like this right now. I can give you"—Big T rifled through a box behind the table—"three cans of beans and a box of pasta." The end of his cigarette glowed red as he turned his gaze to Jimmy.

Now began the dance.

"I can get three times that much a couple blocks over, and you know it, T." That response received a glance of hatred from Ruby.

Ruby leaned across the table and put a finger in Jimmy's face. "Boss-man hears you're taking goods from his territory to his competition, he'll have your head, you runt."

Jimmy buried his desire to roll his eyes. He was at least six inches taller than Ruby. "Is *boss man* going to pay what these things are worth?" Elena's hand found Jimmy's back. Her message was clear—don't press the insults about their boss too hard.

Big T ran a hand through his beard, sending a shower of dandruff-like flakes floating to the table. "Six cans, two boxes. That enough for ya?"

Jimmy leaned forward, placing his hands on the table. He tried not to think about how much of the dandruff was getting on his skin. This was the time for a power move, and he couldn't be distracted. "These threads are the best you've seen in a year. You know it. I know it. And we both know your boss is not going to like the idiot running the next trading house wearing them. Is he? Now, pony up the good stuff if you want us to stay."

Ruby made it halfway over the table before Big T's giant hand caught her across the middle. With a great shove, he forced her back to his side of the table. "Ruby, calm yerself. Kid has a point." Pulling the remaining cigarette stub out of his mouth, he mashed it on the table. Immediately, he grabbed another from his shirt pocket, placed it in his mouth, and lit it with a lighter from his pocket. "Okay, boy. Boss isn't looking for clothes right now, but you're right he won't want someone else to have these. Now listen carefully, cause I'm only going to say this one time, and real low, so the rest of the herd behind you doesn't get any ideas." He leaned in, and Jimmy tried not to choke on the cigarette smoke that filled his nostrils. "Six cans of beans. Six boxes of pasta. And one can of pineapple, a rare find. And that's only because Ruby here is in a good mood."

A good mood? Jimmy didn't want to see her in a bad mood.

Ruby scowled. "Are you kidding, T? That's—"

"My final offer." Big T interrupted. "Take it or leave it, kid."

Jimmy glanced at Elena and Wyatt. It wasn't as much as they'd hoped, but they could live on that for a while. A silent conversation took place between the three of them.

"You're holding up the line, kid. You in?"

Jimmy nodded. With one giant hand, Big T gathered up the entire pile and handed it to Ruby, who eagerly retreated a couple feet to go through the entire find. Reaching into his box, Big T placed the food on the table. Jimmy grabbed the pasta. Wyatt cradled the beans in his arms. Elena examined the label of the pineapple. Big T wasn't kidding. Fruit was hard to come by.

"Pleasure doing business with you, Big T." Jimmy smirked and started walking toward the door.

"See you next week, kid."

"And next time, come back with something the boss can actually use, dirtbags." Ruby sneered at their group as she continued fingering the fine clothes.

Wyatt turned to face her, smugness all over his face. "Yeah, whatever Ruby. If you only knew what we could have traded today, you wouldn't talk so big."

Ruby's features flattened. Dropping the clothes, she approached the table. Her voice lowered to a mocking whisper. "Oh yeah? And what worthless piece of garbage do you think we'd want?"

"It's nothing like you've seen in a long time." Wyatt turned to smile at his friends, looking for their support. Instead, he was met with Elena's expression of shock and Jimmy's glare that communicated he should shut his mouth immediately.

"Huh. Judging by the look on your friends faces, I think maybe you've got your hands on something." Ruby straightened. "Hear that, T? These three have scrounged up something good."

Jimmy knew he had to intervene before Wyatt dug his hole deeper. "Yeah, well, it's something that's cool to us. Not very useful, but it brings back a lot of memories, that's for sure." He prayed she'd buy the line.

Ruby and Big T shared a silent conversation. Big T turned to Jimmy. "Looking forward to you knocking our socks off next time, then. So long, kid."

Jimmy nodded and backed toward the door. Elena stepped toward Wyatt, pinching the back of his arm.

"Ow. What was that for?" Wyatt rubbed at the spot.

"Shut up." Elena whispered.

The three of them walked as quickly as they dared toward the doorway. Elena glared daggers at Wyatt as they walked.

"What were you thinking?" Jimmy snapped at Wyatt as soon as they'd rounded the corner of the next building. He grabbed Wyatt's shoulder.

Wyatt brushed Jimmy's hand away. "What? You're not seriously considering that 'keeper' stuff, are you? It's not real, you know that, right?"

"We don't know what we're going to do, Wyatt." Elena stepped to meet his gaze. "But you don't go telling the likes of them that we have something good to trade before we bring it to them."

"I don't know what you two are all upset about. We're going to trade that thing. We're not running off on some hopeless mission to *save the world.*" Wyatt added air quotes to the last three words.

"That's not what we decided," Jimmy said.

"We? I don't remember *us* deciding anything. Seems like it was all you, Jimmy. Maybe if you'd listened to me, we'd be walking home right now with a lot more than beans and pasta." He stepped toward Jimmy.

Elena jumped between them. "Guys, seriously. We can't do this." She glanced at Jimmy and then met Wyatt's gaze. "We haven't decided what to do…not really. That means we also haven't decided to sell it."

Wyatt huffed. "I wish you'd stop deferring to Jimmy. Let me sell the thing. I can handle Big T and Ruby. I'll show you how much I can get for it and for once be respected as an equal member of this group."

"Where is this coming from?" Elena searched Wyatt's face.

Wyatt's expression softened, and he looked away. "I don't know, guys. I'm just tired of barely getting by. That thing would set us up for a long time, maybe even buy us in to the good graces of Big T's boss. And who knows? Maybe there's a way to get a more consistent meal."

"I'm not working for the likes of them, and neither are you, Wyatt." Jimmy placed his hand on his friend's shoulder. "You are an equal part of this group, and we are making it just fine as scavengers."

"Maybe I don't want to be a scavenger anymore."

Elena threw her arms around both boys. "That's a talk we can have later. For now, we need to get home and figure out what to do."

"She's right, Wyatt."

"I know."

"Guys, that tablet is not safe to have now. We need to figure something out…and fast."

Jimmy turned to both of them. "I have an idea. It's a bit outside the box, but there's enough daylight left to try it. And maybe—" He looked at Wyatt. "Maybe it will come with a hot meal as a bonus."

Chapter Nine

"The military? For real?" Wyatt's disbelief was all over his face as they walked down the road. They'd dropped off the food supplies upon returning to the hideout. Shoving the tablet and red folder in a backpack, Jimmy had ushered them out the door before even explaining where they were going.

"Yes. There's a military post at the power junction a mile east of town." Jimmy strode along, confident this plan would work. "We have to get rid of it, now that Big T and Ruby know."

Elena punched Wyatt in the arm.

Wyatt rubbed at the spot. "Yeah, sorry again about that guys. I only wanted Ruby to know we were better scavengers than she thought."

"Actually, maybe it's for the better because I hadn't thought of this idea until your pride got us in a pickle."

Wyatt raised an eyebrow. "You're welcome?"

Elena punched him again.

"Seriously, I'm going to get a bruise."

"Good. You deserve it." She spoke without even glancing at Wyatt.

Jimmy and Wyatt had been friends for a lot longer than Elena, and it would take her longer to forgive him. Jimmy was confident that, if this plan worked, all would be forgiven.

"Like I was saying, we have to get rid of it. But—and I think Elena will agree—we have to do something about the Lifeboats. We can't ignore what we learned."

"And your answer is the military post?" Wyatt sighed.

"Who better to handle this information than the military? If anyone has the tools to go open the Lifeboat, it's them."

Elena caught up to Jimmy and matched his stride. Grabbing his arm, she squeezed gently. "No one approaches that outpost, Jimmy. You know why."

When Jimmy didn't answer, Wyatt leaned his head in between theirs, startling both of them. "Because they shot the last person who got near."

"But that guy was crazy and had a weapon."

"You don't know that. You only heard it."

It was true. The stories had spread on the trading floor that no one approached the military outpost by the power station. The only reason the city had even occasional power was because what was left of the military guarded key infrastructure. He had to believe, though, that they would want to hear about the contents of the tablet. With luck, they'd be rewarded with a meal or better for their efforts. If rumors were true, the military was still receiving provisions that they might share when they realized what Jimmy and his friends had.

"What could it hurt to try?" Jimmy asked.

"I think a bullet through the chest could hurt a lot, but maybe that's just me." Wyatt caught up to the other side of Elena, and the three walked side by side the remaining half mile.

The report of the rifle halted the three of them in their tracks like their shoes had suddenly glued themselves to the asphalt. In the distance, two Humvees barricaded the roadway. Several heads could be seen peering over the vehicles, rifles trained in their direction. Either the soldiers at the outpost were terrible shots, or it had been meant as a warning.

Behind the Humvees, the power relay sat behind a metal fence topped with razor wire. Tents lined the outside of the relay, with vehicles forming a perimeter around the entire area.

"Do not approach!" The shout came from the peering heads. A low murmur carried over the street to Jimmy and his friends as the soldiers called in the sighting of the threesome into their radios. None of them moved.

"Told you this was a bad idea." Wyatt spoke in a forced tone as though he'd been afraid to even move his lips. "They'll shoot us once they get their wits about them."

"Hold on a second. We don't know that." Jimmy turned his head toward Wyatt while keeping his feet planted in place.

"I'm telling you, the second they get clearance, we're all dead."

"Give this a chance."

"I don't know, Jimmy." Elena's voice was pinched. "They didn't exactly ask who we are."

"Let's just stay put and show them we're not a threat. If this is going to work, we're going to need to meet with someone in charge."

Wyatt opened his mouth to protest, but Jimmy waived off his objection before he could offer it.

"Remain where you are!" The soldier's voice snapped their attention back to the Humvees. "Wait for our approach."

Jimmy smiled. "See what I mean? Now we're getting somewhere."

Wyatt shook his head. "Arrested is where we're getting…and that's if we're lucky."

A soldier emerged from behind the Humvee, keeping his rifle at the ready. With his hand, he reached across his body to activate his radio. More distant murmurs. A second later, the soldier pointed to a second, who also emerged from cover. Rifles raised, and backed up by their companions, the two soldiers cautiously walked in the direction of Jimmy's group.

"If we're going to run," Wyatt offered, "now would be the time."

Jimmy ignored the comment. Instead, he lifted his chin to the men approaching. "We have important information for your superiors."

"Stay where you are."

Okay, the soldiers had exactly one message for them. This was going to take some convincing. A minute later, the soldiers stood about ten paces from them. Jimmy tried to ignore the open barrel of their rifles pointing directly at his chest. One wrong word or sudden movement, and he would be dead. He took a deep breath and resolved to speak in calm tones.

The soldier on the left, whose name plate said Wallace, locked eyes with Jimmy. "This is a restricted area. Civilians are not permitted." The other, named Rodriguez, nodded.

"Okay. We got you." Wyatt raised both his hands in surrender. "We'll leave." He turned to start walking the way they'd come.

"Halt! Do not move." Both soldiers redirected their rifles in Wyatt's direction.

"Okay, man. Be cool." Wyatt's voice betrayed his terror, despite his comment's apparent aloofness.

"We are under orders to bring you three in for questioning. Keep your hands where we can see them." With a nod from Wallace, who kept his rifle trained, Rodriguez shouldered his weapon. Walking up to the group, he ripped the backpack off Jimmy's back. He quickly patted down the three of them.

"Watch it." Elena snapped as the officer searched her.

"I said no speaking." The rifle pointed at Elena, which silenced her.

"No weapons found, sir. Only had this in their possession." He held the backpack up as he rounded their group. Returning to his compatriot, Rodriguez searched the contents of the bag. "No weapons in here, either." He rezipped the bag and after removing the rifle, he shouldered the bag. Once again, two rifles were pointed at the group.

"This way." Wallace directed them up the street toward the Humvees. "Keep your hands on your head where we can see them."

Jimmy, Elena, and Wyatt interlocked their fingers on their heads and walked single file toward Wallace and Rodriguez. Both soldiers parted to the side to allow them to walk through, taking up positions behind them.

The march up the street brought bullets of sweat to Jimmy's brow, keenly aware of the number of firearms pointed at him. He tried not think how easily a single nervous trigger finger could end his life and instead attempted to focus on the potential upside. They'd *have* to be interested in the tablet videos and the Lifeboats.

Arriving at the Humvees, they stepped between the two hoods of the huge vehicles. Two of the other soldiers lowered their weapons, coming short of shouldering them, and took up positions in front of the group to lead the way. All eyes from every direction focused on the threesome as they walked to the fence. A sign that said *Danger High Voltage* hung crooked from a single fastener, and Jimmy wondered if that referred to the power station inside or if the fence itself was electrified.

They rounded the corner and approached a beige tent. The two soldiers leading the pack took positions on either side of the tent doorway. With one hand, the soldier on the right pulled the flap of the tent back, indicating they should enter.

The scent of mud, body odor, and canvas filled Jimmy's nose as he slipped inside. At the other end of the tent sat a small wooden desk, behind which an officer with captain's bars on his collar sat staring at a document. To the left, a map of the city hung from a corkboard. Various pins had been placed on the map with notes next to each. On the right, a radio unit was set up, with another officer listening through headphones. His hand slowly turned the frequency dial like he was listening for something to come over the channels.

Elena stood on Jimmy's left, brushing his hand with the back of hers. Wyatt took position on his right. Rodriguez, weapon now on his shoulder, stood in the corner just behind Wyatt. Wallace moved in front of them.

"Sir, we have the civilians we called in." Wallace stood at attention offering a salute.

The captain glanced at Wallace and returned to his paper. It was clear they would wait until he was finished with whatever he was reading. Several agonizing minutes passed with the entire room waiting in silence for the captain to speak. Finally, he put down his paper and stood, his attention on the threesome.

"These are the uninvited visitors, Corporal?" The captain returned Wallace's salute, who finally relaxed.

"Yes, sir. Caught them traveling east up the highway. Claim they have information."

"Search 'em?"

"Yes, sir. They only carried a bag." With a twitch of his finger, he motioned to Rodriguez. Immediately, he approached the table and dumped the contents of the bag on the desk. Jimmy winced as the tablet struck the table, and he envisioned the screen shattering and their entire story becoming just as useless as the tablet.

The captain scanned the table, randomly picking up one of the spilled documents. He gave it a cursory glance before dropping it on the table. The tablet drew his attention. He touched the screen, absently swiping left and right on the screen. Without even opening any applications, he turned his attention to Jimmy.

"You the leader of this crew?"

"I-I guess. Sort of. Not really." Jimmy's mouth was dry with anxiety.

"Well, which is it. Sort of? Or not really?"

Elena elbowed Jimmy, whose voice cracked. "Y-yes, sir. I guess I'm the leader."

"Care to explain trespassing onto a military outpost?" His gaze bore into Jimmy. His face was clean shaven but appeared worn like the captain had seen more than one sleepless night. "You're fortunate my men didn't shoot you on sight."

"Told you," Wyatt said in a low tone.

"I-I'm sorry, sir." Jimmy couldn't stop stammering. "We needed to talk to someone in charge. You see, we have—"

The captain raised a hand, silencing Jimmy. He glanced at the papers and tablet again. He stopped on the satellite image for a moment, releasing a breathy chuckle. He placed the paper in his desk. With one hand, he rubbed his face as if the entire exercise exhausted him. "Listen, young man. You're not the first person to come here thinking they have some kind of important information for the army to look into. You're not even the first to show up with supposed documents proving their claim."

"But, sir—" Jimmy pointed at the tablet. "If you would just—"

"I know. I know." The captain interrupted. "If I'd only take a look at what you've brought, I'd be convinced and roll out immediately to investigate. I've heard it before. Every few months, someone comes waltzing up to our outpost claiming they have something we must see, and you know what it is…every…single…time? Hokum." The captain let the word hang in the air. "Nonsense, that's what it is. Without exception."

"Sir, the bunker mentioned in the papers is—"

"Enough!" Every spine in the tent straightened at the

captain's shout. He pointed a finger at the three of them. "Now you either made up this malarkey to con your way into a hot meal or for your own kicks…or you stumbled upon some kook's hairbrained ideas they came up with when their mind cracked from the pressure of living in a world that's ninety percent deceased."

"Sir." This time it was Elena's voice entreating the captain. "You need to look at that."

The captain's demeanor softened when he turned to Elena. "Young lady, I believe that *you believe* what you brought me. There have been plenty of rumors of hidden havens where people are surviving this plague. When I had more men, we looked into several of them. Nothing. Always nothing."

Jimmy swallowed hard as Elena retreated a step. This wasn't working. He wouldn't even look.

Their pained expressions must have been obvious because the captain released a long sigh. "Look, I'm not going to keep you. I'll send you on your way with a full stomach, but that's the best I can do. Even if I wanted to look into this, I couldn't. I lose more men each week. At first it was to the virus. Now they're deserting. My own lieutenant disappeared a year ago, and several others have followed. I wouldn't be much of a captain if I allowed my men to be demoralized by the crushing weight of disappointment after a wild goose chase."

"So you won't look?" Jimmy had to ask at least one more time.

"Son, I can't be bothered with it. We were given orders to man this station and protect this section of the power grid. That was months ago before orders stopped coming." He paused to straighten his tie. "In my day, we were taught to obey orders until new ones came down. That is the message I'm giving to my soldiers. We hold this ground and protect it until we are told otherwise." He nodded at Rodriguez. "Private?"

Without another word, Rodriguez began throwing the items into the backpack. Zipping it up, he rounded the desk and handed the bag to Jimmy. He stepped aside and returned to his corner.

The captain straightened as he faced them. "Now you three...I'll see to it you get something to eat on the condition that there be no mention of hidden bunkers or satellite images around my men. What you have there is someone's made up story, and I won't have it here. Understood?"

The three of them nodded their agreement. Jimmy's heart sank into his gut. They really weren't going to listen. He shouldered the bag.

"Corporal, take them to the mess tent and give them an MRE to eat and one for the road."

"Yes, sir."

"Dismissed."

Wallace turned to leave and motioned for the group to follow. Three tents over, the air smelled of some form of cooking, though they could not see what was being prepared. Wallace pulled out three packages labeled *Meal Ready to Eat*. He opened the heater bag, added water, and waited for it to heat up. Placing the entrée into the bag, he handed it to Elena. He repeated the process twice more for Jimmy and Wyatt.

"Give it about five minutes, and it'll be ready." He pulled three more MREs. Twirling a finger, he motioned for Jimmy to turn around. A moment later, the MREs were shoved in the backpack.

Jimmy sat down at a folding table with Elena and Wyatt. He tore open his bag a couple minutes later and sniffed the contents. "What is this?"

"Beef stroganoff. Or so the package says." Elena turned her nose up at the concoction.

"There's also bread and some kind of protein bar," Wyatt exclaimed through a mouthful. He eagerly went in for another bite. "My uncle was military. Said these tasted like armpit, but they give you all the nutrition you need. Probably the most well-rounded meal we've had in ages." He took another bite.

Jimmy tried not to breathe as he stirred the mixture in the pouch with a plastic fork and forced a bite in his mouth. He would never have described food as tasting like *armpit* before, but now he couldn't think of a better description. Across the table, Elena held her eyes closed as she shoved bite after bite in her mouth as though trying not to taste it.

"Come on," Wyatt complained. "It's not that bad."

"It's not that good, either." Jimmy had to swallow twice to avoid gagging on his last bite.

Elena's bag dropped to the table empty, and she let out a disgusted "Ick" as she ran her tongue over her teeth repeatedly. "I'm going to be tasting that for hours, aren't I?"

Wyatt laughed. "And at the speed you ate it, probably burping it, too."

"Gross."

Jimmy pointed his fork at her. "But good for you apparently."

Elena took a swig of water from her cup. A second later, she guzzled the entire cup attempting to wash away the flavor. With a gasp, she slammed the cup to the table. "What now, Jimmy? They won't even listen to us."

The bite in Jimmy's mouth soured at the thought. "I guess we go home and rethink all this."

"You mean trade that thing before it gets broken."

"Wyatt, don't start." Elena sighed. "I'm tired, and I just can't right now."

"I'm serious. You saw how he threw that thing on the table. We're lucky it didn't shatter right there, and we'd be out of the most valuable item we've scavenged yet. I say we show up in the morning when the trade floor opens and let Ruby and Big T have it. If the army doesn't want it, then neither do I."

Jimmy had to admit, the thought of being rid of the thing sounded like a relief at this point. The disappointment of the evening tore into him, and he couldn't imagine another plan that would work. The idea of going out to the Lifeboat, if it really existed, sounded preposterous after listening to the captain. He was ready to agree with Wyatt when his eye caught Elena's gaze.

"We can't, Jimmy." Elena searched his face. "We don't know if the Lifeboat is real, but someone took those pictures. Someone wrote those documents. And whoever the people in the videos were, they believed their story."

"Or made it up as a sick prank," Wyatt snickered.

"No, it's not a prank." Jimmy shook his head. "The body in the car was wearing the same clothes as the man in the video. It was Dr. Sheppard. Whether it's true or not, he at least believed it."

Wyatt leaned in to draw their attention. "You heard the captain. Stories like this are everywhere. Just because Dr. Sheppard believed it doesn't make it true. All those people might have been buying into a delusion."

"He said his family was at the Lifeboat, Wyatt," Elena pleaded her case.

"Or they're dead and believing that they were at some Lifeboat bunker was his way of dealing with his grief. The guy could be mentally broken for all we know."

Jimmy's head hurt with all the conversation. The MRE, as gross as it had been, was hitting his stomach, and he'd be tempted to take a nap at the table if he didn't move. He stood and motioned for the others to do the same. "We need to sleep on it. If we don't leave now, it'll be dark before we get back, and I'm not up for another adventure in the dangerous city."

Elena nodded and pushed her chair back from the table. Wyatt did the same.

"At least *think* about selling it, guys." Wyatt was sounding more reasonable each moment. "After that meal, just think about what we could be eating tomorrow."

Jimmy glanced at Elena who gave him a pained look. He shook his head with a slight eye roll. "We'll think about it, Wyatt. Okay?" That brought an exasperated sigh from Elena.

"That's all I'm asking. Thanks, Jimmy."

Jimmy turned to Corporal Wallace. "I think we're ready to go now. Please tell your captain thanks for the meal."

Wallace nodded and waved that they should follow him. Exiting the mess tent, Rodriguez took up position behind them as they were escorted to the outpost. Returning to the Humvees, Wallace nodded toward the road without a word. Message received. Get walking.

The three of them plodded side by side down the lonely highway, the night sky growing darker as the sun set.

Chapter Ten

Darkness fell as they reached the door to the hideout. Little had been said on the walk home, and Jimmy's mind ricocheted between the options in front of them. He'd hoped the army would have relieved him of both the tablet and the responsibility of the Lifeboats. The idea that the Lifeboats were probably a hoax gnawed at his mind. With each step, the roots of reason grew deeper in his brain. Perhaps they should trade the tablet and enjoy the spoils.

The ring felt heavy on the chain around his neck. What was the better sacrifice? Go off into the world, risking his life and the lives of his friends, to chase down a possible ghost? Or to provide more food than they'd seen in a year by surrendering the tablet to Big T?

Greater love has no one than this...

Jimmy dismissed the thought. He had to focus on survival, and the ring's message held no bearing on this decision as far as he was concerned. Locking the door behind him, he listened as Wyatt and Elena trudged up the stairs. Whatever they decided about the tablet, it was silently agreed they'd start with a good night's sleep. No more discussion tonight.

He turned to the stairwell first. With a finger, he double checked the wire that ran across the stairwell door, and then he followed the wire up the wall to the bag screwed into the ceiling. A good hit on the wire would unzip the back releasing the rocks contained inside. It was Wyatt's invention inspired by one of his favorite movies, and Jimmy thought it was more likely they'd trigger the trap themselves rather than an intruder, but he checked it nonetheless. He'd sleep better knowing it was in place.

Each step up to the apartment felt twice its normal height as the weight of disappointment pressed down on him. Arriving at the top of the stairs, he turned and bolted the door behind him. Wyatt had already retreated behind his blanket, and Jimmy could swear he was already snoring.

Elena rested her elbows on the table, sipping on a cup of water. He pulled a chair over to hers and sat down. They stared in silence for a long moment as Elena ran her finger around the lip of the cup.

"You really going to sell it, Jimmy?" Her eyes studied his, the reflection of the single candle she'd lit on the table dancing in her eyes.

"I don't know. It's not only my decision anyway. We'll make it together."

She shook her head. "It is your decision."

"Just because I found the tablet doesn't mean it doesn't belong to all of us. That's how we do things. We share them."

She reached over the corner of the table and placed her hand over his. "No, it's not. We might talk that way, but it's not what we do. You're the one who looks after us, Jimmy. I may scold you for the risks you take, but I know you take them for us. So does Wyatt."

Jimmy sat quietly. She'd never spoken to him like this before.

"You tried to do the right thing today, and it didn't work out. I wish it had, and I know you do too. But…you showed us where your heart is in all this." She paused. "Wyatt's your friend. In the end, he'll do whatever you say." Her eyes grew glassy in the candlelight. "So will I, Jimmy. I know how much you care about us."

"I do care about you. Both of you."

She squeezed his hand. "Just don't trade it away unless you're sure you can live with that. Your confidence is what keeps you alive when things don't go to plan. I'd hate to see that broken. We *need* you, Jimmy. Promise me you'll be sure before you make your decision."

He thought for a long moment and nodded. "I promise."

"Then I'll be able to live with whatever you decide. For real." Before he could react, she leaned forward and kissed his cheek. Without another word, she stood and disappeared behind her blanket. Jimmy sat there dumbfounded by the kiss.

He was confused before, but now his brain was officially mush. It was too much to process after their long day. He slunk onto his bed and lay staring at the ceiling. He could still feel the warm softness of her lips on his cheek as he slipped into unconsciousness.

A hand clapped over his mouth, jerking him out of sleep. Instinctively, he swatted at the hand until his eyes saw the silhouette of the person leaning over his bed. His eyes came into focus to see the terrified face of Elena. Her eyes were saucers as she brought a finger to her lips and offered a nearly inaudible "shh."

As he settled, her hand slowly pulled away as if ready to clamp down again should he make the slightest sound. Sitting up, he turned to her.

"What's wrong?" Even his whisper made her wince in the silence of the room.

Elena glanced back toward the doorway. "I heard something."

Jimmy turned his ear upward to see if he could make out any sounds. Nothing. He shook his head. "You sure? Maybe it was sounds coming up from the street." It wasn't uncommon to hear voices from people passing their building, up to something nefarious in the middle of the night.

Elena bit her lip and pointed to the door again. "Not outside. Down there."

Clink. Clink.

Jimmy was instantly on his feet at the sound. There was only one thing that made that noise. He'd heard it before when Wyatt had returned early from a scavenge and surprised them. It was the sound of someone trying to open the hideout door.

More silence.

Bam. Crack.

The telltale noise of something large hitting the metal door, followed by the sound of someone pushing it open to break the remainder of the compromised locking mechanism, reverberated throughout the building.

"What? Who? What?" A sleepy Wyatt shot up in his bed.

Footsteps thudded and voices muttered below. There wasn't much to search on the first floor as the real estate company had mostly used an open concept office. It wouldn't be long before they found the—

Crack.

The wooden closet door shattered under the weight of whatever battering ram the intruders were using. A second later the sudden noise of several weighted objects hitting the floor was accompanied by a scream. Cursing followed as someone hollered in pain. The rock trap.

Already, Elena was grabbing the backpack, which still contained the tablet, files, and MREs. Jimmy raced to the window, ripping the blackout paper off the surface. He stared at the drop to the street below. It was a long drop, but they had no choice.

"No, no, no, no." Wyatt was on all fours, cowering as footfalls began to make their way slowly up the stairs. The booby trap had not stopped the intruders, but they were clearly being more careful.

Grabbing a chair, Jimmy lunged at the window. He shut his eyes as glass shattered and fell to the street below. "Guys, we have to jump." Using the chair leg, he knocked out the remaining shards of glass that protruded from the frame.

"What?" Elena stared at him with wide eyes as she slipped the backpack on. "We can't do that."

"We can, and we will. There's no other choice."

The handle to the apartment rattled, and the muffled sound of someone ordering the battering ram to be brought upstairs came through the wooden surface. Wyatt still clutched the floor, frozen.

Jimmy grabbed Elena's hand and pulled her to the window. She resisted, but only partially, as if she was resigned to the inevitable. "Wyatt, get on your feet."

Elena swung her legs out the window and sat on the ledge. "I-I can't do this, Jimmy."

"Yes, you can. Just let your legs crumple as you fall to the ground. You'll get banged up, but you can soften the landing." He placed a hand on the small of her back. "I'm right behind you."

Without another word, he shoved. She screamed his name as she fell to the ground. Her knees buckled, and she collapsed forward to the street. A second later, she stood, only to fall over. A cry of pain burst from her lips, and she clutched her ankle.

Jimmy slung his own legs out of the building just as the door splintered. "Wyatt! Get over here." His friend still lay in a ball on the floor, unable to move. Men poured into the room, pouncing upon Wyatt who didn't fight back.

He swallowed hard as one of the men noticed Jimmy in the window. He took one last look at his friend, who was being forced to his feet by two intruders. He had to leave Wyatt.

He hurled himself forward.

The brief sensation of weightlessness brought his stomach to his throat. His eyes blurred into a sort of tunnel vision as he fixated on the spot of the street where he'd land. His feet struck the pavement as he dropped to the ground. Asphalt tore into his bare arms, tiny rocks imbedding themselves into his skin.

Pushing forward, he reoriented his momentum and rolled over. The back of his head scraped on the road's surface, and he flopped head over heels. His feet struck the ground in front of him and went numb for a moment. The energy of his fall waned, and he skidded to a stop. His vision cleared. Scanning around him, he saw Elena standing next to him.

For a moment, he was relieved that her ankle was better than expected. Then he noticed her feet weren't actually on the ground. They floated a couple inches in the air. Behind her were two giant leather boots. Slowly, he stood, following the large torso of the man behind Elena. At last, he turned to see the massive hand clamped over her mouth.

The face of Big T glared at Jimmy from behind Elena. Big T's tattooed arms held her off the ground. The hand over her mouth jerked away as she bit into it.

"Jimmy!" she screamed.

Big T shook his hand, looking no more hurt than if he'd been bitten by a mosquito. Reaching to his waist with his bitten hand, he grabbed a pistol and shoved it against Elena's temple.

"Now, young lady, there's no reason to be like that." He nudged the barrel a little harder against her head. "You be good now, ya hear?"

Tears streamed down Elena's face as she nodded. Jimmy slowly raised his hands in surrender. Above, he could hear the clamor of their apartment being ransacked.

"Good, kid. This could go down a lot worse than it has if you want it to. Or you can cooperate."

"What do you want?" Jimmy's voice shook with terror, and he could barely get the words out through his tightened throat.

"A little birdie told us you've got a valuable commodity to trade." Jimmy tried not to react to the idea of Big T using the word *commodity*. "Couldn't trust you to bring it in the way you left, and word came down from our boss to come ensure you saw fit to turn it in."

"You're too late, we traded it already."

"Now I hope not, kid. That would be unfortunate. Best way to stay in the good graces of boss man is to stay useful. Get my drift?"

Elena closed her eyes as if awaiting a blow. The bluff was a risk, but Jimmy couldn't simply hand the tablet over. Once they had it, there was no reason to keep them alive.

Shouts and whoops came from the corner of the building as three of the intruders rounded into the street from the alley. Leading the pack was Ruby, who held Wyatt by his hair with one hand and forced a pistol into the back of his neck with the other. She smiled, revealing what was left of her pitted teeth.

"Speaking of the little birdie, here he is now." Big T turned to Ruby, who laughed as she forced Wyatt forward.

"Got us some little rats to throw in a cage." Ruby cackled with delight. "This one didn't even put up a fight."

Without a word, the other two men bracketed Jimmy, grabbing him under his arms. Both held firearms in their free hands.

Big T turned to Ruby and Wyatt, waving the pistol in his hand for Wyatt to see. "Okay, little birdie. Sing for me."

Wyatt winced at the pull on his hair but didn't answer.

The sound of Ruby's pistol barrel hitting the back of Wyatt's head sickened Jimmy. "You heard the man, sing birdie."

"I-I don't know what you mean." That brought another strike from Ruby.

"Now Ruby, leave the boy enough sense to talk." His attention turned to Wyatt. "You made quite a fuss over something you all have."

"Yeah, said it was like something we hadn't seen in a long time. Didn't he, Big T."

"Why I believe you're right, Ms. Ruby."

Ruby smiled and smoothed her hair with her gun-wielding hand. "T, you flatter me with all the *Ms. Ruby* talk." She licked her teeth, and Jimmy thought he might vomit.

Big T paid her no attention. He simply returned to questioning Wyatt. "Now, kid, care to share the location of this item? Tell us, and maybe your little friend here doesn't have to get worse than she already is." He tapped the barrel of his pistol on Elena's forehead, eliciting a slight cry from her.

Wyatt gazed longingly at Elena for a moment. "It's a tablet."

"Wyatt, no!" Elena shouted.

"Working?" Big T asked.

"Y-yes," Wyatt admitted. "Contains information about a Lifeboat."

"A boat?" Ruby sneered.

Jimmy gritted his teeth. Wyatt was offering more information than necessary, and he found himself glad that Wyatt had not watched the videos in case he kept talking.

"N-no. Not an actual boat." He winced as Ruby yanked his hair again. "It's a bunker. People. Doctors. Supplies."

Ruby's eyes widened, and an excited smile spread from ear to ear. She sucked in a breath through her teeth as though her mouth watered for something tasty. "Hear that, T? Supplies just sitting out there."

Big T leaned closer to Wyatt. "Where is this tablet, boy?"

Wyatt hesitated.

"Answer him, runt!" Ruby shook Wyatt violently.

"Backpack," Wyatt blurted. "In the backpack."

Big T looked down at the backpack squashed between him and Elena. Dropping her to the ground, a whimper escaping her lips as her ankle tried to support her weight, he grabbed the backpack and ripped the zipper open in one motion. The red folder and dull gray of the tablet lay exposed in the moonlight.

He straightened. Pulling a cigarette from his shirt pocket, he made a grand gesture of lighting it and taking a drag. Blowing the smoke into the night air, he sighed. He glanced at Ruby who still held on to her wild smile.

"Pack 'em up."

Ruby's face morphed into confusion. "You mean we aren't gonna off them here. We got what we came for, T. Boss said get the goods and *take care* of the kids."

Big T shook his head. "There's more to this, and it's bigger than the boss. This one goes all the way up."

"You mean—?"

Big T nodded. "I mean we go see Mr. Quinn."

Chapter Eleven

The blindfold chafed the abrasion on Jimmy's scalp. The three of them had been loaded in the back of a van, which now jostled as they rattled down the roadway. Though he couldn't see the direction they were headed, he had only felt one turn. That meant they were headed north. Only one thing lay north. The dark sector.

No one spoke outside of Ruby, who seemed to find something amusing as she muttered to herself. Other than the four intruders who'd been in the street, two others had carried the still body of one of their crew to the van. The side of his face was covered in blood from a head wound, and Jimmy guessed that their rock trap had been more effective than he'd considered. The man wasn't dead, but he didn't look good. Jimmy wondered if he'd even make it to their destination.

He did his best to stabilize himself as the van lurched around a corner and rolled to a stop. The sound outside the van changed, and he guessed they'd pulled into a building. The clackety-clack of a garage door lowering confirmed his suspicion.

The van door opened and rough hands grabbed his shirt, dragging him to his feet. Nearby, Elena cried out.

"You'll have to carry that one. Messed up her pretty little ankle," Ruby said, seeming to delight in Elena's pain.

The smell of motor oil and exhaust caught his nostrils. The

floor was smooth under his feet, like concrete. The sounds of people moving and the scrape of their shoes were all around him.

Hands found his upper arms on either side, and he marched forward. A minute later, the sound changed again as they were forced into a carpeted room. With a shove, he was hurled to the floor. A thump on either side of him told him Wyatt and Elena were with him.

Behind him, the door closed, and he could hear a lock click into place.

His blindfold was ripped from his head, aggravating his wound. He rubbed his now uncovered eyes to adjust to the light in the room. Scanning, he could see the first light of day coming through tiny narrow windows high off the floor. Even if he could reach them, they were too narrow to squeeze through.

The room was lined with open lockers. In several, there hung heavy black coats lined in yellow reflective material. Above each, sat a black and yellow helmet, the words *Station 41* emblazoned across the metal badge on the front. A few lockers contained small mementos— pictures of family or girlfriends. An occasional child's drawing was hung in a locker.

He turned to Elena, who still lay curled and clutching her ankle. He slid over to her and placed his hands on her shoulders. She gazed up at him through red puffy eyes.

"You okay?" It was a dumb question.

She shook her head. He followed her arms to her leg. Gently, he urged her fingers away from her ankle. Already, dark purple patches were forming around the swollen joint. He stood and walked behind her. With two hands, he clutched her under her arms and pulled.

Elena yelped in pain as her body shifted, and despite her objections, he dragged her to the wall so she could sit up. Grabbing one of the fireman's coats, he balled it up in a wad and elevated her leg. It wasn't much, but it was the position she needed to be in.

Wyatt had crawled to the other side of the room. He sat, leaning on a locker. His head hung between his arms and rested on his knees.

"Wyatt, you all right?" Jimmy considered approaching him, but when he didn't move, he thought the better of it. Wyatt gave no answer.

Jimmy turned and sat next to Elena. He was hurting all over and sleep deprived from their rude awakening. Outside the locker room, muffled voices could be heard, and Ruby's cackle would occasionally break into the dull sounds.

"What do you think they want with us, Jimmy?" Elena's voice sounded as tired as he felt.

"I'm not sure, but Big T is no dummy. I locked that tablet with a password after we left the army outpost. When they found us, I'd hoped they'd take it and leave us. Big T must have guessed the tablet was locked. Either that, or there is something we don't yet know." He rested his head on the wooden locker behind him.

Elena slid over and rested her head on Jimmy's shoulder. Hours passed as Jimmy slipped in and out of consciousness, each awakening revealing the changing light outside the windows. How long would they be left in here? At some point, he'd wrapped his arm around Elena, and her head rested on his chest.

He rubbed his eyes. The light was getting dim again, and evening must have arrived. He glanced across the room. Wyatt was staring at him and Elena with a dark expression.

The lock on the door clicked loudly, causing Elena to jerk awake. She pulled away from Jimmy slowly, and he withdrew his arm. Elena leaned forward and rubbed gingerly at her ankle. The door burst open, and Big T entered the room. Jimmy wasn't too upset that Ruby was not on his heels.

"Mr. Quinn will see you now, kid." Big T pointed at Jimmy.

"Why just him?" Wyatt asked.

"I think I can tell who speaks for the group. Besides, I'm guessing you already gave up what you know since you couldn't stop running your mouth out on the street." Big T laughed at his own joke and turned back to Jimmy. "Up on your feet, kid."

Jimmy pushed against the locker, sliding his back upward on the wood. As he got his feet under him, his legs complained with stiffness from sitting in one position for so long. He glanced at Elena, whose lip trembled. He let out a long slow breath to calm his nerves and encourage her to do the same. As long as they wanted to talk, there was reason to believe Mr. Quinn and his crew wouldn't kill them.

He walked to the door, and Big T gestured for him to walk in front. Jimmy exited the locker room to find another man waiting, dressed in fatigues. Big T locked the room and nodded at the man to lead the way. Fatigues spun on his heels and started crossing the fire station. Various vehicles lined the room where the fire engines had once sat. On the other side of the room, a staircase hugged the wall, and they started to climb.

The upper level was only half as big as the first floor. A

kitchen lay to the left. A billiard table sat in an open lounge area, where a couple of men in fatigues played a game. Ruby sat on the edge of the table drinking something directly from a bottle of alcohol and eyeing Jimmy as they crossed the space.

The doorway on the other side opened to an office. The door said *Chief* on the outside. Big T rapped on the door three times.

"Enter," called a voice from inside.

The office was more ornate than Jimmy had expected. A large mahogany desk sat in the center with an executive style chair behind it. Bookshelves covered the walls. High, narrow windows lined the ceiling, allowing sunlight to pour into the room. On the other side, an oil painting dominated the wall with two chairs on either side facing the desk.

Behind the desk, a man stood in a black T-shirt and jeans, presumably Mr. Quinn. Glancing at Jimmy, he whispered in the ear of the man next to him, who also wore fatigues. The man nodded and exited the room quickly.

Mr. Quinn gestured to the chairs, and Jimmy sat. Big T sat in the other chair. The first fatigue-clad soldier exited the room and took position outside the door, closing it behind him.

Mr. Quinn sat in the chair and studied Jimmy, his fingers interlaced in front of him. Minutes passed in silence as the man simply stared.

"Jimmy, is it?" Mr. Quinn's voice startled Jimmy, not only because it broke the silence, but it also carried a more sophisticated tone than Jimmy expected.

Jimmy nodded.

"Big T here tells me you put up an impressive fight trying to hide your discovery." He reached over to a drawer in his desk and removed the tablet. He set it on the table in front of him. "This is quite a find."

Jimmy said nothing. Better to wait to be asked a question.

"Tell me, Jimmy. Why didn't you and your scavenger friends trade this for food? I'm sure my people would have paid handsomely for it."

"W-we were going to. Today. We were going back to the trading floor."

Mr. Quinn dropped his gaze to the desk. He offered the tiniest shake of his head before returning to stare at Jimmy. "I'm disappointed. I'd hoped that we could work together in honesty, Jimmy."

Jimmy's stomach lurched. "What do you mean?"

Mr. Quinn stood from his chair and walked to the nearest bookshelf. He ran a hand along the edge of the shelf as if checking for dust. "I believe it was Socrates that said, 'The only true wisdom is knowing you know nothing.'" He turned to Jimmy. "We know you went to the army with the tablet. My people reported your movements to me." He stopped to take in Jimmy's surprise, which he could not hide. "The fact that it never occurred to you that you may have been followed brings me back to my friend, Socrates. Jimmy, you lack wisdom. You think you know what is happening here, but you are mistaken. Welcome to The Brotherhood."

Jimmy swallowed hard. This man was not at all what he expected. The Brotherhood was rumored to be full of criminals, and Jimmy had always assumed that meant gangs and thugs. Mr. Quinn was no thug. There was order in the way his men operated.

He quoted philosophers. Jimmy even believed the books on the shelves were not for show, but that Mr. Quinn actually read them.

"I can see in your expression that I surprise you."

"I-I mean—"

Mr. Quinn smiled with a breathy laugh. "You wouldn't be the first. In some respects, I don't mind the assumption that those of us here in the dark sector are nothing more than mindless criminals that shoot first and, well…that's it." He glanced over at Big T. "I suppose you expected me to look more like him. No offense, my friend."

"None taken, boss."

"It is true that I employ a rougher element, especially at the lower levels of control. It provokes the image everyone expects. Helps people think they know who we are, which gives me the advantage. We are, after all, not uncivilized, but we can't let the people think that."

A ball of anger began to rise in Jimmy. "But you guys invaded our home. You kidnapped us at gunpoint. I think that makes you a criminal."

Mr. Quinn stared out the window. "My friend, I never said that we weren't criminals. Only that we were not mindless ones." He returned to the desk and placed a finger on the tablet. "That is why I'm going to ask you for the password to this device first before *making* you give it to me."

Jimmy fell silent again.

"As I suspected. Perhaps there is more wisdom in you than I guessed. You don't know my intentions and, therefore, won't give up the information. Good for you, Jimmy. You are learning."

A knock came at the door.

"Enter." Mr. Quinn's voice was flat as though not wanting to betray what was about to happen.

The door opened. The soldier who'd received the whispered instructions entered, followed by another, rougher-looking man. He wore torn jeans and a stained white T-shirt. Though probably in his twenties, his unkept appearance aged him at least ten years. Jimmy recognized the man as one of the individual's who'd invaded the hideout. Sweat beaded on his forehead, and he kept glancing back at the doorway.

"Come in. Remind me of your name, young man."

"B-Bill, sir. Billy Walters."

Mr. Quinn paused for a long second. He gazed at the man with unblinking eyes. "Bill, I'm pleased to make your acquaintance. It is my understanding you have been working under Big T here for a month now?"

"Y-yes, sir."

"And in that time, has Big T made it clear that mistakes are not tolerated?"

He nodded, seemingly unable to answer verbally.

"Tell me, Bill, whose job was it to breach the door to this boy's apartment." He pointed at Jimmy.

Billy glanced at Jimmy and then at Big T like he was looking for help. "It was my job. Me and Jason. We breached the doors together. I-I worked the locks, and he used the battering ram."

Mr. Quinn still had not blinked, and his penetrating stare unnerved Jimmy. "And as the one who 'worked the locks,' as you say, was it your responsibility to check for traps."

The jaw muscles on Billy's face flexed several times. "Y-yes, sir. I guess I missed one."

Mr. Quinn's eyebrows rose. "Missed one? Is that your assessment of what transpired? Mr. Walters, I'm afraid it is far more serious than that. Miscounting cans of food would qualify as 'missing one.' What you did was fail in a responsibility, which by your own admission was clearly communicated to you, and it cost me the life of a soldier who has been in my employ for more than a year."

"J-Jason is dead?"

"Passed away an hour ago. Succumbed to his head wound I'm afraid." Mr. Quinn turned to Jimmy. "Rocks in a bag? Primitive, but effective." He walked over to the desk and opened another drawer. Reaching in, he produced a pistol. His gaze returned to Bill. "Your incompetence cost me a valuable resource, and as you already know…mistakes are not tolerated."

"Wait, I can expl—"

Mr. Quinn raised the pistol and fired, causing Jimmy to jerk to one side in fear. Bill was thrown backward to the floor. Crimson blood was spattered on the wall behind him, and a pool began to form underneath his head. Without a word, the soldier in fatigues walked over to Bill's body. Grabbing him under the armpits, he dragged him through the doorway.

"Big T, please see to the clean-up of my office. I won't have that blood setting in."

"Understood, boss." Big T, appearing far too casual for what happened, rocked out of his chair and sauntered out of the room.

Mr. Quinn placed the pistol on the desk. "See, Jimmy, not

uncivilized."

Jimmy breathed deeply to contain his growing panic.

Seeing his fear, Mr. Quinn continued. "A mindless criminal would have simply shot Bill. Instead, Bill got to understand his blunder and the great cost to me. He got to die knowing why it was justified, which is far more civil than someone like him deserved. Don't you think?"

Any words that came to Jimmy's mind wouldn't translate to his lips. He'd seen people mugged or hurt for their belongings or food. It was the way of the world since the virus. To see a man killed in cold blood, with no remorse or anger or any detectable emotion, stabbed fear into the center of Jimmy's heart. Mr. Quinn was evil shrouded in the sheep's clothing of intelligence and eloquent speech.

"Now, as for the matter of this tablet." He tapped the device with a finger as he sat in his chair. "I'm impressed that you went to the trouble of password protection. It was a wise move on your part. Your compatriot confessed there may be a wealth of resources hidden in some bunker nearby and that the information is on this device. I want that information, but you wouldn't be the young man I suspect you are if you gave it up as readily as your friend."

Jimmy's eyes wouldn't leave the pistol still smoking on the desk in front of him. Any moment, he anticipated Mr. Quinn turning it on him. Seeing his gaze, Mr. Quinn slowly reached for the firearm and slid it into the desk drawer.

"There. Is that better?"

Jimmy couldn't speak if he wanted to.

"My friend…and I hope we can come to an understanding

where I may call you that…I can see that talking might be difficult for you right now. You have my compassion. In lieu of talking, hear me out for a moment." He leaned forward in his chair and casually pointed to the window. "Somewhere out there, a group of people have buried themselves under the ground with all the resources we need to survive in this new world of ours. That is, if the information on this tablet proves to be true. However, there have been enough rumors over the years of places of safety and mysterious construction projects that there must be some truth to the idea. The files that accompanied your device have me convinced. I suspect they have for you as well. Otherwise, you would not be so protective of this device."

Standing again from his chair, he rounded the table and placed his hands on Jimmy's shoulders from behind. His grip was firm but not hard. Jimmy had images of the man suddenly snapping his neck without warning. His shoulders tensed involuntarily.

"Jimmy, it's not fair to have a world where survival belongs in the hands of the few unreachable souls. Those of us left here on the outside were not given the privilege of hiding from the pandemic. No, we were left to rot with the rest of the world. What I seek here is justice. A fair distribution of resources. To take back what was taken from us and share it with the rest of the population."

Jimmy tried not to make a face at his use of the word *share*. They had different ideas about what it meant to share with others. Mr. Quinn already ran the city from his anonymous perch in the dark sector. If he got his hands on the resources in the Lifeboat, he would own the city and everyone in its borders.

Mr. Quinn bent down to whisper in Jimmy's ear. "I want to convince you that I'm not the monster that I suspect you're assuming I am. We are not a ragtag operation here. We have order. We have peace, believe it or not." He walked around the front of the chair and sat on the edge of his desk. "I am now down two men. To be fair, one was not worth much as you were able to see. Still, I could use an enterprising and intelligent young man like yourself. Give me a chance. Let me prove to you what we have going on here. I think you'll be more than happy to share the information on this tablet once you see what we're up to here."

You mean once I see you're giving me no choice.

Mr. Quinn reached forward to put a hand on Jimmy's knee. "I would much rather convince you than kill you, but I can see that might take some time to believe."

Nearly all of Jimmy's willpower was required to keep from jerking away from Mr. Quinn. While he couldn't believe that Mr. Quinn was trying to recruit him for his cause, Jimmy allowed a quiet breath of relief. The man could have taken his gun and forced the information from Jimmy, but his ego and desire to win Jimmy to his side bought he and his friends time. He would play Mr. Quinn's game for a while…at least long enough to figure out what to do. He needed to talk to Elena and Wyatt. He wondered how they were faring in their cell.

"I have a request." Jimmy forced himself to speak before he chickened out, but the quiver in his voice was unmistakable.

"If it lets me demonstrate my intentions, let me hear it." Mr. Quinn smiled.

Good. Let him assume I'm buying into his line.

"My friend needs medical attention. Her ankle is hurt and swollen. She needs pain killers and a brace, so she can walk." Jimmy attempted a stoic expression as he looked Mr. Quinn directly in the eye.

"See, we're getting along already. I'll have my men help your friend. Satisfied?"

Jimmy nodded.

"Good. Now please accept my apologies in advance. I cannot have you running around free until we've had a chance to win you over. We will have to return you to your cell. Still, we'll bring you out to show you around soon enough." He walked over to the door and opened it a few inches. Immediately, two soldiers entered ready to escort Jimmy back to the locker room.

Show me your operation all you want, Mr. Quinn. You'll simply be showing this 'enterprising young man' what my options are.

Chapter Twelve

"Jimmy!" Elena's voice was as pained as the expression on her face as she forced herself to stand despite her ankle. Wyatt stood next to her. He held his hands out tentatively like he wanted to help Elena to her feet but was too shy. The door to the locker room closed behind Jimmy, and he could hear the lock being thrown. "We heard a gunshot. We thought that something had happened to you. We thought—" Her lip quivered as her voice caught, but Jimmy could see her gathering her strength not to cry. Elena was as tough as they came. She'd not want to waste energy on tears when they needed to plan an escape.

Jimmy stepped toward her and wrapped his arms around Elena. She melted into his embrace, and he could feel her use his support to take weight off her injury.

He pulled back. "Elena, please sit down. You need to stay off that." He gripped her hands as she lowered herself back to the floor. Wyatt slid down beside her. Jimmy sat cross-legged in front of them both as they sat in a moment of silence.

"What the heck happened?" Wyatt finally asked.

Jimmy caught them up to speed on the conversation in Mr. Quinn's office, his desire to access the tablet, and the execution of Billy.

"So…he wants to recruit you?" Elena's voice betrayed her

disbelief. "Jimmy, I don't think—"

He held up his hand. "I know. It sounds weird. Somehow, he's convinced that giving me a tour of the place is going to show me that I want to be a part of what they're doing here. I plan to play along. At least it will give me a chance to see if there's a way out of here."

"Why not just give him the password to the tablet?" Wyatt asked.

"What? No!" Elena gasped.

"Why not?"

Jimmy sighed. "Wyatt, we can't give up our best bargaining chip to this man. It may be the only thing that keeps us alive. Besides, do you really want the Lifeboat and everyone inside to fall into the hands of someone who will shoot anyone who disappoints him?"

Wyatt's eyebrows lowered and he crossed his arms. "What happens when your hesitation to give him the password disappoints him? What are you going to do when the gun is to your head? Or Elena's? Or mine?"

"We can't—"

"Can't what? Survive? What do you think we've been doing for three years?"

Elena's expression turned cross. "It's not the same, Wyatt."

"Sure it is. Every day we've gotten up and made the decisions that get us to the next day. And the next day. And the next day after that. Now, we have a guy with *all* the power almost literally holding a gun to our head, and I want to make the decision that ensures we get to the next day." Wyatt turned his gaze away from them and shook his head.

Jimmy tried to remind himself that Wyatt's anger was only a mask for his fear, but he couldn't help wanting to slap his friend out of his stupidity. It was clear that cooperating with Mr. Quinn held no guarantees.

"Wyatt, the Lifeboat—"

"I don't care about the Lifeboat." The words filled the room and lingered like a house guest that didn't know when to leave at the end of the night. The three of them sat in silence. Wyatt finally ran his hand through his hair and spoke in a calmer tone. "Look, I know you guys are all concerned about rescuing the people in the Lifeboat and saving the world, but we don't even know that the Lifeboat is there." He paused. "And if it is, what does it matter?"

"It matters. We need to do the right thing."

Wyatt chewed his lip. Elena was still glaring at Wyatt in disbelief at his words. Wyatt shook his head. "Jimmy, I think we disagree on what the right thing to do is. Mr. Quinn is the one who controls everything in this section of the city. He wants something from you. Bargain for our safety. Bargain for food. Bargain for anything that will save us today and make tomorrow better."

"That's what I'm trying to do. I want to help. I am—"

"A scavenger!" Wyatt interrupted. "You're nothing more than a scavenger. None of us are. We scrape the bottom of the barrel every day just to live. What are *we* supposed to do about the Lifeboat?"

Jimmy's hand found its way to his father's ring. With a finger, he felt along the ridges of the engraved words inside the gold circle. Did they really need to do something about the Lifeboat?

Greater love has no one than this…

"We have to try."

"And *that's* where we disagree." With that, Wyatt crawled to the opposite wall and turned his back to them. Elena breathed in like she was about to speak. "Save it, Elena. We both know you'll do whatever Jimmy wants in the end."

Jimmy moved to approach him when Elena's hand found his arm. She shook her head as he turned to her. Silently, she held both hands up in a gesture that said 'wait' and tapped her wrist. He understood the meaning. Give him time.

The lock on the door clicked open, and two soldiers entered the room. One carried a medical bag in her hands. In the doorway, Mr. Quinn stood gazing at Jimmy.

"As promised," Mr. Quinn began, "medical aid for your friend. In exchange, you will accompany me to see our operation. I think you'll be surprised by what you find." He examined Elena, whose eyes were glued to Mr. Quinn. "I can see you have filled your friends in on what transpired earlier. Rest assured, young lady, that I am not so quick to take a life as it may seem. True, I do not tolerate failure, but my goal is order and peace, not chaos. That is what Jimmy is about to find out."

Mr. Quinn didn't say another word, and the message was clear. It was time to go. Jimmy slowly rose to his feet and walked toward the door. He took a glance backward at Elena, who stared at him as he left. Once reaching the door, the medical soldier approached Elena and knelt in front of her. At least she would be treated.

Jimmy's heart sank as the door was closed and latched behind him.

Jimmy stared dumbfounded at the sight in front of him. It felt so normal and so foreign at the same time. Rows of desks lined the room with children sitting at each diligently scratching out the answers to arithmetic problems. At the front of the room, a woman in a soldier's uniform was writing out the beginning of the next assignment, which would be some sort of writing exercise.

"You see, Jimmy?" Mr. Quinn whispered as he leaned into Jimmy. "We seek to create a society here. Families live among us. We provide safety and shelter and food, but we also offer life. Education for children. Work for adults. Purpose. Everything we lost when the virus destroyed the population, we are regaining here."

Something inside Jimmy twisted as he tried to make sense of it all. On one hand, he'd seen this man murder one of his own men without remorse. On the other, he had hard evidence that people lived seemingly ordinary lives. The last time he'd been at school was his sophomore year of high school when finding a date to the homecoming dance and passing a driver's license exam were the most important things. The tiny classroom resurfaced those memories, and he had to swallow hard not to choke on the ball of despair they brought with them. He'd lost so much, but somehow these kids had not. His soul ached for this kind of normalcy.

"I know it's a lot to take in. You're not the first person who I've seen overwhelmed by what used to be taken for granted. I've seen grown men fall into tears in this room." Mr. Quinn turned to Jimmy, his brow furrowed in concern. "I don't think we realize how much the pandemic took from us. Part of our humanity was lost and never regained. We forgot that we deserve to believe that tomorrow is truly coming and isn't out to ruin us. That is why this school is so important. We cannot have a generation growing up believing otherwise."

Some part of Jimmy's mind screamed that he was supposed to be searching for a way out of this predicament, but a part of his heart flooded with a desire to sit against the wall and watch these children learn for the entire day. He didn't want to admit it, but Mr. Quinn was right. A part of Jimmy was lost, and he hadn't felt it until standing in this room.

"But—but you—" Jimmy stammered, unable to fully form the words he was looking for.

Mr. Quinn waved him toward the door, and they stepped into the hallway. "I know. I shot a man in front of you, and you cannot reconcile that with what you're seeing. You have to understand that Billy was directly responsible for a valued member of our community. He failed in his job, and it led to the death of a fellow community member. In the absence of a more formal justice system, I was forced to hand out justice. The punishment was fair. A life for a life."

Jimmy gave Mr. Quinn a doubtful look.

"Okay. I can see you're not convinced. Perhaps our next stop will show you that I'm not only in the business of executing criminals."

Minutes later, they stood in the center of what could only be described as a hospital ward. The former reception hall had been divided by curtain walls to create small spaces, each containing a bed. In some, patients lay. A few were conscious and sipping a bowl of something that smelled delicious. Jimmy's stomach reminded him that it had been some time since he'd eaten. Other patients lay unconscious, fluids dripping into their veins from the IV bags hanging next to their beds.

"We have several physicians and even a head of surgery that have joined with us in our cause." Quinn motioned a hand around the room. "Most common ailments and injuries are still treatable here with the medical supplies we've procured over the years. A few conditions, sadly, are untreatable since cold storage medicines expired. Refrigeration is hard to come by since the military cut off power to our sector."

Jimmy gave him a surprised glance.

"Oh, you didn't know that?" Mr. Quinn smiled while cocking his head. "Military didn't take kindly to our desire to protect our little society here and cut off the power believing it would flush us out. Instead, they granted us the mystique to keep the rest of the city from thinking twice about entering our zone. We still protect our borders, but the fear of this place does most of the heavy lifting now."

Jimmy walked over to the nearest bed where a boy of about eight sat sipping on a bowl of what appeared to be steaming soup. The boy lowered the bowl and gazed up at Jimmy shyly.

"What's your name?" Jimmy asked.

The boy shot a glance at Mr. Quinn, who gave the slightest nod. "Ryan."

"Ryan. My name is Jimmy. Why are you in here?"

Again, a look at Mr. Quinn. "I fell. Bumped my head. Nurse

says I have a kin-cussing."

"You mean concussion, Ryan." Mr. Quinn's voice was soft as he corrected the boy's pronunciation.

Jimmy smiled at the kid. "Do you like it here?"

The boy's eyes grew wide as saucers and again looked to Mr. Quinn for license to answer. "Y-yes. Very much. I go to school, and my mom works for the guard."

"What's the guard?"

"The guard"—Mr. Quinn stepped forward and placed a hand on Ryan's shoulder—"is our next stop. I think we've tired out young Ryan enough for today."

Jimmy stood from the bed and gazed at Ryan. "It was good to meet you, Ryan. I hope you feel better soon."

"Goodbye, Jimmy." The boy resumed sipping his soup.

Mr. Quinn placed a hand on Jimmy's back and began ushering him to the door. "I promised I would show you everything, and I'm a man of my word. The guard is our protective force, and I think you'll be impressed by them."

As they exited, Jimmy turned back to glance at Ryan. The boy sat with his bowl of soup in his lap. He stared at Jimmy, a haunting darkness washing over his face.

Chapter Thirteen

The next several minutes involved stopping at various checkpoints as soldiers in urban camouflage saluted Mr. Quinn and waved him through. As they neared the guard training facility, a large warehouse with a shield painted over the door, an increasing number of soldiers bustled here and there going about their business. Occasionally, a radio would squawk, and several soldiers would pile in a vehicle and take off. Jimmy recalled the vehicle full of soldiers that confronted the two thugs in the park that chased him into the dark sector.

Inside, the warehouse buzzed with activity. Stations were set up around the room, training soldiers in various disciplines. In one, a female soldier with her hair in a tight bun yelled at a rotund, middle-aged man attempting unsuccessfully to climb a rope that stretched to the ceiling. Nearby, several soldiers sat at tables, cleaning and practicing the assembly of their firearms. Still another held a weight area where several beefy guys were bragging about how much they could deadlift.

Most of the activity was in the center of the room. A crowd had gathered and was shouting to the middle of the group. Upon closer inspection, Jimmy could make out two people sparring. On the left, a twenty-something man in camo pants and white T-shirt sported a cocky grin as he circled the ring. His opponent was a black woman, who appeared in her upper twenties, wearing a tank top. Her braided hair was twisted into a tight bun. Toned muscle defined her upper arms. Her expression was dead serious, and she held her hands at the ready as the man bounced around her on the balls of his feet. Various jokes about her size and gender poured forth from his mouth as he repeatedly pretended to lunge forward, producing laughter from several around the ring. Still, the woman remained on her guard.

When one of the jokes fell flat with the crowd, the man cocked his fists and made his move. He leapt forward with a ridiculously telegraphed punch. The woman, stoic and robotic, stepped to the side. Her fist connected with the man's jaw as he passed harmlessly by her. Instantly, the man's knees wobbled. He sidestepped several times attempting to maintain his feet before falling to the ground. Cheers and laughter rose from the crowd as they teased the man for losing in a one-punch match.

"Okay. That's enough," the woman shouted to the crowd. "Get him to the infirmary and checked out."

The crowd began to disperse to the stations around the room. Two soldiers lifted the woozy man from the ground and half-dragged him out the door toward the hospital ward Jimmy and Mr. Quinn had just left. Grabbing a towel, the woman patted sweat off her neck when she noticed the two of them.

"Nedra, it's good to see you still have a way with new recruits." Mr. Quinn smiled broadly as he approached the woman. She saluted, which he half-heartedly returned. "You didn't want to let the man believe he had more of a chance before putting him on his backside?"

"For some I might, but his kind need to be taken down a notch." She nodded at Jimmy. "Who's this? A new cadet for me to train? Care to step in the ring?"

Jimmy's insides turned at the thought of stepping inside a sparring ring with Nedra. Was that why they were here?

Mr. Quinn slapped Jimmy on the shoulder. "Perhaps, though I imagine Jimmy here has more uses than to patrol the border…not that he wouldn't make a fine addition to your crew."

Jimmy wasn't sure what to do with this jovial version of Mr. Quinn. He seemed energized by the activity in the room and especially vibrant around Nedra. He didn't detect any romantic intentions or flirtatious gestures. Mr. Quinn simply appeared genuinely excited by Nedra's presence. It was as if every space in the dark sector brought out a different Quinn. The school produced a soft, almost paternal version. The hospital was the somber Mr. Quinn. Here, he was more outspoken and uninhibited.

Nedra appeared impressed. "A personal tour with the boss? Not everyone gets that privilege. You must have brought something important to the table to earn that level of access."

Jimmy wasn't sure how to respond. The news of the tablet had apparently not made it through the ranks. "My friends and I are scavengers."

Nedra cocked an eyebrow. "Scavengers? Then, I must have been more accurate than I knew. You really must have *brought* something special."

"Let's just say, Nedra," Mr. Quinn began, "that Jimmy has brought potential information that could revolutionize what we are trying to do here in The Brotherhood."

Brotherhood? It was the second time that Jimmy had heard Mr. Quinn use the name. The mysterious name that was only heard in whispers and rumors on the streets felt strange to be discussed as a real entity. It filled him both with a sense of belonging combined with the creepiness of a cult. He still wasn't sure which he'd found himself in. He reminded himself again that this man had shot someone right in front of him earlier that same day.

"So, Jimmy, what do you think of the boss' operation?" Nedra turned to drape her sweaty towel over the back of a chair. "Bit different than out there in the world you scavenge, huh?"

"It's not"—he paused to consider his wording—"what I expected."

Nedra laughed, a bright pleasant laugh like a good friend had told her a joke. A half beat later, Mr. Quinn joined in with his own forced chuckle. Nedra's laugh settled into a sigh. "It's a good thing it's not what you expected. I'd hate to think we all lived in some scary, lawless part of the city. Though I guess the rumors of the *dark sector* have their merits."

Mr. Quinn spoke breathlessly as though he felt the words needed to get out quickly. "Jimmy, what Nedra means is the rumors serve as a protection. If people are scared to come here, then there is less chance that our community will be disrupted. We are peacemakers. Yes, that sometimes means we have to take a life to maintain order, but I intend to bring order to this city which has lost its way."

"It's still pretty crazy out there," Jimmy admitted.

"Yes, it is." Mr. Quinn sighed and crossed his hands in front of him. "The Brotherhood is not yet ready to take what we've built here to the rest of the city. There is simply not enough to go around. The information you have brought me, though, may just change that."

Nedra cocked an eyebrow. "I'm intrigued by this mysterious intel."

Mr. Quinn leaned in, placing his hands on the shoulders of Jimmy and Nedra. "Jimmy has brought us information about a potential hidden cache of resources."

Nedra pulled away, a shocked expression on her face. "That could change everything." She glanced at Jimmy and back at Mr. Quinn.

"Indeed, it could. If it contains what I think it does, then we will have enough to expand the influence of the Brotherhood over the entire city." Mr. Quinn stared off across the room as if playing a scene in his mind's eye. "We could oust chaos and bring order. Our city could become a shining beacon in this dark world of survivors. Humanity could begin living again, not just surviving."

"There he goes again." Nedra laughed. "Dreaming of creating a new world. As for me, I signed up to protect people the one way I know how."

Jimmy gave her a wry smile. "By knocking them flat in a ring?"

"Very funny." Nedra turned to Mr. Quinn. "I like this one, boss." She waved a hand around the room. "Jimmy, well trained soldiers are disciplined soldiers. Discipline will lead to fewer mistakes, and that to fewer deaths. It's one of the many lessons I learned at the academy."

"You were military?"

"Yes, sir." She saluted. "Lieutenant Nedra Davis at your service."

Jimmy recalled the Lieutenant that had left their post by the power station. Could Nedra be the same one? He gave her an inquisitive look.

"I know," she said while nodding. She let out a long sigh and placed her hands on her hips. "Deserter isn't exactly a flattering term, but it applies. Jimmy, I signed up for the military to help people. I went to the academy and became an officer to be certain I had the influence to ensure that others did the same."

"Then why are you here instead of a military post?"

"Because, my young friend," Mr. Quinn interrupted, "Nedra has seen the incompetence of the military to prevent the descending chaos. They are far more concerned with obeying orders from a now unresponsive Washington than adapting to the changing needs of our world."

Nedra offered a half-hearted smile. "That's right."

A soldier approached with a clipboard. Mr. Quinn held up a finger to Jimmy. "One moment, son. I need to address this. Nedra, if you would—" He motioned for her to stay with Jimmy. Stepping aside, he turned his back, pulling the soldier away from them to talk privately.

Jimmy started as Nedra's hand was suddenly on him. Her grip was like a vice as she yanked him in a circle to place him between her and Mr. Quinn in the distance. Her eyes bore into him with a glare that could halt a wild animal. When she spoke, it was in a raspy whisper with a note of desperation.

"Jimmy, listen to me. You cannot, under any circumstances, give that intel to Mr. Quinn."

Chapter Fourteen

Jimmy sat motionless in Mr. Quinn's office. The blood from Bill's execution had been thoroughly cleaned, and the smell of disinfectant hung in the air. The moment with Nedra had been quick, enough only for her single plea, but it had his stomach in a knot. The school. The hospital. The order. It all made the Brotherhood seem so benevolent.

Nedra's glare still burned in his memory. Her confidence and laughter had melted away faster than a spilled ice cream cone on a hot summer day. Genuine fear had washed over her. Who Nedra was and why she was here was a mystery, but there was clearly a hidden underbelly to this operation. He rehearsed her words in his mind again.

You cannot, under any circumstances…

"Jimmy, are you still with me?" Mr. Quinn asked.

Jimmy snapped to attention. Mr. Quinn sat at his desk, reclining in his oversized executive chair. His hands were folded neatly across his middle, and he gazed at Jimmy as though expecting an answer.

"Excuse me? What?" Jimmy shook his head in confusion.

"I asked what you thought of our little tour of the Brotherhood. Impressive, huh?"

"It was something. You got that right." Jimmy silently chided himself for not playing the part better.

Mr. Quinn leaned forward, placing his hands on his desk. "Jimmy, you know how the virus began, right?"

He nodded. "They were trying to protect crops. Instead, they got a virus."

"That's right." Mr. Quinn jabbed a finger at the air. "Scientists, for the good of humankind, modified plants to protect them from a pest. For a time, they were successful. Food was grown in abundance. A great surge of prosperity was about to wash over the world. That is until—" He paused, waiting for Jimmy to fill in the blanks.

"Until the aphids mutated?"

"Right again. You've studied up. I'm guessing this has something to do with it." He tapped on the tablet with a finger. "The pest got stronger, so the plants got stronger, and the virus was born. Within months, most of the world was dead or dying. Do you know what I did before the pandemic?"

"Militia leader?"

Mr. Quinn laughed as though genuinely amused. "That's humorous. You might think that, but no. I was actually a professor of mathematics. Statistics were my specialty. I loved it because it is how the world works. Probabilities reveal predictabilities. That was the problem with the new crops. Too much defensive thinking, which created the very predictable response of the aphid mutation. It's like when nations are at war. One nation, to protect itself, will make bigger and better guns under the delusion that it will end the conflict. Instead, and very unsurprisingly, the other nation will get even greater weapons. Eventually, the conflict will escalate until one side sacrifices the accuracy of directed weapons for those that simply create mass devastation, like a nuclear missile."

Mr. Quinn was nearly bouncing in his chair explaining his theory. "The process is always the same. It can be forecast with almost unquestionable certainty as it all breaks down into numbers and percentages. In essence, the virus the plants created was their 'nuclear missile,' a weapon so generalized that it not only took out the aphids but also destroyed all life within its radius. Instead of helping the plants develop bigger guns, so to speak, they should have figured out a way to remove the aphids all together. No enemy. No escalation. No virus."

Jimmy stared at Mr. Quinn. Where was he going with this?

"I know you have not liked all that you've seen since being here. But I hope that seeing the good we are doing has left you more open-minded to consider what I'm telling you. I am seeking to do what the scientists didn't."

"You want to kill aphids?"

Mr. Quinn let out a single breathy chuckle as he glanced down at his desk momentarily. "In a manner of speaking, yes. A war is coming. Make no mistake. Resources are dwindling. People are becoming desperate. Bigger 'guns' will be developed. We will destroy ourselves as a species unless we can change the formula."

Jimmy couldn't help but be a little intrigued. "And how do we do that?"

"Instead of circling the wagons and protecting what little we have, we go on offense. We take control of all the resources. We remove the enemy of individuality and so remove the conflict all together. Do you know what that will leave us with?"

Starving people? Jimmy didn't dare suggest what he was thinking. He opted for silence instead.

"Order. Pure, unadulterated order. With order comes predictability. With predictability comes a peace that can be measured, maintained, and structured." He laid his hand on the tablet and gazed at it like it was sacred. "That is why I need the information on this tablet. A flood of resources such as this tablet promises will allow the vision of the Brotherhood to come to fruition. Our city can have peace and provision again without the pest of individuality to threaten it."

Without freedom and choice, you mean.

Jimmy's insides tangled into a knot of confusion. Despite the craziness of it, some of what Mr. Quinn said rang true. He'd lived on the streets long enough to know that things were not getting better. Criminals were getting bolder and more violent. Living as a scavenger had an expiration date. Eventually, he'd need to compromise his morals to survive. Order and peace and a full stomach sounded tempting.

Still, Bill's now invisible bloodstain loomed heavy in the room. The acrid fumes of cleaner burned his nose, reminding Jimmy of the kind of man that would take control of it all if he had the choice. Not to mention Nedra's warning.

You cannot…

"I-I need to think about it."

"I'd expect nothing more from a young man as bright as yourself."

Chapter Fifteen

The door to the locker room closed and latched again behind Jimmy. Before he could react, he found himself smothered in Elena's arms, who squeezed the breath out of him. Wyatt slowly stood to his feet in the corner.

"Where have you been? It's been hours." Elena pulled away and searched Jimmy's eyes.

"Mr. Quinn has been giving me the grand tour of the place. There's a lot to share. But first, how are you standing?" He examined Elena's leg. A snug wrapping had been placed around her ankle and halfway up her calf over which a black brace gave her ankle the support it needed.

"Well, they know their first aid. I'll give them that." She lifted her foot and gingerly flexed her ankle a couple times. "It's been nice to move around again."

Jimmy turned his attention to Wyatt, who still remained in the corner with his hands in his pockets. "You okay?"

Wyatt's face flushed red. "Look, I'm sorry, bro. I shouldn't have blown up at you guys like that."

Jimmy nodded. "I get it. We're under a lot of pressure here. Now when we get out of here—"

"Jimmy, stop. I said I'm sorry for blowing up, but that doesn't mean I've changed my mind. I'm tired of surviving. If that means joining up…"

"Okay, before you go down that road, I need to tell you what's happened." The three of them sat on the floor in a tight circle as Jimmy quietly relayed Mr. Quinn's tour to them—the school, the hospital, the training center, and Mr. Quinn's 'probabilities' lecture. "The guy is clearly crazy. Even Nedra must see it. We need to get out of here."

"Why?" Wyatt asked. Jimmy and Elena gave him quizzical looks. "I get it. He shot a guy, but he did it because the guy put others in danger. He wants to help people, and I don't know if you've been paying attention, but the world could use a little order. Even if it means sacrificing a little freedom. And it's not like it's the first person we've seen killed since the pandemic."

"But what Nedra said—" Elena started.

"—is nothing more than a few words from an army deserter we know nothing about," Wyatt finished. "We at least know what this Mr. Quinn is about. We trade the password on the tablet for positions in The Brotherhood, and we're set for life. We can bargain for what we want. And how do we know he won't help everyone, including those in the Lifeboat?"

"So you're back to assuming the Lifeboat is real?" Jimmy asked.

Wyatt bit his lip. "I know what I said earlier. Truth is, I could hear bits and pieces of those videos you watched, even from the other room. People wouldn't do what those people on the tablet did for something that isn't real. The point is, I think we give Mr. Quinn what he wants."

Jimmy rolled the ring around his neck in his fingers. "So, we try to escape and save everyone. Or we stay and save ourselves."

Wyatt huffed. "No. We stay and save everyone I care about instead of a bunch of strangers. They're fine in their Lifeboat. I don't need to trade my chance, so they can come out early. That's how I see it." Wyatt stood and pounded on the door to the locker room. "Hey, go tell Mr. Quinn that he's got a new recruit. I want to join up."

"Wyatt, you can't!" Elena scrambled to her feet.

"I can. I am. And I hope you guys come with me." He stared at the floor. "I care about you, Elena. You may not see it, but I'm doing this for you."

The door opened a minute later. Mr. Quinn stood outside with two guards. He frowned when he saw it was Wyatt at the door but quickly switched to a smile. "So, you want to join The Brotherhood?"

Wyatt nodded. "I've heard enough about this place to know I want a part of it. I'm tired of surviving and scraping by."

"That is wise, my young friend. What about your compatriots? Is my friend Jimmy in agreement?" His eyes found Jimmy and stared.

Elena turned to Jimmy. Her eyes searched his face. The meaning was clear. *Go with Wyatt.*

Jimmy turned to Mr. Quinn. "Still undecided, but I can at least start the process. I'd like to check out the guard a little more."

Mr. Quinn smiled from ear to ear. "I predicted your sensibilities would help you see the wisdom in joining us, though your choice of the guard is unexpected. While I am eager for you to divulge the knowledge of the tablet, anyone is eligible to seek membership in the Brotherhood. Perhaps by participating you will be more open to sharing. Very well, the guard it is—for both of you. If anyone can convince you of the worthiness of our cause, it's Nedra. She's as loyal as they come."

Are you sure about that?

"What about me?" Elena asked. "I don't exactly want to be locked in here by myself."

Mr. Quinn nodded. "No, that wouldn't do. You cannot train for the guard in your condition, but let it be considered a gesture of my goodwill to allow you to accompany your friends to the training center. I want them to see that I am for you, not against you."

Minutes later, the three of them found themselves in the guard training warehouse. Jimmy watched as his friends gaped at the operation, taking in the various stations still busy with activity. Nedra approached the three of them, nodding to their escort that they were dismissed.

"Nedra, this is Elena and Wyatt. They are my friends."

Nedra nodded to each of them in turn. She breathed in to speak.

"Before you say anything," Jimmy interjected, "you should know that Wyatt is sold on Mr. Quinn's cause. He is *all in*. Elena and I are still figuring out where we stand."

Nedra forced a smile on her face. "Sounds good. Wyatt, glad to have you with us. Let's see if we can't convince your friends to stop hesitating." She shook Wyatt's hand. "Let's get you guys suited up. Those street clothes will not do to train in." She offered

Jimmy a knowing glance.

She ushered them to a corner of the room. Uniforms hung on racks around the station with two changing tents set up nearby. Each of them selected a T-shirt and camo pants in their size. Elena retreated into the far tent to change. Jimmy and Wyatt entered the closest one.

"And you thought that Nedra lady was trying to warn you." Wyatt smirked as he worked the T-shirt over his arms. "Seems loyal to Mr. Quinn to me. You know what I think?"

Jimmy buckled the pants around his waist. "What do you think?"

"I think that was a warning not to *give* Mr. Quinn the information. She thinks like I do. You should bargain with it. Don't give it away."

"Yeah, maybe." Jimmy inwardly breathed a sigh of relief. He couldn't have Wyatt blowing Nedra's cover, whatever she was covering for, and it would work in his favor if Wyatt believed his own words. "You're probably right. Seems a little unlikely that she'd be warning me away. It's not like she knows me. Guess I just wanted to believe what I wanted to believe."

Wyatt walked over, appearing too comfortable in his new clothes. He patted Jimmy on the shoulder. "That kind of thinking will get you killed, my friend. We're survivors, and this"—he tugged at the shoulder of his T-shirt—"is a no-brainer survival move." He exited the tent.

Jimmy took a long breath before throwing the flap of the tent aside and stepping out onto the warehouse floor. Standing outside the other tent, Elena stood with one arm across her body grasping her opposite elbow. She scanned the floor as if searching for her place in all of this.

"So, where you guys starting?" Wyatt bounced on the balls of his feet. He appeared ready to take off running in his excitement.

"I-I think I'll go to—" Elena hesitated and glanced at Jimmy. "I don't know. Maybe first aid training. I should learn to change this dressing at least." She pointed to her ankle.

Jimmy caught her gaze. *Don't leave me.* "I'll go with her." He turned back to Wyatt who watched them with pursed lips. "And you?"

"Headed straight for the main stage. The sparring ring." Wyatt's lips spread into a smile. "Sure you don't want to come see me beat up on the competition, Elena?" He waggled his eyebrows at her.

Elena returned his gesture with a dark expression. "I don't think so."

Hurt washed over Wyatt's face at Elena's rejection. "Fine. Go have fun playing with Band-aids. I'm here to make my mark." Shoving his hands in his pockets, he turned and stomped off toward the center of the warehouse.

"What was that about?" Elena asked.

Jimmy placed a hand on her shoulder. "He's got a thing for you, Elena. He always has. Guess he'd hoped to impress you by joining up."

"I don't know how he can't see how insane this place is. It's like he's brainwashed."

Jimmy thought about their conversation in the tent. "I guess he wants to believe what he wants to believe." He sighed.

Elena's hand was suddenly resting on his shoulder. Heat washed over his face, and he had to resist the instinct to pull away in embarrassment. Her fingers of her other hand wrapped around his. "Jimmy, I don't want to be here, but if I am going to have to be, I'm glad you're here too." Without warning, she turned and wrapped her arms around his neck. He hesitated a moment before allowing his arms to tighten around her middle. It wasn't the 'I'm glad you're okay' type of hug that he'd received so many times before. She held him close with a tenderness that made his heart skip a beat.

For years, the two of them had been close friends with an unspoken agreement that they could never—should never—be anything more. Survival meant setting that aside, especially with Wyatt's growing interest. Hints of feelings had been there, but Jimmy had been too scared to make a move. Now she had. Perhaps it was the uncertainty of being captured by The Brotherhood, or maybe it was because Wyatt seemed to be drifting into loyalty with them. Perhaps their group of three was becoming two, and she felt more freedom to act on what had been there for a long time.

A flood of relief washed over his soul. He couldn't help it. Elena was special to him, more than any other human being on the planet. He'd dared to hope that she felt the same way, but it had not been hard to talk himself into believing he was deluded. Her embrace confirmed all he hoped.

Still, the relief quickly gave way to dread as he stared over her shoulder and found Wyatt halfway across the warehouse. He'd stopped and turned back to look at them. Even from this distance, Jimmy could see the anger washing over his features. As far as

Jimmy knew, Elena had never given Wyatt any reason to believe she returned his affections, but there was no other way to describe what Wyatt's glare communicated…betrayal.

A week passed, and they hadn't spoken of it. Wyatt had kept to himself, quickly making friends among the other guard members. The days had been busy with physical training, weapon maintenance, and for Wyatt, of course, sparring. The three of them still remained imprisoned in the locker room at night, but exhaustion was the convenient excuse to keep the conversation to a minimum. Wyatt had protested being locked up the first night, but promises that accommodations would improve when he was fully initiated had quelled his distaste…that and the meals Wyatt had been invited to with fellow guardsmen. He'd returned to the locker room full each evening, while Jimmy and Elena had been given only leftover scraps. Whether Wyatt was more offended at being locked up or being in the same room as Jimmy was unclear.

Jimmy sat in a chair in the training room with his hand extended outward. Elena practiced wrapping his wrist in a bandage, following the instruction of a middle-aged woman who'd served as a nurse before the pandemic. Elena occasionally glanced up and met his eyes. He flashed her a smile each time, but he had no idea what to say. They'd shared a moment, but now it was awkward. They were so in the habit of being nothing more than friends that it felt weird to entertain something more.

Not to mention the image of Wyatt's seething anger burned into his memory.

A roar from the sparring ring caught their attention. The awkward tension broke as they both looked to see what the commotion was.

"You think that was Wyatt?" Elena raised her eyebrows in concern.

"He's a scrapper. More than one bully tried to push him around in middle school only to find out he was more trouble than he was worth."

As they turned back to their task, their glances caught. Each of them offered the other an embarrassed smile. Jimmy placed his hand on hers, stopping her task.

She sat back in her chair, releasing the bandage and slipping her hand from his. "Jimmy, I—" She paused. "I'm sorry. I shouldn't have done that the other day."

"Why not?" Now that the conversation was open, it was not the approach he'd expected.

"Because we can't get confused. It's not time for any of that. We need to get out of here. We need to convince Wyatt not to join these people. Lifeboat or not, we can't stay…and that's what we need to focus on right now."

Somewhere inside, his heart shattered. Whether out of wisdom or fear, she was pulling away. He wanted to reach out to her…to recreate the moment they'd shared. He resisted, knowing it would be artificial. She wasn't wrong to focus on their escape plan, but to hit the brakes so hard felt like a denial of what they both now knew existed.

"Elena," he whispered.

She held up a hand, stopping his words. "Whatever you want

to say, I think it's best not to. I care about you Jimmy, but I'm not going there."

Another roar from the crowd at the sparring ring. Whatever was happening had the guard riveted. Elena returned to the bandage on his wrist, though she moved with less gentleness, rushing through the motions. Several minutes passed without a word between them.

"Jimmy?" He turned to find Nedra staring at the two of them. She nodded to the bandage. "Hope that's just for practice."

Jimmy ran his hand over the wrist bandage. "Oh yeah. This is nothing. I'm not injured."

"Good to hear it. You're going to want to be at full strength."

"Why is that?" Elena straightened again in her chair.

"Jimmy here has just been challenged."

Jimmy raised his eyebrows. "Challenged?"

Nedra bit her lip like she didn't want to share the news. "Yep. In the ring. And one of the unspoken rules in the guard is that you don't refuse a challenge."

"But who would—"

"He didn't." Elena closed her eyes.

"Who?" Jimmy searched her face and then Nedra's. It felt like they knew a secret that he was not in on.

Nedra sighed. "Jimmy, you've been challenged by your friend, Wyatt."

Chapter Sixteen

Jimmy anxiously unwrapped the wrist bandage as they walked across the warehouse behind Nedra. Elena offered nervous glances but didn't say a word. Why had Wyatt challenged him to a fight in the ring? While the answer seemed obvious, he hoped Wyatt had another motive. He secretly wished that Wyatt intended to use this as cover for their escape somehow.

But he knew the truth.

The crowds around the ring parted as Nedra waved her arms to the sides. In the center of the circle, Wyatt stood fixing the athletic tape on his knuckles. A sweat ring covered the collar of his t-shirt, and his hair stuck to the sides of his head. A single spot of blood could be seen on the front of his shirt. Guardsmen occasionally patted Wyatt on the shoulder, and it was clear he was making a name for himself in the ring.

Jimmy gathered himself to prevent his stomach from flipping in anxiety. The last thing he needed was to lose what little he'd eaten for breakfast in front of everyone. Most people didn't know how to fight. The ex-military members in the guard surely had training, but the average person off the street had little idea how to properly fight another person. Unless they'd had experience in a fist fight, most people would swing wildly and telegraph their moves.

Jimmy had been in his share of scrapes over the years, and Wyatt had been a part of them. They'd looked after one another in school, and more than one bully had discovered that messing with one of them meant messing with both.

Jimmy could throw a punch. So could Wyatt. Jimmy knew full well that Wyatt was far tougher than he appeared when pressed to the wall. He was docile until cornered, and then he was like a wounded animal…vicious and desperate. Knowing that only added to Jimmy's apprehension of fighting his friend.

A guard approached Jimmy with a roll of tape. As if he'd done it a hundred times before, he began taping Jimmy's knuckles like he was prepping a boxer for a prize fight. A couple of minutes later, the guard grabbed Jimmy's hands in his to give the taping one final inspection.

Elena grabbed his arm. "You don't have to do this, Jimmy."

"Yes, he does." Wyatt's voice, after a week of barely speaking to them, startled Jimmy. "We're members of the guard, and we don't walk away from a challenge." A murmur of agreement spread through the crowd.

"We're not part of the guard. Not yet. We haven't officially joined."

"Yet you train and learn among them?" Wyatt allowed the question to hang in the ring. Nods came from around the circle of guardsmen. His days in the ring had won more respect than Jimmy had anticipated. The crowd was fully behind him. "Elena, you're about to see why I'm right in joining The Brotherhood…and why you should join me." He rolled his shoulders and shook his arms, loosening himself up for the fight.

Jimmy swallowed hard. He couldn't back down. If the guard became convinced that he had no intention of joining The Brotherhood, their relative freedom to train among them would be taken away along with their ability to study the compound for an escape. He hated to think what Mr. Quinn would do if he concluded that Jimmy couldn't be won over. He had to play the part.

Flexing his taped fingers, he reminded himself to keep his thumbs tightly tucked and not to strike too hard on a bone. Hitting the wrong target could easily end with a broken hand.

Wyatt paced on the other side of the ring, eyeing Jimmy and psyching himself up for the fight. Jimmy stood at his full height. He had a couple inches on Wyatt and wanted to at least remind him of that. He brought his hands up to a guard position.

Nedra stepped in between them. "Okay, fellas. I want to remind you that this is a sparring ring, not a boxing match. We're here to train and better our abilities, not to kill each other."

Fat chance. Wyatt appeared eager to get things going.

"Go!" Nedra waved an arm announcing the start of the match.

Wyatt stopped bouncing and calmly stepped toward Jimmy. Several days of non-stop sparring had made him far too comfortable in the ring. He circled Jimmy, who stepped to match the movement. Jimmy kept an eye on Wyatt's footwork, trying to anticipate his move. Their circle grew tighter. Then, light flashed without warning in Jimmy's vision as Wyatt's jab found his lip. He tasted blood. Wiping his mouth with the back of his hand, he could see a red streak on the white tape as he pulled his hand away.

"Feel better?" Jimmy asked, hopeful that maybe that was all it would take to calm Wyatt's anger.

"Hardly." Another jab, this one short of the mark. "Been picked on all my life, or have you forgotten?"

"I haven't." Jimmy thrust his fist in Wyatt's direction. He ducked, and the blow met only air. They continued to circle.

"Good. Never expected the latest to come from my friend."

Jimmy side-stepped to dodge another testing jab. "How's that?"

Wyatt stopped and took a step back. "Really? You don't know? My parents always reminded me that I didn't measure up. Teachers always felt the need to make me feel stupid. And you…here we are surviving in this hellish world, and you have to establish yourself as the leader of our group. Everything's on *your* terms." Wyatt held his hands out motioning to the crowd around the ring. "I finally belong somewhere, Jimmy. You could, too, but it threatens your control. Because you are too scared to not be in charge, Elena sits on the sideline following your lead. Well…no more."

Wyatt launched himself at Jimmy. The move was not unexpected, but the ferocity was more than Jimmy had anticipated. Wyatt's fist found Jimmy's stomach, expelling all the air from his lungs. Jimmy gasped, trying to regain his breath. He doubled over and stumbled backward. A second later, Wyatt's other fist found Jimmy's cheek. The world spun, and Jimmy felt his breakfast start to rise. He forced himself to straighten and put up his hands in defense.

Seeing Wyatt's face, Jimmy stepped forward and threw a woozy punch. Too slow. Wyatt knocked the blow aside. Another blow to the jaw, and Jimmy's legs buckled. The concrete bruised both knees as they hit the floor. Jimmy began to tip forward, but Wyatt caught his shirt in one fist. His vision blurred, but he could see Wyatt turn to Elena.

"See this, Elena? Think he can protect you? Think he's got the right plan?" Wyatt shook Jimmy violently. "He'd have you do whatever he wants. Here, *I* can take care of you. Here *I* am learning to be strong. Here, *I* can keep you safe."

Jimmy blinked hard a couple times to clear his sight. Elena had tears streaming down her face. Her watery eyes were wide with shock, and she stared at Wyatt like she didn't recognize him. Whatever reaction from her Wyatt was expecting, this was apparently not it.

"No. You can't still want to be with him." Wyatt's voice tipped into desperation. "I'm the one you should want, not this weakling." Wyatt pulled Jimmy in closer and leaned over to whisper in his ear. "You can't protect her like I can. Not anymore."

Wyatt reared back his fist. Elena screamed. Nearby, Nedra protested that the match was won. Jimmy's vision flashed as Wyatt's fist found his jaw. Then, the world went black.

Jimmy's eyes fluttered open. The smell of antiseptic and starched sheets filled his nose. Late-day sunlight poured in horizontally through the windows casting bright squares of light on the opposite wall. He opened his mouth to speak, and that's when the pain hit. He could feel the puffy swollenness of his face with each movement of his jaw. His lip was cracked, and he swore a tooth was slightly loose—and the headache…it was brutal.

He'd lost the match. No, he hadn't lost. He been beaten soundly without landing a single punch. Strangely, he wasn't mad about that. Hitting his friend didn't sit right with him, and he found himself glad that he wouldn't have to live with striking Wyatt.

He groaned. A nurse nearby turned to him and stepped quietly in his direction.

"Look who's come to," she said with a soft smile. "I've been telling Nedra that she's pushing the limits of what she allows in that accursed sparring ring, but this is going too far."

"Elena?" It hurt too much to speak, and he could only get the name past his lips before grimacing, which only produced more pain.

"Is that the young lady who came to visit you?" She furrowed her brow in concern. "Yes, she was here, but only for a bit. Guards took her away. Something about 'train or be locked up.' She spat at one of them, and they hauled her off."

Jimmy imagined Elena being locked alone in the locker room. He hoped that was all that was happening. The urge to stand and find her forced him to roll to the edge of the bed. His head exploded in pain.

"Oh, no. I'm afraid you should stay down, young man." The nurse placed a gentle hand on his shoulder. "You may be concussed and need rest."

"I-I can't. Need to go…see…Elena."

"You can't." This voice was different. Jimmy turned to see Nedra walking up to his bedside. "You've been called to Mr. Quinn's office, and I've been sent to collect you."

Despite the protests of the nurse, Nedra won out. Each step down the hallway felt like a jackhammer was going off inside his head, and he stopped more than once to gather himself. Nedra patiently waited for him to recover each time. Her hardened exterior was a constant visage of determination and steadiness, but the slightest crease in her brow betrayed something else. If he didn't know better, he'd think she was concerned.

"What does Mr. Quinn want, anyway?" The words came out as a groan as they stepped into the sunlight, which forced Jimmy to scrunch his face, setting off pain receptors in every bruise.

The jaw muscles on Nedra's face flexed as she grit her teeth. She breathed heavily through her nostrils, giving away the intensity of whatever she was feeling. She grabbed the sleeve of his shirt and turned him forcefully to meet her. He let out an involuntary grunt as his headache throbbed from the sudden maneuver.

"You remember what I told you when we first met?" Nedra's eyes darted back and forth, searching their surroundings for anyone who might be paying attention. She shook him slightly. "Do you remember?"

You cannot, under any circumstances...

He took a long slow breath. "I remember. And don't shake me. My head feels like it's about to split open." He rubbed at his temples with two fingers.

"I'm sorry." She let him go and stepped backward. "But you need to get over how you are feeling and focus. Your hand is about to be forced, and you need to decide what is most important."

"What do you mean *forced*?"

She bit her lip. "I can't tell you more, especially not here in the open, but you'll find out soon enough. Just…remember what I told you before you make your decision."

Jimmy's mind raced through all possible scenarios. Was he about to be threatened? Hurt? Was someone else going to be hurt? His heart skipped as he worried this might involve Elena, but he didn't dare ask more with the other people moving about the buildings of The Brotherhood compound.

Nedra returned to her stoic expression, even stowing away the crease in her brow. Jimmy wasn't quite sure of her agenda, but he could tell she was practiced at keeping her sentiments to herself. Nedra made a show of grabbing his arm and forcing him forward as they entered the firehouse where Mr. Quinn's office was housed. Soldiers and other members of The Brotherhood froze in place to watch the march through the garage. Their expressions all communicated the same thing…they were glad not to be him.

Two guards flanked Mr. Quinn's office door. Nedra waved a hand, and both nodded to her. She knocked on the door.

"You may enter." Mr. Quinn's muffled voice came from the other side of the door, and it lacked its usual optimism.

Pushing open the door with one hand, Nedra guided Jimmy inside. Mr. Quinn sat at his desk, his hands neatly folded in front of him. Next to his hands lay the tablet. In the corner of the room, Big T leaned against the wall, his huge meaty forearms folded across his chest. He ran his upper hand through his beard as though in thought. Nedra closed the door and took her position in the corner opposite Big T. Jimmy took in these details only through his periphery vision. His focus was on who was sitting in the chair facing Mr. Quinn's desk.

Wyatt.

He expected a situation where he or one of his friends was threatened in order to force him to give up the information on the tablet, but the room did not read that way. Wyatt seemed too confident…almost smug. Cocking his head, Wyatt looked up at Jimmy with a half-smile.

"Hey, Jimmy. How's the face?" The half-smile spread to a grin.

The hesitation to punch his friend in the mouth disappeared, and Jimmy bit his tongue to avoid getting baited into a war of words. His face grew hot with anger.

"I had heard that young Mr. Wyatt here had beaten you soundly in the sparring ring, Jimmy, but until now, I hadn't believed it." Mr. Quinn let out a long sigh. "I trust my staff at the medical wing has treated your wounds with care?"

Jimmy nodded, still not taking his glare off Wyatt.

Mr. Quinn pointed to the other chair next to Wyatt. "Have a seat, my friend. I can understand that this encounter is upsetting, but I trust we can handle it like men." Jimmy slowly slipped into the chair, finally turning his attention to Mr. Quinn. "Good. Young men such as yourselves can indeed find themselves at odds with each other, especially when a young lady is involved."

The flash of heat spread over Jimmy's face again, this time from embarrassment. He opened his mouth to speak and then shut it.

Mr. Quinn chuckled, momentarily breaking his serious tone. "Yes. Yes. It is not hard to see what Ms. Elena means to you." He nodded to Wyatt. "To both of you."

Jimmy shot a glance over at Wyatt, who now stared at the floor. Wyatt's intentions with Elena had always been sort of obvious, but it was still startling to hear them said aloud. An unspoken understanding existed in their group that such things would not be acted upon, yet it was clear the closeness they'd shared meant something different to each of them.

"Yes, Jimmy. Wyatt has been fairly forthcoming in his intentions with the third member of your party." His somber appearance returned. "I must admit that the situation has me concerned. What happened today in the sparring ring was unacceptable. I pride myself on creating a community of order and predictability, and the kind of unhinged mayhem that happened between you two has no place here. I have already spoken to Nedra about maintaining better control over the sparring ring."

Nedra shifted in the corner. Jimmy rubbed his sore jaw. The desire to protest being lumped in with Wyatt's lack of control rose up inside him, but he tamped it down. Angry or not, Wyatt was still his friend. He wouldn't throw him under the bus for Mr. Quinn's sake.

"I live my life, Jimmy, by a set of rules. But one of those rules stands out above the rest, and it has proven its worth over and over. Can you guess what this most important rule is?"

Jimmy shook his head.

"In any calculation, keep track of all the variables." He paused to let the words hang in the air. "Do you understand? It means don't lose sight of each moving piece. Only then, can you correctly predict the outcomes."

Mr. Quinn stood and walked to the window. "When Wyatt was brought before me to answer for his lawlessness, the situation became clear. You are not the first two young men in history to feud over the affections of a woman, and you won't be the last." He turned with a fierce glare. "But I won't have it here. So, I am left to decide what to do with the two of you."

Wyatt twitched in his seat. He wrung his hands in front of him as though nervous about what was coming. Did he know what Mr. Quinn was going to do?

Mr. Quinn returned to his desk and placed his hand on the tablet. "Your party was brought here because of this piece of technology. Jimmy, I showed you respect in an effort to work together. I treated you as someone welcomed in our community. I treated your friend's wound. I allowed all of you to begin your training, even before fully committing to The Brotherhood." Darkness washed over his face. "And my repayment? Disorder. A lack of moderation. No doubt your excess in the ring is already the talk among the men and women under my command, so I am forced to respond. My patience has worn out, Jimmy, and I want the information on this tablet. I believe it's time to test how strong the friendship between you two remains."

There was the threat…the forced hand. Wyatt or the tablet. That was the choice. Jimmy could feel Nedra's eyes boring into the side of his head. Whatever was coming next, she clearly didn't want Jimmy to give in.

You cannot, under any circumstances…

Mr. Quinn took a deep breath and seated himself in his desk chair, the momentary flash of anger retreating to a controlled response. Wyatt waited for his hand to slide to the drawer to produce the pistol and threaten Wyatt. Instead, he stared coldly at Jimmy.

"Jimmy, your friend has offered us a deal."

Chapter Seventeen

"Excuse me?" Jimmy straightened in his chair. Had he heard that right? Next to him, Wyatt shifted nervously, all but confirming what Mr. Quinn had said.

Mr. Quinn sighed heavily. "Yes, my friend. Wyatt, when confronted with his recklessness, offered to give us what we've wanted all along. It seems, though he has no knowledge of the code to unlock the tablet, he claims to have overheard the majority of the information. He is willing to give it to us."

Nedra swallowed hard in the corner but otherwise didn't so much as twitch an eyebrow.

Jimmy glared at Wyatt. "What are you thinking? We talked about this."

Wyatt met Jimmy's eyes with a deadpan expression. "No, you talked about it. You told us what we were going to do with the videos on the tablet."

"That's not how it went down, and you know it." Jimmy couldn't help the rising tone in his voice.

"I want to be here."

"That's it? You want to be here, so you'll make this decision for us? Sounds like you're guilty of the very crime you accused me of in the ring. So, we give up the information and all live happily ever after with The Brotherhood?"

Mr. Quinn cleared his throat. "I'm afraid, Jimmy, that is not the whole picture." He paused, making sure he had Jimmy's full attention. "Wyatt has not negotiated for you three to live with The Brotherhood. Only he and the young lady…Ms. Elena."

The revelation hit Jimmy, stealing the breath from his lungs. Wyatt had left Jimmy out of whatever deal he'd made. The betrayal seeped through his veins, darkening every corner of his soul. How could Wyatt do this? He turned to gape at his…friend.

Wyatt's gaze slowly rose from the floor to meet Jimmy's wide-eyed stare. His face was expressionless, showing no signs of remorse or relief.

Jimmy raised his eyebrows as if to communicate 'say something.'

Wyatt's chest rose and fell as he took a deep breath. Without breaking his gaze, he spoke. "You can't protect her anymore. Not like I can. As long as you're around, she'll never see that."

In his mind, Jimmy launched from his seat and hurled himself at Wyatt, pummeling him with blows. In reality, he sat glued to his chair, unable to move. Silence weighed heavily in the room. Jimmy's heart slammed into the back of his ribcage.

Mr. Quinn blinked slowly as he rolled his head back and forth. "These kinds of conversations give me such tension in my neck." His eyes opened, and he offered Jimmy a bored look. "I'm afraid those are the terms your…er…friend made."

"And I'm supposed to what? Just leave here and never come back?"

Mr. Quinn sighed again. "Jimmy, you have been in this office before. I believe you know how this ends. You have seen and learned too much about The Brotherhood to simply be let go."

The muscles in Jimmy's legs fired, and he shot up from his seat. At least, that was the intention. He made it hardly more than halfway to standing before the massive hands of Big T grabbed his shoulders and shoved him back into the chair. He wriggled and fought against Big T's grip, but the man was too strong and had far too much leverage for Jimmy to do more than futilely struggle. After a minute, he ceased his fight and stared at Mr. Quinn. The breaths came quickly, and he thought he might pass out from hyperventilation. Any second, Mr. Quinn was going to reach for that pistol in the drawer, and that would be the end.

Mr. Quinn held up a hand. "Jimmy, relax. What you think is about to happen is not going to."

That got his attention.

"Wyatt made a deal with us, and I took it because it was a good one...with one exception."

At that statement, Wyatt's head shot up. "Exception?"

"Yes, Wyatt. An exception." He leaned back in his chair and crossed his arms. "Despite your efforts to fit into the mold of The Brotherhood, you have missed one of our most core values. It is a value that provides for the order and predictability I so crave. Can you guess which value I'm talking about?"

Wyatt stared in dumbfounded silence.

"Loyalty, young man." He paused and allowed the word to hang in the air over the desk. "A loyal soldier is a predictable soldier. You will know who he defends and who he defends against...every time." He nodded his head at Jimmy. "As I understand it, Jimmy is a longtime friend. Not an hour ago, you offered me information if I would arrange to dispose of your friend and leave the girl to you. Tell me, how is that loyalty?"

"I—er—uh," Wyatt stammered. He was on the edge of his chair now, and Big T moved to place a hand on Wyatt's shoulder. "I didn't think you'd kill him." He turned to Jimmy. "You got to believe me, Jimmy. I only thought they'd kick you out. I—I just wanted to have a chance to show Elena how much she means to me. I—I—"

"Young man, stop your blathering. It's tiresome."

Wyatt stopped talking, but the hand wringing returned in full force.

Mr. Quinn rubbed the bridge of his nose. "I'm getting a headache, so I'm going to cut to the chase. Wyatt, if your loyalties are so fickle that you'd submarine a friend to gain something for yourself, I have difficulty trusting that you would support The Brotherhood when it mattered most. Yes, we offer a lot for you to gain right now, but what happens when you are faced with hardship down the road? I need to know that your fortitude is strong enough to withstand temptation. I need to know you'd be willing to sacrifice for The Brotherhood."

"I will. I mean, it is. I mean—"

"That's enough out of you." Mr. Quinn's voice resonated through the room with such command that Wyatt shot back fully into his seat. "Now, Jimmy, not all is lost here. Though I struggle with the lack of devotion your friend has shown you, what he offers is more than acceptable. And I"—Mr. Quinn shot Wyatt a look—"am a man of my word. Should I take Wyatt up on his offer, he will be given a full pass to join The Brotherhood guard with all the privileges that come with that. The same would be true of your friend, Elena.

"However, while we have agreed on the terms of the deal, we have not actually signed the bottom line, so to speak." Mr. Quinn leaned forward, gripping the tablet with both hands. "Jimmy, I like you. From the moment we met, I was impressed with both your social posture and your intelligence. You have looked after your friends for years and have remained consistent in that stance, even under the pressure of being our guest. You have been slow to sign on to The Brotherhood, and I respect a man who thinks things through. It's what I would do."

Jimmy swallowed hard. Next to him, Wyatt was in full panic mode, though quietly so as not to disobey Mr. Quinn's orders.

"Jimmy, I'm going to offer you the very same terms I have with Wyatt. You and Elena can stay here as full members of The Brotherhood. In fact, I believe you have earned a fast track to leadership here. In exchange, you will give me the code to this tablet and anything else I need to access the information it contains."

"What?" Wyatt could not contain his outburst. Big T's hand shot over his mouth, and it was Wyatt's turn to attempt to uselessly fight the bulk of Big T.

Jimmy shook his head violently. "You can't ask me to make that decision. I might be angry at Wyatt. In fact, I'm furious he would cut me loose like that, but I can't betray him. I can't do to him what he just did to me. I won't sign his death warrant." He did his best to meet Mr. Quinn's gaze without flinching.

Mr. Quinn's lips spread into a wide smile. "And that, my friend, is why I'm offering you this deal. You have character."

"What about loyalty? Isn't asking me to betray Wyatt violating your core value?" Jimmy almost felt smug in finding the hypocritical knot in Mr. Quinn's logic.

Mr. Quinn nodded his head thoughtfully for several seconds. "You are right. This decision does not fit perfectly into our values here, but your accusation is misdirected. It is not I who painted us into this corner but Wyatt. I'm seeking the best exit from a morally compromised situation. Frankly, I will take what I can get at this point...and I'd like to get you."

Wyatt let out a whimper. He was no longer fighting Big T, but the man had not released his hand over his mouth.

"But can you trust me to join The Brotherhood after betraying my friend? Isn't that what you just said to Wyatt?" Something inside Jimmy was screaming at him to stop arguing, knowing that Mr. Quinn could tire of the back and forth and simply take Wyatt's deal. Still, he had to try. He could not live with himself if he didn't.

"My trust in Wyatt is broken, but this is apples and oranges. There is a great difference in choosing to cut a man loose to his face than there is to stabbing him while his back is turned, or in your case while unconscious in the medical ward. Wyatt is guilty of the latter, and I cannot trust him unless I'm left no other option. You have a chance to do the former, so I can at least trust I'll know where I stand with you."

Mr. Quinn was nothing if not logical.

"I-I can't make this decision." Jimmy's mind scrambled for a way out, but he couldn't find one. "I need to think about it."

"I expected nothing less, my friend." He turned to Wyatt. "Despite what you think may happen here, I honestly do not know what your friend will choose. Wyatt, you will be allowed to roam free at the compound with one objective—prove to me your loyalty. I have my doubts after your display today, but perhaps you are a statistical outlier and will show me otherwise. Perhaps you'll surprise me. I'm willing to give you a week to do so. Make no mistake, you are being watched. Leaving the grounds will mean your life is forfeit. Understood?"

Wyatt nodded as Big T slowly removed his hand from Wyatt's mouth. While he could not hide the fear from his face, a look of determination began to form in his expression.

Mr. Quinn returned his gaze to Jimmy. "You have the same time span to decide if you want to take my deal."

Chapter Eighteen

"Where have you been?" Elena threw her arms around Jimmy. "They told me you'd awoken in the medical ward, but they wouldn't let me see you again. Kept saying you were 'in a meeting.'"

Jimmy sighed. How could he burden Elena with the knowledge of what had transpired in Mr. Quinn's office? "Wyatt has joined The Brotherhood…fully. He won't have to stay with us in here anymore. Mr. Quinn wanted to talk to me about doing the same." It wasn't the full truth, but it wasn't exactly a lie either. He hated being anything less than transparent with Elena.

She studied his eyes, which probably appeared terribly puffy and bruised. "There's something more. What is it?" She could always read him.

He broke eye contact and pulled away from her. "It's—it's nothing."

She shook her head. "No, it's not. Did they get access to the tablet?"

"Not yet, but it's only a matter of time. One way or another, they'll get what they want." Wyatt's betrayal pierced his heart anew, and he leaned against the wall and slumped to the floor. "Right now, I just want to get some sleep."

Elena's gaze held his periphery for a long moment, but she

didn't say anything further. She grabbed a blanket. *When had they gotten blankets?* Mr. Quinn's gesture, no doubt. She slid down the wall next to him and curled up.

Grabbing his own blanket, he did the same. A sleepless hour passed as he contemplated his options. Either way, he was thankful that Elena was safe. How could he choose? His own death or the death of his friend. Despite what Wyatt had done, he still could not bring himself to sacrifice his friend. There was no solace either in the idea of leaving Elena living with a lie but telling her the truth about Wyatt would only make her do something rash that would get her killed.

Escape was the only choice. But how?

A hand clamping over his mouth startled him awake. In the darkness, he could make out a silhouette and the shape of a pistol but nothing more. Grasping the forearm of his attacker with both hands, he tried to force the muzzle away from his face.

"Shh. Jimmy, it's me." The voice was Wyatt's. "Don't wake Elena. We need to talk."

Jimmy calmed down and motioned that he would be quiet. Wyatt cautiously removed his hand from Jimmy's mouth. Only then did Jimmy realize the door of the locker room was wide open, allowing a soft light to illuminate the corner of the room.

Wyatt stood and waved his hand that Jimmy should follow him. He held a finger to his lips as he pointed at Elena. Jimmy nodded and rose to his feet. The two of them slipped outside the door, and Wyatt quietly shut the door behind him.

Searching the area, Jimmy saw no one outside the locker room. "Where's the guard?" He turned to Wyatt and froze in place.

Wyatt pointed a pistol at his face.

Slowly, Jimmy raised his hands halfway up in surrender. Wyatt swallowed hard and motioned with the pistol that Jimmy should start walking.

"Wyatt, where are we—?" Jimmy's words were cut short when Wyatt straightened his arm, bringing the barrel of the pistol closer. "Okay. Okay." He turned and started walking the hallway.

Once out of earshot of the door, Wyatt started whispering. "We don't have long. Told the guard I'd be someone important when I gave Mr. Quinn the information he wanted, and he gave me five minutes with you and this gun." He paused and wet his lips before talking again. "Jimmy, I can't let you do this."

"Do what?" Jimmy dared to ask, though he was confident of the answer.

"I can't let you take Mr. Quinn's deal. I'm not going to die here."

Anger burned inside Jimmy, and he whirled on Wyatt. Wyatt stepped back and raised the pistol an inch. Jimmy stopped his advance, but he could feel the heat of fury on his face. "So you want me to die? I should just fall on my sword because you're tired of there being three of us?"

Wyatt glanced away. "You have to believe that was not the deal I struck. I told them to let you go. All I wanted was you out of the picture. I never wanted you dead."

"And you thought they would just go along with that?"

The muscles on Wyatt's jaw flexed several times. "I'm not

sure what I thought. All I know is this is the first place since the world went crazy that I feel like I won't have to wonder if I'm getting to eat tomorrow. I want to be here. I wanted *all* of us to be here, but I knew that you'd never agree to it. I could see it every day as we trained with the guard. You'd find a way to escape and take it—and her—with you."

Jimmy relaxed a little. Wyatt had shown the kink in his armor. "Wyatt, she doesn't—"

"Shut up!" Wyatt shook the pistol at him. "She only doesn't see me because you are in the way. If you weren't here, she'd care for me like she does for you."

Jimmy held his breath as he stepped forward. He reminded himself to speak calmly. "Wyatt, she doesn't feel that way about me. Or if she does, she won't act on it. She told me just before we fought."

"You're lying. I saw you two the other day."

"Yes, you saw us, but she put on the brakes and said it couldn't happen again. She wants to survive and doesn't want to get confused about that. And she's probably right." As the admission passed over his lips, Jimmy winced at the sting it left behind.

Wyatt's brow lowered. "I'm supposed to believe you simply because you said so?"

"No, you're supposed to show Elena a little respect and ask her yourself." Jimmy was surprised at the firmness in his voice despite the presence of the pistol still aimed at him. "You made this decision without even talking to us. I can sort of understand that you might be mad at me, but if you really feel about Elena that way, why wouldn't you talk to her?" He could see that the words pricked at Wyatt, and Jimmy could only guess at the conversation going on in Wyatt's head.

Wyatt lowered the pistol slightly. His eyes searched the floor. Then, he shook his head and straightened the gun. "No, she can't have a clear conversation with you around."

"You're not giving her enough credit."

"You. Blind. Her." Wyatt jabbed the pistol barrel at the air with each word. "You deceive her and string her along to meet your own ends. For all I know, you're the one that *put on the brakes*." He signaled quotation marks in the air with his free hand. "You're controlling her, and she follows blindly. And it's going to get us all killed."

Rage boiled inside Jimmy as he listened to the story Wyatt was telling himself. His feelings for Elena aside, he'd completely gone off the deep end with his logic. All fear melted away as the anger rose. "So your solution is to kill me? Is that what we're doing here?" His surrendered hands flopped to his sides.

"It's not like that. I told you I didn't want you dead. Stop saying I do." Wyatt spoke through gritted teeth.

"So says the guy holding the gun in my face."

Wyatt pursed his lips and shook his head. "There you go again, assuming everything. I needed you to listen, that's all."

Jimmy glanced back in the direction of the locker room. "Your five minutes are running out. I'm listening."

Wyatt met his eyes with determination. "Leave. Escape. Tonight, by yourself."

Jimmy scrunched his brow. "What?"

"There's a guard change in ten minutes. That should leave you enough time to sneak over two blocks. As the guards chat it up, you can make a break across the street into the shadow of the next building. From there, you can travel unseen out of here." He paused to take a breath. "I don't want you dead, Jimmy. Just gone."

"Then you stay on here lying to Elena with some tale about how I abandoned you guys? You really think she'll buy that?"

"She'll have to. She wants to survive…remember? She'll choose to believe the lie because it's her best chance. That means she picks me."

Jimmy laughed derisively. "You're sick, Wyatt. What happened to you?"

"Ninety percent of the world's population died, and I was left behind to survive. That's what happened. Choosing to live among people who can keep me safe with the girl I want to be with doesn't sound so crazy when you consider everything we've been through."

Jimmy didn't recognize his friend anymore. The taste of supposed security among The Brotherhood had poisoned his thinking. Jimmy searched Wyatt's face for any glimmer of his old friend, and the only discovery he found was pity. He had to make one last effort to reach his buddy.

"Wyatt, let's leave together. All three of us. You say we have ten minutes. Let's grab Elena before the guard returns and escape tonight. We've survived this long scavenging. We can move to another part of the city that Mr. Quinn doesn't control and keep going." He stopped to consider what would convince Wyatt. "I promise that I will include you more…in everything. Come on, we can be out of here tonight."

The slightest tremor appeared in Wyatt's grip on the pistol before he gathered his resolve. "No, Jimmy. We can't go back to what we had. Too much has happened. Leave. Now. I'm not going to ask again."

"If I don't? Are you really going to shoot me?"

Wyatt offered a shy smile. "No, I'm not. I don't have to. All I have to do is walk away, and you find yourself on the outside of your cage. You'll either run as I think you should, or you'll get caught and look like an escapee. I suspect Mr. Quinn will revoke his deal after that. Either way, I get to stay here with Elena."

They stared at each other in silence for a long moment.

"Run, Jimmy." Wyatt lowered the weapon by his side.

It was the opening Jimmy needed. He sprang at his friend, driving his right palm into Wyatt's cheekbone. With his left hand, he grabbed the barrel of the pistol and wrenched it against Wyatt's loosened grip. The gun broke free of Wyatt's fingers, and Jimmy swung the weapon like a club, striking Wyatt in the temple.

Wyatt let out a grunt as he stumbled backward, reaching for his head which was bleeding. Jimmy didn't wait to see what would happen. He sprinted back up the hallway to the locker room. A yawning guard was retaking his place at the door, and he never saw Jimmy coming.

Throwing his full force at the guard, Jimmy brought his forearm up to the guard's jaw, forcing his head backward as they slammed into the locker room door. The crack of the guard's skull striking the metal door sickened Jimmy, but the move had the desired effect. The guard slumped unconscious to the floor. Jimmy shoved the pistol into his waistband, making certain to click the safety on, and grabbed the guard's legs to drag him away.

"Jimmy? Jimmy, where are you?" The muffled voice of Elena came from inside the locker room. The impact on the door must have awoken her.

Jimmy threw the latch and opened the door. He rushed inside and pulled a weary Elena to her feet.

"Jimmy, what's happening?" She rubbed her eyes as they stumbled out of the locker room into the light. Her gaze caught the unconscious guard on the floor, and she gave Jimmy an expression of amazement. "Did you do that?"

"No time to explain. We're getting out of here…right now."

Chapter Nineteen

The two of them slipped out the door of the firehouse and scurried through the vacant streets of the compound. Elena gave up asking more questions, probably from the urgency in Jimmy's voice. It was only when they stopped to catch their breath that she finally spoke.

"Where's Wyatt? Why isn't he here?"

Jimmy swallowed between breaths. "He's not coming." He wanted to explain more, but anything else would take time, and a partial answer would only confuse her. They couldn't afford to slow down. If Wyatt had been correct, Jimmy estimated the guard change was only a couple minutes away.

They hugged the wall of the building, and Jimmy whispered a prayer of thanks that the clouds were blocking most of the moonlight. Reaching the corner of the building, he peered around the edge. A half block away, a guard station had been set up in the middle of the road. Concrete barriers had been moved into a circle that blocked the majority of the roadway. Two guards stood in the center. The occasional crimson glow of a lit cigarette was visible in the silent darkness. From their vantage point, the guards had a clear view of the street for blocks in either direction. The barrels of two rifles poked up from the barrier against which they were propped.

"You better tell me you have another one of those. I'm not going to sit out here all night without something to smoke." The voice came from a third guard that emerged from the street a block up. He and a companion moved into the dim light, each with a rifle slung over their shoulder.

"I've got one left if you want it." The guard in the circle extended a crumpled cigarette packet to the approaching guards as they swung their feet over the concrete barrier. He took it and promptly lit it, taking a long drag.

"Man, who did I tick off to pull this watch?"

"What are you talking about? The 3am shift is the best, especially since I get to sleep through it." The first guard laughed as he clapped the replacement guard on the shoulder. The other three took up the laughter as they huddled together. Various insulting comments, the kind that guys throw around among friends were shared. The conversation slipped into what female member of The Brotherhood had caught each of their eye, which brought more jesting.

Jimmy turned to Elena. "This is our chance. Next time they burst into laughter, we cross the road."

Elena nodded.

"Dude, did you see Chambers yesterday?" The replacement guard nearly shouted to get his friend's attention. "The guy nearly shot himself in the foot at target practice. Man can't handle his weapon. Nedra was so mad she about took his head off."

The four men erupted in laughter at their compatriot's expense. A couple of them doubled over in their fit as they continued to making comments about their fellow guard. Jimmy waved to Elena behind him. In a half-crouch, they padded across the street in near silence beyond the cover of the next building. Jimmy stopped and peered around the corner.

The men, overcoming their fit of laughter, slapped each other on the back as the two new guards slipped their rifles off their shoulders, leaning them up against the concrete. The others shouldered their rifles and hopped the barrier, retiring for the night.

Jimmy turned to Elena. "I don't think they saw us." Only then did he notice the tears in her eyes.

"Jimmy, why isn't Wyatt with us?"

He reached for her hand and squeezed it. "I promise I'll explain once we're out of here. You have to know I tried to get him to come."

She nodded and sniffed.

Keeping her hand in his, Jimmy stood upright. The two of them hurried down the street, careful not to make noise. With each passing block, he breathed easier knowing The Brotherhood was farther behind them. The relief of escaping the compound flooded over him, yet there was an ache deep down in his soul that would not be dismissed.

He'd left his best friend behind to fend for himself. It was possible that the knowledge Wyatt had might be enough to save his life when Mr. Quinn learned of their escape, but it could also be viewed as another breach of trust. As soon as their guard described that Jimmy had attacked him from outside the locker room, Wyatt would have to explain himself.

Any deal Wyatt had with Mr. Quinn might be cancelled, even if he gave up his knowledge of the Lifeboat. Jimmy's gut turned at the thought of his friend being killed the instant he told them what he knew. Mr. Quinn was too logical to see Wyatt as anything other than a liability.

His one solace was that Nedra was still there, and she had no desire for Mr. Quinn to learn what Wyatt knew.

An hour later, they found themselves standing outside the door to their former hideout. A lifetime had seemingly passed since the last time they'd stepped through the door of their home. The door sat ajar on broken hinges. Jimmy let out a long sigh.

"Not sure we're going to find much here, but let's see if there's anything left."

Elena nodded, and even in the dim light Jimmy could see the glassiness of her eyes. She was struggling to keep her emotions from overwhelming her. Admittedly, so was he. This had been their home, the most secure location they'd ever lived in as a group since the virus had forced them to scavenge.

Stepping inside, he noted the secondary door was also broken. Rocks lay strewn about from their traps. A dark stain on the floor betrayed where one of the invaders had been mortally wounded. Jimmy's stomach lurched at the thought that the trap had taken a life. Each creak of the stairs echoed, emphasizing the emptiness of the place.

Their collective breath caught when they entered the apartment above. Everything they'd owned had been tossed around the room. The Brotherhood Guard had gone through every inch of the place. The food stores were empty. Anything of value was missing. The worst was discovering that the drone was missing from its hiding place. Jimmy had hoped to at least recover it, so they could resume their scavenging once they'd relocated. Now they would have to search by hand, which was both exhausting and far more dangerous.

"They went over this place with a fine-toothed comb after you were captured." The voice from the shadows startled both of them. Elena emitted a tiny yelp. Jimmy's heart found his throat, and he fought the instinct to bolt, reminding himself that he needed to protect Elena. One of the curtains from their sleeping quarters pulled back.

Nedra stood there, watching them in the darkness.

"What? How?" Jimmy stammered. "How are you here?" He raised the pistol he'd taken from Wyatt, but he could not control the tremor in his hand.

She stepped toward them, and Jimmy moved protectively in front of Elena. Nedra held up a hand. "I'm not here to hurt you, Jimmy."

"Then why are you here?" Elena asked with surprising firmness in her voice. Jimmy never ceased to be amazed at the amount of courage Elena could have.

"And how did you get here so fast?" Jimmy asked.

Nedra let out a long breath as she ran a hand down the length of her face. "Being captain of the guard has its privileges, including being able to leave the compound at night whenever I want. I knew you'd probably do something desperate after your meeting with Mr. Quinn, so I stopped by your cell only to find your guard unconscious and locked inside. Seems I was right. Wasn't hard to figure out why you'd left when you did—the changing of the guard. Clever. I only had to requisition a vehicle to get ahead of you. I knew you'd come here."

"That doesn't explain *why* you're here." Jimmy did his best to jab the barrel of the pistol in the air in her direction. Even he wasn't convinced by the maneuver.

"Are you really going to shoot me, Jimmy?" Her lips curled into a wry smile. "I'm not sure you're that type of person. Besides, the safety is on." She stepped forward and gently pushed the barrel of the pistol downward. Jimmy didn't fight her. "There, that's better."

Jimmy felt his face flush as he checked to see that the safety was indeed on. He tucked the pistol back into his waist and shoved both hands in his pockets. "Nedra, what are you doing here?"

"We're not going back with you," Elena added.

Nedra shook her head. "I'm not here to make you go back. In fact, I'm here to make sure you move on. I noticed your handiwork in the hallway outside your cell. If I guessed that you came here, you can bet they will too when they realize you're gone. Desperate people tend to run to what is familiar, and Mr. Quinn is too logical not to guess that would be here. The second that guard comes to and starts pounding on the door to the locker room, you can bet that someone is going to figure it out."

Jimmy's heart skipped a beat as he realized that she was right. Mr. Quinn and his goons would be on their way soon if they weren't already.

"Then we need to leave." Jimmy took a step toward the door.

"Wait, Jimmy." Elena placed a hand on his arm. "Let's hear her out."

Nedra gave a slight nod to Elena and reached behind her. Slipping her backpack off, she lowered it to the floor and unzipped the top. She reached in and pulled an object from the bag.

It was the tablet.

"When you go, take this with you." She placed the device back into the bag and offered it to Jimmy.

Dumbfounded, he froze in place until Elena prodded him from behind. He reached an unsteady hand toward the bag and took it from Nedra. "Why are you giving this to us?"

"I told you. Mr. Quinn cannot get his hands on the information on that device. Your friend, Wyatt, might be able to tell him a few things, but I'm guessing there's a lot more on that tablet than what Wyatt overheard."

Jimmy nodded.

"That's what I thought."

"How did you get it from Mr. Quinn?" Elena asked.

"Like I said, being captain of the guard has certain privileges. I have access in places many do not."

"And you don't think he'll put it together that it was you who took it?"

Nedra sighed. "It's a possibility, but it seems a smaller logical leap that you found a way to swipe it rather than betrayal by his trusted guard captain."

"Why are you his guard captain? Why don't you leave that place?" Elena stepped forward toward Nedra, her brow furrowed in concern.

"I joined the Brotherhood because I was tired of sitting at a military post waiting for new orders that would never come. I went

AWOL to investigate some of the rumors of havens outside the cities, but I found none. When I came back to surrender myself to my Captain, I was intercepted by The Brotherhood. Mr. Quinn showed me what they were doing, and I was initially entranced."

"I know the feeling," Jimmy said.

"The school. The hospital. The resources. When you only look at the surface, it's hard to distinguish between absolute control and organized benevolence. I joined up immediately and found a home among the guard. Quickly finding I was the most experienced military officer in their ranks, I proposed new training regimens and systems. Mr. Quinn was impressed, and I quickly became one of his insiders."

"Then why betray him?"

"You've seen what he is capable of. Once inside, I realized who he is. He's drunk with his own power and wants to control the entire city." She pointed to the backpack. "Whatever is on that tablet, if he's that interested in it, he can't have it."

Elena placed her hand on Nedra's shoulder. "Nedra, come with us. I know we're young, but we know how to survive in this city. You don't have to go back."

A tear collected at the rim of Nedra's eyelid, and she tilted her chin upward to blink it back before it fell. "It's not that easy. Mr. Quinn"—she paused to swallow hard—"takes out insurance on all his most trusted followers, usually in the form of another person. Had Jimmy joined up, he would have used you, Elena, as his insurance to guarantee loyalty." She nodded at each of them in turn. "He talks a lot about loyalty and trust, but the truth is—Mr. Quinn trusts no one."

"And he has someone you care about?"

Nedra nodded, swiping at another tear. "I have to go back and play my part."

Elena wrapped her arms around Nedra, and the two women held each other in an embrace for a long silent moment. Jimmy stood silently with his eyes on the floor, honoring the moment. When they pulled away, Jimmy noticed that the tears had finally been allowed to escape Nedra's eyes.

Nedra sniffed and wiped her cheeks with a hand. "It's been a while since anyone has shown me that sort of kindness." She pointed to Jimmy. "That information needs to be as far from here as possible. The cache that is described on that tablet—find it if you must—but get out of here in the next half hour. If Mr. Quinn gets his hands on it, he *will* control this city and everyone in it."

She hugged Elena a second time and even embraced Jimmy before retreating down the stairs. Jimmy gazed at Elena in the darkness of the apartment. The silence in the room weighed heavily as the realization of the task in front of them became clear.

"We have to open the Lifeboat before the Brotherhood finds it." Jimmy spoke in a whisper, afraid to upset the delicate balance of peace and responsibility in the air.

"The satellite image had the coordinates removed, remember? Besides, that picture was taken by the army captain." Elena sighed. "All we know is the direction Dr. Sheppard was heading. Who knows how far he needed to go."

"Actually, that's not true." Jimmy bit his lip. "There's something I noticed when looking through the videos of Dr. Sheppard. I took a screenshot to see if I was right."

Jimmy opened the tablet and breathed a sigh of relief that the battery still had some charge on it. He opened the photos and scrolled through several screenshots he'd taken while watching the videos of the various keepers. He found the one he was searching for and showed it to Elena.

"Check out the background."

Elena examined the picture, and her eyes grew wide. "Is that—?"

Jimmy nodded. In the background behind Dr. Sheppard was the satellite image. With two fingers, he zoomed the photo in on the picture to the corner where the coordinates of the Lifeboat were—unredacted and clearly readable. He flipped over to a map application and entered the coordinates, needing to go back and forth from the picture to the application a couple of times to get the numbers right. A pinpoint appeared on the map in the middle of a green blotch on the map. Jimmy pinched the screen to zoom out to see the bigger picture. He pointed to a spot just a few miles from the pinpoint.

"That's where Dr. Sheppard's car was. It wasn't that far to get there, and the Lifeboat isn't much farther."

"Which means—" Elena paused as if wondering if she should say it.

Jimmy smiled at her. "Which means we can get there and open the Lifeboat."

Chapter Twenty

Jimmy cinched the backpack straps tighter as Elena returned from the roof access of the building. In her hand, she held two crumpled water bottles that she filled from the rain barrel they'd placed on the roof a year earlier. She slipped them into the backpack and zipped it closed.

Without a word, they descended the stairs and went out the doorway. The sun was rising, and birds were singing in the trees nearby. A few years ago, this would have been a pleasant morning to take a walk or head to the local coffee shop. Instead, the weight of their task bore down on them, and the daylight made them feel exposed. Still, it was safer than traveling at night.

"You ready for this?" Jimmy turned to Elena, offering her an unsure smile.

She took his hand in hers. For a moment he couldn't breathe. It was the first affection she'd shown him since that moment in the guard center, but he reminded himself that she was not willing to have a relationship while they needed to survive. He smiled at her and squeezed her hand.

"I'm ready." Elena ran her thumb across the back of his hand. "And maybe if we can pull this off—" Her words cut off, and she glanced downward. Her face flushed. "Well, if the Lifeboat is really there, the world could change." She squeezed his hand.

Sparks of energy coursed through Jimmy's chest as he realized her meaning. The Lifeboat had the potential to restore the world and save the remaining population. In that moment, though, that purpose was lost on Jimmy. The only world he cared about saving was the one with Elena in it.

Walking to the edge of the alley, he peered around the corner of the building to see if anyone was on the street. No one was visible. Across the street lay the edge of the city where city streets quickly gave way to neighborhoods and ultimately country roads out of town.

He smiled at Elena and nodded his head in the direction they were headed. She returned his nod and grinned. Crossing the street, they disappeared and left their former hideout behind.

They took a more circuitous route to the county road, steering themselves far away from the edge of the dark sector and The Brotherhood compound inside. The path took an extra two hours, but with the Brotherhood now likely on high alert, they didn't dare get anywhere close. They walked in silence, their ears tuned to every sound. More than once, they ducked into an alley or abandoned home when they heard an unfamiliar noise. Luck was with them, and they encountered no one. If The Brotherhood was out searching for them, they were looking in the wrong place. The ease of it all filled Jimmy with trepidation.

His hand found the ring still hanging around his neck. He'd

surprisingly not thought much about it while with The Brotherhood, but its message came back to him in a wave of guilt.

Greater love has no one than this...

Should he not have left Wyatt behind? The reality of what awaited Wyatt this morning as the truth was revealed turned Jimmy's stomach in a knot. His mind involuntarily listed all the things he could have said to Wyatt to persuade him to come. He even considered whether he should have forced Wyatt to come when he got the jump on him in the hallway. Should he have used the pistol to force Wyatt to escape The Brotherhood? Something about *that* scenario didn't sit right with him. Still, the thought that he'd not done everything he could to save his friend weighed upon him. He'd failed his friend.

As if sensing his internal conflict, Elena whispered to him, breaking the silence of their journey. "Wyatt made his choice, Jimmy. I'm terrified of what will or may already have happened to him, but he *chose* to stay behind."

"I could have left. Yeah, he would have lied to you about why I left, but you'd both be alive. I could have been okay with that."

Elena stopped and grabbed his arm, turning him to face her. "Don't say that. You heard Nedra. Mr. Quinn was going to use me as insurance for your loyalty. He would have done the same with Wyatt. I would have lived every day with Mr. Quinn's noose around my neck, waiting for the moment to decide he didn't need Wyatt anymore. That's not living. That's a long, excruciating death sentence."

Jimmy nodded and glanced at the pavement beneath his feet.

Elena placed a hand on his cheek and made him look at her. "I'm serious. There was nothing you could have done differently. Wyatt wasn't going to come willingly, and I wouldn't have wanted to be left behind."

The warmth of her hand on his skin made Jimmy's heart melt. The uncertainty of his choice faded as he gazed into her eyes. He drank in the moment and gave her a shy smile.

"That's better. You can't doubt yourself." She paused. "I don't doubt you."

Her hand left his cheek, which felt cold and empty without her presence. His hand was still wrapped around the ring, and he realized he'd sacrifice anything for Elena. She was his family, whether they were able to entertain a relationship or not. As his father had done and then his mother, he would live out the message of the ring for her.

An hour later, they stood motionless on the same bend in the road Jimmy had visited before. This was the place their journey had started. He pointed farther down the road to where he knew the car lay hidden.

"That's where Dr. Sheppard is."

Elena sucked in a breath as if taken aback by the realization that Dr. Sheppard's remains lay nearby. "He almost made it to his family. He was so close."

Jimmy tugged at the strap of the backpack. "At least we have his message to give to them. Nedra didn't realize that she was giving us more than information when she returned the tablet. His last gift to his family is recorded on that."

They stared at the road in front of them. Only a few miles separated them from the Lifeboat. Only a few miles until they could potentially change life as they knew it. It didn't feel completely real, and yet part of him wanted to take off in a run to get there faster. He reminded himself that Elena was still healing and dependent upon her ankle brace to walk.

He gazed upward at the sun, which was almost directly overhead. "We should arrive by sometime this afternoon if we don't stop."

"Then what are we waiting for?"

Chapter Twenty-One

The hillside was covered in scrub brush and weeds. Somewhere, within yards of their position, lay the entrance to the Lifeboat. The miles from Dr. Sheppard's car to here had been uneventful. A single dirt road, exiting the main road, had led them to this hill. It was only at that moment that Jimmy realized that he had no idea how they would get inside.

Would they be able to open the door?

Would someone come out to meet them?

What if they were unable to communicate with anyone inside?

The realization that this would all be a waste of time if they could not get the Lifeboat open slammed into Jimmy. His heart raced, and part of him wanted to frantically start searching for the opening. Instead, he took a deep breath and turned to Elena.

"I have no idea what we're looking for. It must be near here, so why don't you go left, while I go right."

Elena nodded with an excited smile and began walking along the edge of the hill. Jimmy did the same in his designated direction. Occasionally, he would stop to pull back some brush or the weed growth to examine the ground beneath. Every time, he was met with nothing more than a bare rock face. No sign of a door or opening presented itself. The afternoon sun beat down on him and sweat began to soak into the collar of his shirt. He sat down on a rock under a tree and wiped the sweat off his brow.

He scanned the area. The dirt road had simply ended at the edge of the hill, and he'd hoped that would have been the entrance. Did they have the right place? Was there another hill nearby?

"Jimmy! Come here. I-I think I found it!" Elena's voice sounded electrified with excitement.

Jimmy hurled himself off the rock and sprinted to her location. Catching up to her, he found her frantically pulling away weed growth from the side of the hill. Without a word, he began to assist her, having no idea why she thought she'd found the entrance. Yank after yank produced handfuls of centipede grass. With each tug, more of the rockface beneath became bare. That is when Jimmy saw Elena's discovery.

A bronze seal, affixed to the rock, about six inches in diameter stared back at them. What had likely been a glossy surface now bore a dull patina with the embossed edges already turning green with exposure to the air. An insignia of a globe wrapped in a sling that bore a rescue cross was encircled by the words *Global Rescue Coalition Lifeboat Two*. Somewhere beneath the rock was a community of people with the tools to save humankind.

Elena stood back and covered her mouth and nose with her hands. Tears welled up in her eyes, which creased in the corners from her hidden smile. "It's real, Jimmy. It's really here."

Jimmy's fingers trembled as he ran them across the letters of the seal. His doubt washed away in a flood of hope, and for the first time, he believed their world might change for the better. He turned suddenly and wrapped his arms around Elena, who initially stiffened at his hug. After a moment, her body relaxed into his, and she returned the embrace. Tears and laughter and sighs of relief were exchanged as they held each other.

They'd found it.

"Hello?" a voice crackled from behind them.

Startled, the two of them turned their heads to the sound. Forgetting for a moment they still were in a partial embrace, they stared at the bronze seal as though it would talk to them.

"Is someone there? I can't see you." The voice came from above the seal. Jimmy stepped forward and grabbed a clump of weeds. With a tug, the weeds broke free of the hill. Beneath the plant-life, an indention was carved into the rock. Recessed inside the indention, a speaker was mounted to the left. To the right, the glass lens of a camera turned as it attempted to focus.

"That's a little better. Instead of a dark blur, I'm now getting a bright blur." The voice seemed encouraged to be talking to them. "Can you see if the camera lens is broken or blocked?"

Jimmy examined the lens. Years of dust and dirt clung to the glass. Grabbing the tail of his shirt, he wrapped his finger in fabric and wiped the surface of the lens. A couple of strokes later, he had the camera mostly cleaned.

"That's better. Thank you, young man."

"You-you're welcome, I guess." Jimmy stepped back by Elena's side and stared at the camera as if he could peer inside to see the person on the other end. "Who are you?"

"Unfortunately, I'm not authorized to answer that until I confirm who you two are."

Elena straightened at the realization of being acknowledged. Whoever was on the other side, the camera was clearly operating. She stepped forward a half-step, and the camera lens whirred as it adjusted to focus. "M-my name is Elena. This is Jimmy."

"Elena. Jimmy. It's good to meet you."

"And you are?" Jimmy asked again.

"Once more, I'm not authorized to answer that until I can confirm your identity."

Jimmy sighed in frustration. "We don't exactly carry ID on us. Not much use for it the way the world is."

The voice coming from the speaker chuckled. "No, I don't imagine there would be, though I'd love to hear more about what the world is like out there. Let me rephrase my question. I'm less concerned about who you are and more about *why* you are here. How did *you* find us?"

Finally, a question that felt like they were getting somewhere. "We know Dr. Sheppard." Jimmy hesitated. "Well, we didn't know him. We found him—what was left of him. Er—." Jimmy bit his lip. This wasn't coming out right at all.

"Sir," Elena said with more confidence than Jimmy, "we found the remains of Dr. Sheppard. His tablet contained a message from him asking anyone who found it to come here." She unzipped the backpack on Jimmy's back and pulled the tablet out. She held it up to the camera. "He said you needed to know that it was time to open the Lifeboat."

Silence came from the speaker for a long moment. "Did you s-say the remains of Dr. Sheppard?"

Elena nodded with a slight frown. "Yes. I'm sorry. He had a

car accident on his way here. H-he didn't make it."

"Oh no." The voice sounded genuinely upset and kept going as if forgetting to turn the microphone off. "Who's going to tell Cyndi? Oh, this is going to grieve her so. Oh my. And the children—"

The distraught ramblings of the voice went on for some time, and Jimmy began to feel awkward listening in. "Sir, I'm sorry for your loss. He wanted whoever found the tablet to bring his information here, and that is what we've done."

Again, silence from the speaker. After a minute, the voice returned with an edge to it. "H-how do I know you are telling the truth? How do I know this isn't some kind of cruel prank or just a means to gain entry in here?"

Jimmy let out an exasperated groan.

Elena grabbed his arm and whispered. "He's upset. He's lashing out. Be patient." She opened the tablet and pulled up the video of Dr. Sheppard. Walking up to the camera, she held up the tablet and pressed play. Dr. Sheppard's shaky voice produced a gasp from the person on the other end of the camera.

My name is Doctor Harold Sheppard. I was on my way to the Lifeboat when a deer struck my car. I-I've been in an accident. My car flipped, and I'm stuck in here. S-something must have struck me as the car rolled. As best I can tell…

The video went silent. Elena turned the screen back to herself and pressed the power button. "That's the end of the battery." She sighed heavily. "But hopefully it's enough to prove that we're telling the truth."

Jimmy stepped up to Elena's side and gazed into the camera

lens. "Sir, whoever you are, we're telling the truth. We have all of Dr. Sheppard's messages and notes on this tablet. I hope you can charge it because they explain that it's time to come out of the Lifeboat. The other keepers are dead, too." He pointed to the tablet. "It's all on here, I promise. Please, there's just two of us. Can you come out? Or let us in?"

They stared at the speaker, which sat wordless. No response. For several minutes, they heard nothing from the nameless voice on the other end.

"Sir? Sir, are you there?" Elena asked.

Nothing.

"What are they doing in there?" Jimmy wondered aloud.

"Wait there, please." A new voice squawked over the speaker. This one was calmer and carried a greater sense of command. Several minutes passed before they were convinced that was all they were going to get.

"I guess we wait?" Elena turned to Jimmy, the tablet clutched in both hands.

"Apparently, so." Jimmy turned and leaned against the rock. He slid down to the ground and rested his head on his crossed arms. Elena sat next to him, leaning onto his side.

They waited.

Hours passed. The sun began to get low in the sky, and the shadows of the trees grew long. The hot summer air began to cool. Insects began to buzz as the shade increased, and the forest around them became alive with the sounds of animals moving as dusk approached.

"Stand back, please."

The voice over the speaker, the same authoritative voice that had told them to wait, startled them. Both of them jumped, Elena releasing a small gasp of surprise. Jimmy had nearly dozed, and his head swam as adrenaline rushed through his body. He stood, his achy legs complaining after so little movement. With a hand, he helped Elena to her feet. They retreated several steps and turned to face the camera.

Click. Click. Click.

Thud.

Mechanical sounds emanated from the rock. Dirt and debris on the hillside shook and began to tumble to the ground. A vertical crack formed in the rock. Not a natural split in the earth that might form in an earthquake, but a perfectly vertical crack with clean edges, save for the random bits of plant-life that clung to the edge. The gap widened as the rockface slowly swung outward, scraping along the ground. Hydraulics hissed as the behemoth door opened, and puffs of dust and dirt were blown outward as the atmosphere inside equalized with the outdoors.

Jimmy waved his hand in the air as the cloud of debris blew in their direction. Through his squinted vision, he could see three shapes emerging from the doorway. He couldn't make out the faces of the individuals, but the shape of the rifles in their hands was unmistakable. In seconds, they had taken up flanking positions with their firearms raised. Instinctively, both Jimmy and Elena raised their hands in the air. Elena still clutched the tablet in one hand, and Jimmy wished they'd tucked it away. The dust began to clear, and the faces of the soldiers came into focus.

Two others emerged from the door. The first was a large man. He wore a military uniform, his collar bearing two stars. His hair was grey and cropped close. The other man was slight in build, had curly brown hair, wire-rimmed glasses, and was dressed in khakis and a blue polo shirt. Both approached Jimmy and Elena.

"Hand over the tablet." The military man glared at Elena with his hand held out.

"Just a second, General." Polo shirt held a hand up in protest. "You are not in charge here."

The general glowered at the slight man. "In matters of security threats, I am in charge."

"We have yet to determine there is a threat here. Two teenagers hardly seem threatening, especially when your men are holding them at gunpoint."

"They carry intel belonging to the Global Rescue Coalition—"

"—which they have made clear they intend to turn over to us," Polo Shirt interrupted. "No, General, you are not in charge of this situation. Please order your men to lower their weapons."

The general's jaw flexed several times before he nodded to his men. Jimmy only realized he was holding his breath when the rifles lowered. He sighed in relief.

The man in the polo shirt smiled. "Now, let's start again. My name is Dr. Reginald Clay, and I'm in charge of Lifeboat Two."

Chapter Twenty-Two

The stainless-steel table in the middle of the kitchen felt cold under Jimmy's hands. Elena sat to his right, her hands folded in her lap. Despite the general's protests, Dr. Clay had ushered them inside the Lifeboat after exchanging introductions. There had been a tense moment of disagreement between Dr. Clay and General Thurston regarding what room to host the newcomers, and Jimmy and Elena had to wait awkwardly until the two had finally agreed the kitchen posed the smallest security risk. Once seated, the general had left but made a show of posting two guards by the door.

Dr. Clay turned in their direction with two steaming mugs in his hands. "Here you go. While our accommodations down here are rather spartan, I was insistent that we would have good coffee." He placed the mugs in front of Jimmy and Elena.

The scent of freshly brewed coffee bathed Jimmy's nostrils, taking him back to days of meeting with his high school study group at the local grind. It had been forever since he'd enjoyed a cup. The first sip filled his mouth with buttery richness that melted into the bitter bite of coffee. For a moment, he forgot the world was in chaos, that The Brotherhood was out to control the city, and that ninety percent of the population was dead. Then the moment was gone.

Dr. Clay grabbed his own mug from the counter and sat

across the table. He took a deep breath and locked eyes with both Jimmy and Elena before speaking. "As you can see, there are a lot of nerves about your arrival. One of the paramount measures we put in place was the secrecy of the Lifeboat. It's why we kept the knowledge of these bunkers to a handful of keepers. If the surviving population discovered we were here—well, you can imagine."

Elena gave Jimmy a knowing look. Jimmy swallowed hard. "Dr. Clay, there is something you need to know in addition to the information on the tablet."

Dr. Clay's expression fell. "Someone else knows we're here, don't they?"

"Yes. They don't know your exact location, but they know the Lifeboat exists."

"And I take it these people are not the sort we would want here."

"Not unless you want armed and dangerous people at your door."

Dr. Clay nodded. "I'm surprised, and admittedly impressed, that you led with that knowledge, given the general's reaction to you two showing up."

"We want to be fully transparent," Elena said. "We're not here to hide anything. We only wanted to deliver Dr. Sheppard's message to you." She slid the tablet across the table to Dr. Clay. "No strings attached."

Dr. Clay placed his hand on the tablet and stared at it for a moment. He closed his eyes as if silently grieving the loss of Dr. Sheppard. Then, he took the tablet to the counter where he plugged it into a charger. He turned and leaned against the counter with his arms folded.

"Look, I am inclined to believe you. You have Dr. Sheppard's tablet after all, and your story will hopefully check out when we can view the entirety of the files on it. I am a man of science, and I believe in the Lifeboat project. Everything needed to start over is underground here with us. One day, we will have to open the doors and try to make that happen."

He reached over to the table and grabbed his mug. Taking a sip, he continued. "There are those like the general that are wary of the world out there, and I'm sure it's with good cause."

Jimmy nodded his agreement. "It's dangerous out there, for sure."

"If the general and those like him had their way, we'd live out the full ten years underground here and not worry about the population out there."

"That's horrible." Elena gasped. "How can they want to forget everyone out there?"

Dr. Clay sighed. "It's easy when you're detached from everything I'm certain is happening out in the world to place security above humanity. If we go above ground to attempt to rebuild without the proper precautions, the entire project could be ruined if our resources fell into the wrong hands. Does that make sense?"

Jimmy and Elena nodded. "It's a good thing you have the general and his guards then. You can protect yourselves." Jimmy chuckled.

Dr. Clay bit his lip and glanced at the floor. "It's not that simple. And frankly, it's my turn to be transparent. Our compound once boasted hundreds of scientists, educators, farmers, soldiers, and leaders. Despite all our screening and quarantine efforts before populating the Lifeboat, someone asymptomatically carried the virus in here. In the first year, our numbers depleted rapidly. President Williams, most of our military guard, and almost all of my colleagues were among the victims. We were lost for quite a while without leadership. Now, only a few dozen of us remain."

"All with Type B blood?" Jimmy asked.

Dr. Clay's eyebrows rose. "So you know?"

Jimmy pointed to the tablet. "You'll want to watch Victoria Clarke's video."

A smile spread across Dr. Clay's face. "It's just like Vicky to figure it out on her own. Not surprising that she kept studying the virus after the Lifeboats were locked up." His face darkened. "I can't believe Vicky is gone, too."

"Was she a friend?" Elena asked, her brow furrowed in concern.

"Sister, actually." Dr. Clay removed his glasses to wipe a tear.

"I'm sorry."

He smiled. "Thank you. She knew the risks. We all did. Despite my best efforts to persuade her to take up refuge in Lifeboat One in Great Britain, she refused. She said someone with their head screwed on straight needed to oversee the Keepers." He sniffed and took another sip of coffee, regaining his composure. "The point is, not many of us remain here in Lifeboat Two. The general would kill me for admitting this to you, but our guard are few in number. Our main security measures are the secrecy and protection of this bunker. Only the lightest security was provided because we couldn't have too many mouths to feed that only filled a single role."

"So that means—"

"If someone from the outside comes in force, we cannot stop them. So let's hope you two are right that these people don't know the location of this place…at least until we have a plan."

Did you find your accommodations acceptable?" Dr. Clay asked as he approached Jimmy and Elena. It had taken a couple hours for the Lifeboat staff to view the videos on the tablet and discuss their authenticity before deciding Jimmy and Elena were who they claimed to be.

"You're really okay with us staying here?" Jimmy asked, running his hand through his wet hair. "Because I can get used to having hot showers again."

"And clean clothes," Elena added.

"Actually, it's one of the stipulations required by General Thurston. The only thing worse than having you two find this place is having you two out there able to tell others where we are." Dr. Clay laughed, seeing their expressions. "That's right. The man who wouldn't let you in now won't let you leave. Ironic, isn't it?"

Elena was still twisting her hair into a long braid. "Still, it kind of makes us prisoners, doesn't it?"

Dr. Clay frowned. "Are you wanting to leave?"

"Not exactly."

"Then, it's semantics, really. Yes, you are not permitted to leave, but since you don't want to anyway…everyone's happy." His frown changed into a warm smile. "For the record, no one here—with the exception of General Thurston—sees you as prisoners. As for him, well you'll notice his guard is not here. In fact, the place is a buzz of activity since you arrived. I've not seen my team this motivated since we were on a deadline to prepare this place before lockdown. We're glad you arrived."

"So that means—?" Jimmy began.

"Yes. Dr. Sheppard's video confirms that the virus has run its course, and it's time to attempt to set up above ground and begin the process of rebuilding. It will take about a month to get everything ready for transport, especially with our depleted numbers, and you two can stay with us until then. In fact, when is the last time you had a hot meal?"

Jimmy's stomach growled at the thought of food. In truth, they'd barely eaten since leaving The Brotherhood. "I could use a bite."

Dr. Clay turned with a wave of his hand. "That settles it. I want to give you a full tour of the place, but I'll start only with the things that are on the way to the cafeteria. We'll get you something to eat."

The three of them turned into the main corridor which travelled the length of the facility. The walls were rough stone, and the ceilings felt uncomfortably low, betraying the haste in which the bunker had been created. Doors lined either wall. Most of the doors closest to the entrance belonged to the guard, including a heavy-duty door with a large lock labeled *Armory*. This was followed by offices and the staff kitchen they'd waited in initially.

Dr. Clay stopped and turned to them, his hand motioning to the door to his right. "Now this you'll want to see."

Jimmy eyed the door, which read *Greenhouse*. "Is that—?"

"It's where we keep our heirloom crops, and where my team spends the bulk of our efforts. Since the virus started in the food supply, we needed to preserve a wide variety of food crops that had not been genetically modified. It's the crops in this room that will ultimately restart our ability to provide food for the surviving population topside. More than anything else in the Lifeboat, this room is the key to restoring life as we once knew it."

Dr. Clay slid his key card through the magnetic reader, which produced a quiet tone. The door lock clicked open, and he pulled on the handle. Bright light poured into the corridor from the room inside. "After you."

Jimmy and Elena stepped into the room, which was lined with white coveralls. Dr. Clay removed two and handed them to Jimmy and Elena. "We are cautious about contamination in this room, so you'll need to wear cleanroom suits."

Jimmy stepped into the coveralls and zipped the front all the way up. Dr. Clay, wearing his own suit, handed him a hair net and shoe covers. He slipped the gear on and looked at Elena, who was tucking her braid into her own hair net. Her lips spread into a grin when she saw him in the getup. He could tell she was suppressing a laugh.

"What? You don't like my new style?" Jimmy mocked a runway walk, complete with turn and too-serious expression. He popped a hip to the side, placing his hand on it, and posed.

Elena couldn't contain her laughter. She doubled over, her

arms crossed across her middle. Jimmy laughed with her.

"Not the most fashionable wear, for sure." Dr. Clay smiled at them, slipping on his own hair net. "Honestly, it's been a while since that kind of laughter has been heard down here. It's good to hear."

Jimmy recovered from his fit and slipped his shoe covers over his sneakers, a grin still wide across his face. Dr. Clay crossed the room to a white metal door. Sliding his keycard again, the new door clicked open. A bluish glow, as if something unearthly awaited them in the next room, spilled through the opening as he pulled on the heavy door. The three stepped into the space beyond. All laughter stopped, replaced by the silence of awe.

Through the door, a naturally cavernous chamber stretched at least the length of two football fields. Greenhouse lights, mounted in rows the length of the rock ceiling, bathed the entire space in a blue violet glow. Row upon row of plants stretched skyward on aeroponic and hydroponic columns boasting every manner of vegetable. The individual trickles of water running over the plant roots inside the columns joined together to create a rushing sound that made Jimmy swear he was in the jungle for a moment. He even thought he could see several fruit trees in the corner. Elena walked over to the column in front of her and ran her finger down the skin of a bright red tomato.

The kaleidoscope of colors and smell of plant life was almost too overwhelming. Jimmy had to remind himself to take a deep breath.

"This, my new friends, is my life's work." Dr. Clay caressed the leaf of a vine in front of him. "It's why I was chosen as one of the lead scientists for Lifeboat Two."

Elena squatted down at the base of one of the columns. "You can grow plants without dirt?"

"Yes, we can. In fact, it's more efficient and allows us to isolate each plant in its own contained ecosystem should one become diseased and need to be removed. There's no soil to pass a fungus or infection to the next plant."

Jimmy's mind could not connect a coherent phrase to all the thoughts racing through his brain. To think that all of this fresh food had been right here for the last three years. A flood of jealousy coursed through his consciousness only to be quickly overcome by hope. Soon, the world outside would be able to benefit. Dr. Clay and his team had the means to save the suffering world above. The gravity of what they'd done by delivering Dr. Sheppard's message hit him, and his knees began to shake.

He sat down, right in the middle of the floor, and rested his face in his hands.

"Jimmy, you okay?" Elena placed a concerned hand on his shoulder as she sat behind him.

"I-I just can't take this all in."

"I know." Elena wrapped her arms around him from behind, and the two sat for a moment.

Dr. Clay approached and squatted down next to them. "I can't imagine what it has been like out there to struggle every day to find food and safe shelter." He held up his hand, which contained a crimson tomato. "This one is ripe and would have been picked in the harvest today. Have a taste."

Jimmy looked up at Dr. Clay. With a trembling hand, he took

the tomato. The weight of it surprised him as he ran his finger over the delicately firm skin. His nostrils filled with the smell of natural ripeness. He glanced backward at Elena, who offered a soft grin and a slight nod. With two hands, he brought the tomato to his mouth and bit.

His teeth penetrated the skin and sank into the meat of the fruit. Juices burst from the insides of the tomato and ran out the corners of his mouth to his chin. Pulling the fruit away from his lips, he savored the taste for a moment before he began to chew. The sweetness of the body of the tomato mixed with the tartness of the natural acid. He swallowed, and he could feel tears welling in his eyes.

Handing the tomato to Elena, he wiped the juice from his chin with one hand. Elena took her own bite, and her eyes rolled with delight at its flavor.

"That has to be the most delicious thing I've ever tasted." She took a second bite before even swallowing the first.

An ear-to-ear grin spread on Dr. Clay's face. "Just wait until you taste what our cook can do with these. I'm serious, if everyone from outside has that reaction to fresh food, these next few months are going to be a lot of fun once we're up and running."

The three of them stood and strolled among the columns of fruits and vegetables. Beans and lettuces. Raspberries and blueberries. Melons and squash. Everywhere they looked was a veritable Eden of natural deliciousness.

"All the ripe fruits and vegetables are harvested and brought to this end of the floor." Dr. Clay pointed as they approached the side wall of the room. Baskets and barrels lined the floor, filled to the brim with food. "These are organized. Some are harvested for seeds. The rest are sent to the kitchen over there to feed those living down here." He pointed to a doorway next to a large window. Several cooks were hard at work preparing the evening meal. "Quickest way to the cafeteria is through the kitchen."

They crossed the space toward the kitchen door, when a large red button caught Jimmy's attention. It was recessed and mounted to the wall behind glass. Warning signs and lights surrounded it.

"Dr. Clay, what's that?" He pointed with his chin in the direction of the button.

"That is our failsafe," Dr. Clay answered with a sigh. "Something I'm glad we never had to use."

"Failsafe?" Elena asked.

"You've seen the videos on the tablet. You know the virus began when genetically modified foods attempted to defend themselves against aphids. One of the greatest unknowns of the Lifeboat project is if that virus would somehow spread to the heirloom crops we were bringing underground. If that happened, the entire population down here would be at risk"—he paused to take a breath—"or so we thought before we understood the immunity of B-type blood carriers. Every Lifeboat was installed with these fail safes that would kill the entire crop in the room to prevent the virus from infecting the population. It uses a highly concentrated non-selective herbicide that damages the plants beyond repair in minutes. Trust me, you wouldn't want to be in here more than a few minutes when that happens. Thankfully, the crop never developed the virus, but that didn't stop our community from being decimated by the virus anyway." Dr. Clay took a long breath and rubbed the bridge of his nose.

"I'm sorry. That must have been devastating."

Dr. Clay nodded and spoke in a whisper, barely audible above the running water noise. "Yeah. Those buttons are on every wall of the room. You can't walk the perimeter of this space without being reminded of how careful we thought we were being. In the end, it didn't matter."

Elena stepped in front of him, halting his gait. She reached up and wrapped her arms around Dr. Clay's neck. Dr. Clay straightened, startled by the gesture, but then leaned in to return the embrace. They held each other a long time before he let out a long sigh, as though breathing out the sadness he felt.

"Thank you, young lady." Dr. Clay smiled and held his glasses up to wipe his eyes.

"We've *all* been through a lot," Elena said. "Now we *all* get to make it worth it."

Dr. Clay nodded with a smile. "Right you are." He held a hand up toward the kitchen to indicate they should resume walking. "Now if I could treat you to a meal, I would be much obliged."

Chapter Twenty-Three

The kitchen was a cloud of spiced aromas and tendrils of grilled goodness. Jimmy had almost been tempted to pick a piece of grilled bell pepper right off the hot surface before thinking better of it. Within minutes, a hot plate of food was placed in front of each of them. Grilled vegetables over a bed of rice sat next to two warm rolls.

"Where do you get the eggs and milk for making bread?" Elena asked.

"That would be from our chicken coop and dairy cows." Dr. Clay let out a chuckle when he saw Jimmy's shocked expression. "Yes. They're at the other end of the compound. We live a fairly vegetarian lifestyle down here, but our population of chickens and cows provide enough eggs and milk for a few luxuries."

Jimmy couldn't help but imagine a grilled steak sitting in front of him. His mouth watered, despite the incredible taste of the food in front of him. "But you don't get to eat—"

"Meat?" Dr. Clay shook his head. "No. Unfortunately, not. Feeding animals for consumption was too impractical, so we focused on providing more sustainable foods. Besides, we need our population of animals to hopefully breed a new stock once we are topside. I'm guessing most of the world's livestock was hunted or died in the first year without the farms running."

Jimmy picked one of the rolls off his plate. The warm, spongey bread yielded under the pressure of his fingers, melted butter dripping out of the middle of the roll. He took a bite. Until that moment, the ripe tomato was the greatest thing he'd ever tasted. The bread melted in his mouth, and he couldn't remember the last time he'd enjoyed food this much. The canned and packaged goods they'd survived on were nothing compared to the buttery goodness he was eating.

"Enjoying that roll?" Elena giggled.

He opened his eyes only to realize that he'd been savoring the roll with his eyes closed. His face grew hot with embarrassment.

"Should we leave you and the roll alone for a minute?"

Dr. Clay shook with silent laughter. Elena made no attempt to contain hers. The giggles turned into chuckles.

"It's just so good," Jimmy said, his mouth still full of roll. The moment he said it he realized that the statement only made him appear more ridiculous.

Elena nearly spit her food out as her laughter increased. She held a hand to her mouth to keep from expelling the forkful of rice she'd eaten. Even Dr. Clay allowed his laughter to become audible.

The three of them laughed until Jimmy's stomach hurt.

A pang of guilt struck Jimmy as he sighed to end his laughing fit. The last time he'd laughed this much had been with Wyatt. What had become of his friend? What would it have been like to share this meal with him? Everything Wyatt wanted, a full stomach and safety, was here at the Lifeboat.

If only he'd stuck with them a little longer...

Elena gave him a knowing look and nodded as though able to

read his thoughts. She offered a sympathetic smile and resumed eating.

"Excuse me. I was told you two were the ones who brought the tablet to the Lifeboat."

Jimmy turned to meet the woman speaking behind him. She was blonde and middle-aged, wearing a t-shirt and jeans. Next to her were a teenage boy about his own age and a girl who appeared to be about thirteen. The girl's eyes were red and puffy as though she'd been crying. The woman was still dabbing furtively at the corners of her eyes with a tissue. He instantly recognized her from her photo.

"Yes, we are." Elena answered when Jimmy hesitated.

"My name is Cyndi Sheppard. Harold was my husband."

The realization that he was meeting the family of the deceased Dr. Sheppard hit Jimmy square in the chest, and he had to focus to take a breath, so he didn't choke on the bite of roll still in his mouth. He quickly chewed and swallowed. Standing from his chair, he turned to meet Cyndi Sheppard.

He wasn't certain what to say. "I-I was the one who found the tablet with your husband."

Without warning, the woman lunged at him, throwing her arms around his neck. She squeezed until he could barely breathe. Tremors overtook her body, and he could tell she was crying again.

"Thank you." She spoke in muffled sobs at his shoulder. "Thank you for bringing his final words to us. We might have never known what happened without you."

Jimmy peered over her shoulder to see her glassy-eyed son place an arm around his sister, who'd begun to weep again. Cyndi pulled away with a loud sniff.

"I-I'm sorry to be so forward. Here I am hugging you before even asking your name." She wiped at the tears on her cheeks.

"I'm Jimmy. This is Elena." He motioned to Elena, who stood and circled the table to offer an embrace to Cyndi.

"It's nice to meet you both. This is my son Matthias and my daughter Vanessa." She gestured to her children with a hand. Cyndi paused, seemingly hesitant to go on. "Can you tell me how you found him? How did you know how to look for him?"

Jimmy knew this next bit of news was going to be hard to hear. He took a deep breath. "We didn't know it was your husband until we found the car. We are—er—were scavengers, trading useful items for food. When I found your husband's car with my drone, I only thought it would be something to check out." He sighed realizing how recently he'd stumbled upon the vehicle with his drone. It felt like years had passed.

"Where was his car?"

Jimmy swallowed. "Just a few miles from here. He was on his way here…to be with you."

Cyndi's lip quivered as she slowly lost the battle to maintain her composure. Her head twitched in a barely perceptible nod, as if too much motion would break open the floodgates of emotion. She sniffed hard, her voice choking as she spoke. "Thank you for telling me. Dr. Clay and the others were somewhat cryptic in that detail. It's nice to know that he hadn't forgotten about us. After years of not hearing anything, you begin to wonder." She stopped, dabbing at her eyes again. "You may not have intended to find my husband, but you did. I'm grateful to you for it."

Her children took positions at her sides, and they wrapped their arms around their mother. The three turned and plodded off to exit the cafeteria, their heads hanging as they walked.

Jimmy turned to Dr. Clay. "I'm sorry. Maybe I shouldn't have shared that."

Dr. Clay shook his head. "No, it's all right. We weren't sure when to let her know that he was so close. We thought it might be salt in the wound, but perhaps it's best that it's out in the open. Truth is always best in the end."

An hour later, Jimmy leaned against a railing overlooking the greenhouse from above. The height of the plants and the entire operation still amazed him, but he found his mind wandering away from that to another topic. His fingers found the ring hanging from his neck.

Greater love has no one than this…

"What is it, Jimmy?" Elena stood at his side, her arms resting on the railing. He could feel her eyes studying the side of his face. "I can tell something is eating at you."

"Wyatt should be here."

Elena's face darkened. "Jimmy, you have to stop beating yourself up about that. I'm sad that he's not with us, too, but as I said, he made his choice."

"I know, but I could have done more. I *should* have done more." Jimmy rehearsed his last conversation with Wyatt in his mind. "I should have made him listen or knocked him out or…something."

"As you've told me, you only had minutes to get me and get out while the guard was changing. I don't think you could have done all that while dragging Wyatt's unconscious body."

Jimmy nodded. Elena was right. Her logic was sound, but the thought still burrowed into his soul. "Everything he was looking for…everything that made him sign on to The Brotherhood, he could have found here. Food. Safety. Community. He just wasn't patient enough to wait for it."

Guilt threatened to tear Jimmy apart from the inside, and he straightened with a loud sniff to hold back the tears. His friend was gone, left to the mercy of The Brotherhood's rage, and he was standing here looking at the abundance of the Lifeboat. Their future was full of hope, while Wyatt might not even be alive. No, the message of the ring didn't seem to work in this world.

"He liked you, you know."

Elena turned her gaze toward the greenhouse. "I know."

"He may have even loved you."

She shook her head, still fixated on the rows of plant towers beneath them. "No. He didn't love me. He may have thought he did, but love does not force the other person's hand. He wanted you to leave and deceive me into thinking…well, I don't know what he would have said. He might have claimed you were dead. Or that you abandoned us. Either way, he would have tried to deceive me. That is not love."

"You may be right." Jimmy joined her in gazing at the towers.

"I know I'm right." Elena turned to Jimmy, placing her hand on his. "It's like the ring around your neck says. Love chooses to sacrifice for others. It doesn't hoard what it wants. It doesn't lie to get what it wants. It does what is best for the other person, despite the cost to oneself."

Jimmy glanced down at their hands before turning to meet her eyes. The deep brown of her eyes twitched slightly as she gazed back at his features. He smiled at her, shyly at first before allowing the full warmth of his feeling to spread across his face. His heart fluttered as he considered what he wanted to say to her in that moment. He thought of Dr. Clay's words. *Truth is always best in the end.* He should tell her the truth—the full truth. He took a breath to speak.

"Jimmy,"—she spoke quickly, as if trying to get the words out before he could make his confession—"you sacrificed. I know you believe that you've failed. The truth is you risked everything to get me away from the Brotherhood. You've spent the last three years putting yourself in harm's way to provide for us. Whenever there was something we could salvage, you never hesitated to offer to go after it. You did it for us…to take care of us. To take care of me."

Jimmy's confession lodged in his throat, unable to come out. Her gaze melted his insides. Her touch made him want to tremble and relax all at the same time. His mind raced for something to say. "I-I thought you hated it when I went out scavenging." He chided himself for choosing something so dumb to say in the moment.

She smiled, laughing slightly to herself. "I know I fussed at you a lot, but it's because I was afraid that something would happen to you, and you wouldn't return." Her gaze dropped to the floor. "I was scared I would get left behind like Dr. Sheppard's wife."

The analogy took Jimmy by surprise. What was she saying?

"Elena, I—"

"One second," she interrupted. "I need to say this before I chicken out. For three years, we have watched out for each other. Both of us got left behind by parents who didn't make it through the pandemic. We've been surviving from one day to the next, sometimes only barely making it. I thought there was no real future to hope for." Tears found the edge of her eyelids, threatening to fall. "I couldn't entertain anything except to help the three of us get from one day to the next, but the truth is—" She paused, appearing unable to go on.

Jimmy gently placed a finger under her chin, encouraging her to meet his gaze. "What is it?"

She stared at him, a single tear escaping her eye and running over her cheekbone. "The truth is…I love you. I have for a long time. Now that it seems we have the chance for a future—" She glanced again at the plant towers before returning to him. "A future that could mean some kind of life together—I wanted you to know. I *needed* you to know. I love you, Jimmy."

The words ignited a flame inside Jimmy's heart. Not the slow, soft burn of a match, but the vibrant phosphorus brilliance of a firework exploding within him. The sensation shot a buzz of electricity that reached the ends of his limbs and vaporized any fear he had. His entire body felt alive as if newly born. The air, though they were far underground, smelled sweeter than after a spring rain. In an instant, his mind replayed the moment over and over. The shape of her lips as she spoke. The softness in her features. The creases at the corners of her glassy eyes. In milliseconds, he'd relived the moment a hundred times, each filling him with as much warmth as the last.

Elena loved him.

"Elena—" He paused, the awkwardness of the moment increasing the more he hesitated. How could he not make this sound cheesy or trite? He thought of all the ways he could answer, and his mind only came up with movie quotations.

You complete me.

I know.

As you wish.

None of those were right for the moment. He had only seconds before awkwardness became hurtful, so he opened his mouth and said the next thing that came to mind. "You win."

Elena pulled back slightly and gave him an inquisitive expression. "I win?"

Stupid, Jimmy. So stupid. "Uh, yeah. You win. I've wanted to tell you I loved you for so long, but of course you beat me to it. So I guess you win."

For a second he thought he'd blown the moment. He'd had an opportunity to finally confess his heart, and he'd said the dumbest thing possible. Any moment, her smile would disappear, and she'd feel hurt that he'd not said it right.

Then, she smiled. It was an expression of pure joy mixed with amusement. "Jimmy, that has to be the weirdest way to tell me you love me back." She paused, letting out a small laugh. "But I'm glad you do."

Not wanting to mess up the moment any further, he rested his hand on the back of her neck, his fingers intertwining in the strands of her ebony hair. He gently pulled her toward him. She didn't resist.

Their lips met.

He drank in the moment as her lips caressed his in soft warmth. Her arms tightened around his middle, and he embraced her with his other arm. A kiss lasting only seconds stretched into a moment containing years of connection and fondness and growing love.

When they parted, they rested their foreheads against each other. She blushed as she peered upward at him and let out a breathy chuckle. He smiled and returned the laugh. Elena's hand slid upward to find his, and she held it against her cheek as she leaned into him.

They held each other in the purple-blue haze of the greenhouse as the trickling water echoed off the walls. For a moment, the world was not crazy. They experienced a second of peace in which they did not need to consider their survival or the fate of the world. All that mattered was each other.

Then came the explosion.

Chapter Twenty-Four

The ground shook beneath Jimmy's feet, and he needed to let go of Elena with one hand to grab the railing. Lights flickered throughout the room, and bits of rock sprinkled downward from the ceiling. A low *boom* followed an instant later, momentarily buffeting their eardrums.

Screams and panic could be heard from the workers below. People began rushing, though Jimmy couldn't imagine where they were going.

Another explosion. More flickering lights. More bits falling. This time, a plant tower cracked in the middle, and water began escaping from the side slapping the concrete floor with each droplet.

"What is that?" Elena gasped, unable to hide her fear.

Jimmy didn't answer. He grabbed her hand and ran for the main corridor. The hallway was filled with people darting from one room to the next. A few tried shouting instructions. Parents held their hands over the heads of children in the vain hope of protecting them should the rock begin to cave in. One worker was shoving hard hats into people's hands.

Boom!

Jimmy stumbled as the ground moved beneath his feet, bringing Elena down with him. She yelped and clutched her ankle, which still sported the brace given to her. Scrambling to his feet, he grabbed her hands and pulled her to a standing position. She took a step and cried out when she attempted to put her weight on her ankle.

Wheeling around to her other side, he ducked his head under her armpit. Tucking her injured leg behind her, the two hobbled up the corridor until they reached the door of Dr. Clay's office.

Dr. Clay burst from the office, the door clanging loudly as it hit the wall unrestrained. His eyes were wide as saucers, and he stumbled back, startled by their presence. He stared as though unable to recognize them.

"Dr. Clay, what is happening?" Jimmy exclaimed above the shouts and cries.

Dr. Clay shook his head as if clearing mental cobwebs. It was only then that Jimmy noticed the blood trickling down from his scalp. Something had struck his head, and he was confused.

"They-they-they're outside," Dr. Clay stammered.

Jimmy grabbed Dr. Clay's arm and shook him. "Who's outside? Where can we go to see what's going on?"

Dr. Clay still didn't seem to register Jimmy's face. "S-security office. Cameras."

Elena let out another whimper, and Jimmy tightened his arm around her. "Where is the security office? Dr. Clay…can you lead us?"

Dr. Clay touched his head with this hand. Pulling it away, he marveled at the blood that covered his fingers.

"Yes, you're hurt. You need help. Perhaps there is someone who can help at the security office. Which way is it?"

Dr. Clay's hand trembled as he continued to stare at the blood. "N-near f-front offices. Th-that way." His eyes didn't leave the blood as his other hand pointed farther up the hallway.

Jimmy wrenched Dr. Clay's arm to spin him in the direction of the security office. Still supporting Elena, he urged Dr. Clay forward with a hand on his back. The three shuffled forward, occasionally being bumped by someone running the other way.

Boom! Another explosion rocked the facility. This time, the lights went out for a full three seconds before kicking back on.

Dr. Clay fell to the floor. With a strained cry, he covered his head with both hands and curled up against the wall. Jimmy helped Elena support herself against the wall as he slipped out from under her arm. With both hands, he lifted Dr. Clay.

"Dr. Clay! We have to keep moving!" He shouted above the commotion. He was so close to Dr. Clay's face that spit from his mouth hit Dr. Clay in the cheek. He didn't seem to notice.

Dr. Clay trembled and covered his face, overwhelmed by fear.

"I can't carry both of you. Now walk!" Jimmy shoved Dr. Clay back into the center of the hallway. He hated treating him like this in his injured state, but he had to help Elena.

He slid back under Elena's arm. Several excruciating minutes passed as they trudged forward, and Jimmy wondered if Dr. Clay had misled them in his confusion. Up ahead, Jimmy made out a doorway with a bright red label. White letters were inscribed on the label, and Jimmy breathed a sigh of relief when the word *SECURITY* became readable.

Stumbling forward, he urged Dr. Clay and Elena to the door. He yanked the handle, and the heavy door swung outward.

The interior of the security office was a buzz of activity. At the center of the room, General Thurston stood with his arms folded and barked orders. Screens displayed various grayscale views of the exterior of the bunker. Several showed vehicles of all makes and models lined up at the edge of the trees. Men and women stood behind the hoods of the vehicles in camouflage fatigues with their rifles trained in the direction of the bunker.

Another screen showed the entrance that Jimmy and Elena had entered. Chunks of rock were strewn about the ground. Two men crouched by the doorway working on attaching something to the massive entryway. A second later, they scrambled away from the door. On every screen, people ducked behind their vehicles. A brilliant flash lit up the entry.

Boom!

Lights and a couple screens flickered but stayed on this time.

"Backup generators are holding, sir," a soldier called out to the general.

"Is the welcome party in place?" General Thurston roared. "If they manage to open that doorway, I want a hail of bullets ready to punish anyone who dares to enter this facility."

"Alpha Team is nearly in place."

"Radio again and tell them I want them in position yesterday!"

"Yes, sir."

General Thurston let out an exasperated grunt as he ran his hand over his closely cropped hair. In that moment, he noticed Jimmy's party standing in the doorway. He allowed a curse to fly. "Boy, what are you doing in here?" He glanced at the screen again. "These friends of yours?"

Jimmy ignored the question. "Sir, it's Dr. Clay. He's hurt."

The general's attention snapped to Dr. Clay, and for a moment concern washed over his face. "Winters, grab that med kit and help the doctor." He jabbed a finger at one of the soldiers.

"Yes, sir. Right on it." A uniformed woman rushed over, a red cross emblazoned on her sleeve. She helped Dr. Clay into a chair and began inspecting his wound.

"She's hurt, too," Jimmy said, helping Elena into another chair.

"I'm fine. Help Dr. Clay first." Elena spoke through gritted teeth as she sat next to Dr. Clay.

Relieved of his two injured companions, Jimmy turned back to the general, who stood staring at him. His lips were drawn tight and veins pulsed at his temples.

"Now, boy, you care to share what you know about the people outside attempting to blow a hole in our bunker?"

Jimmy gazed at the screens. He'd guessed who was out there, but he longed to find any evidence that he was wrong. Instead, his eyes locked on a familiar face. A man stood wearing a loose-fitting jacket, his upper body peeking out the sunroof of a sport utility vehicle. His arms were crossed and resting on the roof of the car. He wore a bored expression.

Mr. Quinn was right outside the Lifeboat.

Chapter Twenty-Five

"What's the point? They know that we're here," Jimmy protested. He and the general had been going back and forth for several minutes since Jimmy had identified the people outside. The general was pressing him for 'intel' on who he was facing. All the while, Jimmy watched with one eye as Mr. Quinn's soldiers prepared another explosive on the bunker doorway.

General Thurston glared at him red-faced as he pointed an angry finger at Jimmy. "Your suggestion is really to let him in the building? To compromise the safety of everyone in here?"

"All I'm saying is that he's going to break through that door anyway. We can't stop him." Jimmy clenched his fists, exasperated. He understood the general's desire to protect his people at all costs, but people had already been hurt by the blasts. "General, I understand that you are in charge—"

"You're darn right I am, boy."

"—and I know you're concerned with the safety of everyone in here."

"Get to your point."

"Sir, I know Mr. Quinn. I've seen his soldiers in action. They are trained and well equipped. Mr. Quinn is too calculating to attack this place unless he felt he could get inside."

Another blast. The screens flashed white and flickered as the backup power threatened to disconnect.

General Thurston's lips spread into a smug grin. "Son, that door is several inches of steel, able to withstand being rammed by a vehicle at high velocity. I don't think whatever improvised device your *Mr. Quinn* has concocted in his kitchen can breach that wall."

As if on cue, Mr. Quinn started pointing at his men on the screen. They opened the back of a delivery van and pulled two boxes marked with military stencils. "Whatever he has in there, doesn't look homemade."

General Thurston squinted at the screen as the boxes were opened. Inside, stacks of wrapped bars lined the interior. The labels were unreadable on the security screen, but the general's wide-eyed expression told the story even before he opened his mouth. "Dear God, where did he get military grade C-4?"

"C-4?" Jimmy asked.

"Composition Four. Plastic explosive."

"Probably got it from the military."

General Thurston glowered at Jimmy like he'd spoken heresy.

Jimmy swallowed and continued. "Ninety percent of the world is dead. Military posts are abandoned all over the place. And"—Jimmy hesitated, knowing the general would not like the next part—"many of Mr. Quinn's forces are military."

"Defectors?"

"Survivors," Jimmy corrected. "They couldn't sit around waiting for orders from Washington that will never come."

The bars of C-4 were being fixed to the bunker door. It

wouldn't be long before Mr. Quinn blew the doors off the place, causing untold injuries to those inside.

"General, he's coming in whether we like it or not."

General Thurston glanced at the floor and shook his head. "It's not in me to surrender."

A groan came from Dr. Clay whose bandaged head turned in their direction. His lips parted as if it hurt him to speak. "But it is in you to protect the lives of those in this shelter."

Dr. Clay's voice caught both of them off-guard, and several people in the room paused to turn to the wounded doctor. Jimmy was relieved to see Dr. Clay had calmed down from his earlier panic.

The doctor slowly raised a hand to gently touch the bandage on his head. He winced the moment his hand made contact. "I'm still a little foggy, but I'm catching up. General, please consider what a confrontation will cost. You don't have a third of the men this force has, and that is just what I can see on the screen."

General Thurston sighed. He stared at Dr. Clay, not with the hardened glare he'd been giving Jimmy, but a softer expression that carried the weight of the years they'd lived underground and taken care of the Lifeboat survivors together. Walking over to the console, he repositioned a microphone that jutted out from the panel. He pointed to an illuminated button next to the microphone. "Press this here, young man. Talk to your friend outside."

Jimmy stepped backward. "Me?"

"This Mr. Quinn knows who you are. Perhaps you can get him to stop for a moment to listen."

Jimmy approached the microphone. The entire security room was frozen with their eyes fixed on him. He tilted the end of the microphone to his lips and cleared his throat. His finger hesitated over the button that activated the microphone. On the screen, the vehicles were being motioned backward, preparing for the larger blast that the plastic explosive would cause. It was now or never.

<hr>

"M-Mr. Quinn?" Jimmy couldn't hide the tremor in his voice. For a second, nothing changed in the behavior of the men and women on the screen. He tried again, louder. "Mr. Quinn."

Mr. Quinn waved his hands at his men from the roof of his sport utility vehicle. Soldiers turned to their underlings and made slashing gestures at their throats, instructing all vehicles to cut their engines. Mr. Quinn disappeared into the sunroof and emerged from the door of his car. He walked forward to the bunker door, seemingly confident and unfazed. His eyes scanned the door until he located the camera in the corner. For a long moment, he stared into the camera. It unnerved Jimmy, as though Mr. Quinn could see him through the lens.

"Jimmy, my friend, is that you?" Mr. Quinn smiled as if excited to hear from Jimmy again.

Jimmy turned to the general and Dr. Clay. The general stopped whispering in the ear of one of his men and pointed at the microphone. "Keep him talking." He turned again to the soldier to his left, who nodded and exited hurriedly from the room.

"Uh, yes, it's me. Jimmy."

Mr. Quinn smiled at the camera. "I thought the voice sounded familiar. I'm glad to see you're okay, my friend. It's a dangerous world out there…or should I say out here."

"Yeah. I suppose." Jimmy mentally scrambled to find something to talk about. He needed anything that would elicit a response from Mr. Quinn. "Where's Wyatt?" The words crossed his lips before he could think twice about them.

Mr. Quinn's smile dissolved into a frown. "Oh, he's here." He motioned with his head to the group behind him. Jimmy scanned the cameras, but he could not see Wyatt in the group. "I must say, Jimmy, that I was disappointed you didn't take me up on my deal. I think we could have worked well together to create something amazing with The Brotherhood. Still, Wyatt offered me enough information to keep him around for now."

"I want to see him…to make sure he's okay."

Mr. Quinn raised an eyebrow. "Really, from what I understand you knocked your friend…er, ex-friend…out cold during your escape. Doesn't sound like you're all that concerned about his welfare."

Jimmy answered with silence.

"No, I don't think you'll be seeing your friend until we can speak face to face. Why don't you make things easier and let me in? Then, maybe you can see Wyatt."

Jimmy silently cursed. Only a moment ago, he'd been eager to have the general let them in, but now it would look like Mr. Quinn controlled him. He needed to change the subject.

"H-how did you find this place?"

"Why don't you ask what you really mean, Jimmy? You want to know how I found this place with the limited information I received from Wyatt, don't you?" There was a long pause as if he expected Jimmy to answer. "That's what I thought. True, young Wyatt did not get to view the maps that led to this location, but his information was enough to convince me you hadn't stumbled upon a fool's errand."

"Then, how did you get here?"

"Simple. Your other friend. Elena, is it? She led us right to you."

Chapter Twenty-Six

Jimmy's gaze shot to Elena, who straightened in her chair. A look of shock or fear—he couldn't be certain—washed over her face. In an instant, the general and one of his officers drew their sidearms and pointed them at Elena. She cried out as her hands instinctively rose to her face in protection. Jimmy lunged in her direction, placing himself between Elena and the pistols.

"What are you doing?" he shouted.

"Placing her under arrest," the general barked. "She betrayed our position."

"You don't know that." Jimmy held both arms out to his side to keep them from flanking his position.

The general pointed to the screen. "He just said—"

"Exactly." Jimmy interrupted. "*He* said. Let's hear what she has to say before we're turning our guns on her."

The general's shoulders eased slightly, and the muzzle of his pistol lowered halfway to the floor. He nodded at his officer to follow his example, but neither holstered their weapon.

Jimmy lowered his arms cautiously and turned to Elena. She cowered in her chair, her face buried in her arms. Jimmy gently pried her hands away, and she jerked backward trying to escape his grip. Tears flooded her cheeks, and her lips trembled.

"I-I didn't do anything. J-Jimmy, h-he's lying." The words

came as whispered gasps. All the while, her saucer-like eyes stared at the guns. "I-I didn't."

Jimmy knelt in front of her, taking both her hands. "I believe you," he whispered. He turned to the general and raised the volume of his voice. "I believe her."

"That's nice, but her face reads guilty." The general rolled his eyes.

"Her face reads that she just had two guns pointed at her!" The words came with such force that Jimmy surprised himself. Even the general took a step backward. "Now put the guns away."

"General Thurston, I don't think the girl is a danger," Dr. Clay interjected.

Both men holstered their pistols, a look of shame passing across the officers' face.

A slow, steady chuckle came from the speakers. Everyone turned to the security screen to see Mr. Quinn's ear-to-ear grin. He was laughing.

"Awfully quiet, aren't you Jimmy?" He laughed again. "Let me guess. My revelation caused quite a stir. I'm guessing someone in charge of security immediately thought the worst of poor Elena. You, being the ever-chivalrous friend, intervened on her behalf, and I'm now interrupting a bit of a standoff. Am I right?"

Jimmy refused to move from Elena's side.

"I'll take your silence as an affirmative. You see, Jimmy, I know you. I know all of you. It's not hard to calculate what kind of people are on the other side of this camera. Government is so predictable." Mr. Quinn sighed and crossed his arms. "I'm guessing there is a mix of science types and military types, who probably have a very fragile truce with each other. It's a truce I'm certain I've upset. There may even be a political figure or two adding complexity to the dynamic in there. That is if the virus hasn't wiped them out. We could all be so lucky."

He was correct, and that made Jimmy's stomach turn. Mr. Quinn could seemingly predict any outcome, and Jimmy grasped that he was here with a plan. He eyed the general, who seemed taken aback by the accuracy of Mr. Quinn's description.

Jimmy stood slowly. He glared at the general as he gestured toward the microphone. The general nodded. Message received. *Do not mess with Elena as I go back to speaking to Mr. Quinn.* He squeezed Elena's hand as he moved away, his eyes riveted on the general.

Leaning into the microphone, he spoke. "Mr. Quinn, you don't know what you're talking about." He winced at the simplicity of the words, but he had to try to throw the man off.

Mr. Quinn frowned. "Please, Jimmy. I thought we chose to quit lying to each other already. No, I'm guessing your lovely friend is sitting in a pile of tears and denying she's had anything to do with our discovery of your little *Lifeboat.*"

Jimmy's gut knotted at the accuracy of his words. *How did he know so much?* He turned to Elena, who still had tears dripping from her cheeks.

"I promise, Jimmy. I didn't," she rasped, her voice hoarse from her crying.

"Maybe she is and maybe she isn't," Jimmy said.

"Oh, she is. Tears. Denial. Swearing she didn't do it." He paused, a wide grin again spreading across his face. "And she'd be right."

"What do you mean?" Jimmy asked the question a little too quickly, showing his hand.

Mr. Quinn smirked. "See? I'm right. I always am. You want to exonerate her, so you can't help but want to know what I'm getting at. Well, I'll humor you. She *did* lead us to you, but she didn't *mean* to. In fact, she had no idea she was helping us." He paused. "Jimmy, can you figure it out? Or do you need a hint? Let's see if you are as intelligent as I thought."

Jimmy gazed at Elena, who still shook her head in denial. He scanned her until his eyes locked upon the wrap around her ankle. Without warning, he dove to the floor in front of her and began unwrapping the swollen joint. "Sorry," he whispered as she winced.

Layer after layer of the wrap peeled away. Near the bottom of the dressing, a small device clung to the wrap material. He didn't need to understand the technology to guess its purpose. "They tracked you."

Elena leaned forward to see the device, her mouth agape. "When did they—?"

"Mr. Quinn's medic applied this wrap when Wyatt and I were out. You were in pain, and it would have been easy for him to slip this in there without you noticing." Jimmy cursed under his breath. "He's one step ahead…always."

"I think I speak for all of us when I apologize for the misunderstanding, Elena." The words felt empty coming from Dr. Clay instead of the general, but Jimmy was at least thankful they'd been spoken. The medic pulled out a fresh wrap and applied a new brace to Elena's ankle.

"Jimmy? You still there?" Mr. Quinn's voice sounded hopeful. "Did you find the device?"

Jimmy sprang back to the microphone. Fury coursed through his veins. His insides boiled, wanting to rage at Mr. Quinn for his deception that nearly brought harm to Elena. He wanted to punch the general for being so quick to turn a weapon on her. And he hated himself for not being more careful to check the dressing they'd put on her, which ultimately put her in danger.

"Jimmy, I don't have all day." Mr. Quinn sounded impatient.

"What do you want?" His tone betrayed his anger. He couldn't resist.

"Well said. I agree it's time to get down to business. I've had my fun and proved my point. You can't fool me, Jimmy, so it's best you hear me out."

"I'm listening."

"Good. I have enough plastic explosive attached to the doors of this facility to blow them off their hinges twice over. I suspect you are turning now to confirm this fact with the military people in your presence."

Jimmy was indeed looking at the general, and he hated Mr. Quinn for knowing that.

"If what Wyatt tells me he overheard is true, then these Lifeboats were formed prior to the discovery of the B-type blood immunity. That means there is a high statistical chance that the population of this bunker has been decimated over the last few years, leaving their security forces depleted to a fraction of their size."

"You don't know that for certain. We may have dozens of

security waiting to gun you down the second you enter."

Mr. Quinn offered a sympathetic expression. "It's probabilities, Jimmy. The chances that an asymptomatic carrier of the virus passed through their inevitably hasty quarantine measures is extremely high. One person in a confined population would spread the infection quickly."

Dr. Clay let out a long slow breath as though reliving the horror the Lifeboat community had gone through.

"There's no such thing as chance," Mr. Quinn continued. "Only probability, and the chances that I'm right on this one are about the same as finding any needle in a stack of needles."

"Don't confirm anything," the general whispered.

Jimmy nodded. "So then what? You enter here and murder us all?"

Mr. Quinn shook his head and looked down. "Jimmy, I'm hurt. You really think that lowly of me? I know full well that this bunker contains valuable resources, some of which are personnel. Yes, those who oppose me will unfortunately have to be neutralized to keep them from becoming a nuisance, but I intend to offer everyone present the same deal. Join The Brotherhood. Live and learn and contribute to *our* community."

"And leave you in charge? Let you rule over the city as a dictator?"

Mr. Quinn frowned in apparent impatience. "I think you'll find that most people prefer such an existence to death. Look around you. Even those in the room with you are questioning their loyalties."

Jimmy glanced around him. A few of the other soldiers in the room appeared overly fixated on the task in front of them as if trying to hide their inner conflict.

"As for you, Jimmy, you get a rare treat. For the first time in my life, I'm offering a second chance. My students at the university called me 'the hammer' because I never hesitated to drop a failing grade when it was deserved. No second tries. You will be the first to get a second opportunity to strike a deal with me. Surrender, and you will be back in my good graces."

"And if I don't?"

"I don't think I need to explain myself any fur—"

A shot rang out over the speakers. Mr. Quinn's body crumpled to the ground.

Chapter Twenty-Seven

The screens erupted with activity as gunfire littered the air outside the bunker. Brotherhood members scrambled for cover behind vehicles, taking aim to return fire against the unknown assailant. One member of The Brotherhood made an attempt to reach Mr. Quinn only to have bullets find their mark. He lay bleeding out on the ground, blood soaking into his uniform.

Despite the chaos on the monitors, Jimmy couldn't take his eyes off the wounded Mr. Quinn. He lay on his back writhing in pain and clutching his chest. In the corner of his vision, he swore he noticed General Thurston offer a small fist pump. Turning to the general, he found the man smiling ear to ear.

"What did you do?" Jimmy asked.

The general's smile morphed into a smug grin. "Thank you, young man, for buying my men the time needed to put an end to this foolishness."

"What do you mean? How did I—" Jimmy froze as the realization came to him. "You sent your men out there? To take him out?"

"Security is my top concern, boy. I don't expect you to understand the weight of responsibility I bear. That man was a danger to our community and needed to be stopped. Sent my men out the secondary hatch to take position on the high ground."

"But they outnumber your men at least five to one." Jimmy shook his head, turning back to the war outside. "How do you expect to win this?"

"Cut the head off the snake, the body will eventually die. Give it time. Without their leader, those people outside will eventually give up."

Sure enough, things seemed to be turning in favor of the general's men. Whatever vantage point they had secured, it was allowing them to pin down Mr. Quinn's soldiers. Sparks emitted with each bullet that hit the vehicles. Occasionally, he'd see one of The Brotherhood drop to the ground wounded. One lay sprawled over the hood of a Jeep, blood trickling down the front of the vehicles. The scene made Jimmy sick, yet part of him was hopeful that perhaps this was the end of the danger.

Mr. Quinn flipped over and crawled toward the base of the hill behind a large boulder. How he was moving with a bullet wound dumbfounded Jimmy. He turned to another screen that gave a better camera angle. Mr. Quinn took refuge behind a large boulder. Out of the line of sight of the general's men, he sat up with his back against the rock. Ripping open his shirt, he fingered at a dark material underneath, inspecting where the bullet had struck him. Jimmy leaned in trying to figure out how this man was so mobile.

"Kevlar. He's wearing Kevlar!"

"What?" The general lunged at the screen to inspect the image more closely. He released a string of curses. Grabbing his radio, he began barking orders for a detachment of his men to reposition and hunt down Mr. Quinn.

"What is it?" Elena was at Jimmy's side, hopping on one foot to keep from further injuring herself. "Is he not dead?"

"He's wearing a Kevlar vest. The bullet struck him. He's wounded. Maybe even broke a few ribs and lost his breath for a minute, but the round didn't penetrate…not if he's moving that well."

Indeed, Mr. Quinn's head flopped back onto the rock as if relieved by his inspection of the bulletproof vest. He took several deep breaths, wincing and grabbing his ribs with one of his hands. His relief transformed into a scowl. Turning his head, he glared at the camera. How did he seem to know Jimmy was watching him? Reaching for his radio, Mr. Quinn spat out three words that made Jimmy's stomach turn.

Blow the door.

Moments later, the screen showing the front of the bunker flashed into brilliance followed immediately by the concussive report of the explosion. Lights and screens flickered, and the entire mountainside seemed to rock with the force of the blast. Speakers for the surviving microphones outside blared feedback as the excessive volume of the blast clipped out the audio system. The monitor for the camera over the door showed nothing but static, and the others were a haze of smoke and dust.

"Breach! We have a breach!" One of the soldiers to Jimmy's left began shouting into a radio.

The muffled sounds of gunfire came from the hallway—from inside the bunker. The dust on the still operational screens began to thin, and the shapes of Brotherhood soldiers approaching the gaping wound in the side of the mountain became visible. Several soldiers, appearing to be General Thurston's men, writhed on the ground. Wherever they had taken cover, the explosion had taken them out.

The Brotherhood moved toward the door, exchanging gunfire with the remaining security forces located inside. With each report of the bullets, Jimmy swore the number of shots decreased. Before long, the gunfire stopped. Whatever men the general had left to guard the doorway, they were dead, wounded, or captured.

All resistance gone, The Brotherhood flooded the building. Jimmy returned his attention to the camera that displayed Mr. Quinn.

With some effort, Mr. Quinn pushed himself into a standing position. He closed his eyes and held a hand to the left side of his chest where he surely had broken ribs. His face scrunched in pain as he gathered himself. Letting out a breath, his right hand pulled at the Kevlar vest. Clutching his chest, he marched to take position behind his men at the bunker entrance before disappearing into the breach.

Chapter Twenty-Eight

A terrifying silence fell over the control room. The tension suffocated Jimmy, and he had to remind himself to breathe. Elena's hand squeezed his shoulder. Placing his hand over hers, he scanned the room. Two soldiers sat at their stations in stunned silence. They no longer examined the screens but rather seemed to stare into nowhere. The medic who had been helping Dr. Clay silently leaned over to grab her bag as if mentally preparing herself for the number of wounded that awaited her.

A slight click drew Jimmy's attention to the door where the general leaned on the entry while chambering a round in his sidearm. He wore an expression of robotic focus as years of training appeared to kick into gear. He eyed the two soldiers sitting at the screens.

"On your feet, men. That's an order."

The dazed men reluctantly stood from their chairs and pulled their pistols from their holsters. One mimicked the general in chambering a round. The other simply stared at his weapon like he'd never seen it before.

Dr. Clay grunted as he stood from his chair, his concussive headache certainly pounding on the inside of his skull. "General, I don't think we should—"

"You no longer have authority, doctor." The general glared at

Dr. Clay. "This is now a combat operation, which firmly places me in charge of the facility."

Dr. Clay held a hand out to ease the tension. "I understand, General. But it doesn't have to be."

"Don't be a fool."

"Please…hear me out." Dr. Clay slowly approached the general who appeared ready to storm the hallway at any moment. "In a minute or two, those men will find this room, and we will be left with a choice. We can run out there, guns blazing, and take out as many as possible. Their numbers will overwhelm us, and we will succeed in only getting ourselves killed. Or…" He paused to take a breath and hold his aching head. "Or we can make an attempt to negotiate for the lives of everyone under our care."

"Yeah, right. We walk out there with our hands raised, and that crazed cult leader shoots us dead where we stand." The general checked the safety on his weapon.

"General," Elena said as she hobbled over to him, "I think you should listen to Dr. Clay." She teetered for a moment, and Jimmy rushed to catch her.

"She's right." Jimmy ducked under Elena's arm. "Mr. Quinn is a lot of things. Crazy? Yes. Willing to kill? Absolutely. A liar? No."

That caught General Thurston's attention.

Jimmy continued. "He offered a deal, and I think he'll make good on that promise. We've ticked him off for sure, but he's too calculating to simply murder everyone in the building. He came for resources, and like he said, that includes manpower."

Sounds of commotion came from the hallway. Whimpers and

screams could be heard of people being pulled from various rooms and hiding places. Mr. Quinn's men were rounding up the survivors.

"He's taking prisoners. You can hear it."

The general eyed Jimmy, then Elena, then Dr. Clay. "It's not in me to stand down."

Dr. Clay smiled at the general as one would an old friend. "It's been a long three years. Together we have tried to protect and care for the population of this place. We fought to get this place assembled in a hurry and in secret. We battled the spread of the virus when it took out many of our people. We stood strong with the grieving in the aftermath. Together, friend, we have met every challenge we faced head-on. What if caring for them doesn't require a show of force this time?" He took another step toward the general and placed a gentle hand on his forearm.

General Thurston released a long, slow breath and clicked the safety back on his pistol. The other two soldiers followed suit and quickly holstered their weapons. "We're dead men."

"Maybe so. But perhaps our people will not be."

The general nodded.

Bam. Bam. Bam. "Open up!" The command came from outside the doorway.

"I hope you're right, doctor." General Thurston holstered his weapon and slowly grabbed the handle of the door and twisted it. "We're coming out peacefully. Hold your fire." In one fluid motion, the general eased the door open and filled the space, so he was the only target. He raised his hands in surrender. "We're coming out. No resistance."

For a moment, nothing happened. Then, a hand grabbed the general's shoulder and yanked him forward into the hallway.

A shockwave of pain shot through Jimmy's knees as The Brotherhood soldiers threw him to the floor. Half bent over, he knelt on the floor and took a quick assessment of those around him. Elena knelt next to him trying not to cry out in pain from her injured ankle, on which the soldiers had forced her to walk. Dr. Clay sat backward onto his feet on the other side of Elena. His eyes were closed tightly as if fighting the pain in his head. On his other side, Jimmy could see the general and the two control room soldiers on their knees with rifles pointed at the backs of their heads. The slight metallic clatter of a firearm being adjusted in someone's grip told him he, too, had a gun pointed at him from behind.

The trickle of water and the smell of green plant life came from all directions. Mr. Quinn walked quietly through the towers of growing vegetables, admiring the bounty in front of him. He'd removed the Kevlar vest and donned a fresh shirt. More than once, Jimmy noticed him hold his ribs. Reaching up, Mr. Quinn plucked a crimson tomato from its vine. He admired the plump vegetable and inhaled a lungful with it pressed to his nose.

"Such an impressive display of ingenuity and care." Mr. Quinn bit deeply into the tomato, juice running down both sides of his mouth. For a moment, he chewed with his eyes closed, savoring the mouthful. He wiped at his chin with his fingers and stared at the juice on his hands as he rubbed his thumbs against the pads of his fingers. "Three years since I've tasted something so delicious."

Members of The Brotherhood stood silently watching as their leader examined the gardens around him. Jimmy searched the faces, but most were only vaguely familiar from his time at the compound. He started when Mr. Quinn suddenly squatted in front of him.

"Jimmy. Jimmy. Jimmy." Mr. Quinn croaked out the name in slow repetition. His breath smelled acidic from the tomato. "You are my greatest puzzle."

Jimmy turned to meet the man's gaze and straightened when he found him only inches away. Mr. Quinn's lips were curled into a slight grin, and tomato juice still clung to one side of his chin. He took another bite of the tomato, slurping as he did so.

"You know why I find you so puzzling?" Mr. Quinn asked. "You consistently resist me and yet I find you so helpful. The harder you try to keep me from reaching my goal, the closer I seem to get…with your assistance." He cocked his head to the side to meet Jimmy's eyes. "I should have killed you a long time ago, and yet I'm compelled to keep you around. Isn't that strange?"

Mr. Quinn's steadiness unnerved Jimmy. He'd rather the man be raging. At least that would feel consistent with the psychosis that must be going on underneath.

"I can't figure you out, my friend. And yet"—Mr. Quinn stood as he raised his voice—"when I offer you the chance to peacefully surrender, you and your new pals here send men to shoot me." He was shouting now, a red flush spreading across his face.

Jimmy changed his mind. The rage was not better.

Mr. Quinn grabbed the sidearm from a soldier's holster nearby. He jammed the muzzle into Jimmy's forehead. "Tell me, Jimmy. Why shouldn't I be done with you right now? Huh?"

Jimmy shook involuntarily. He wouldn't dare to speak.

"Quiet now, are we? You had plenty to say when you were distracting me as your executioners crept into place." He stepped to the side and placed the pistol against Elena's head. She released a small yelp before biting down hard on her lip. "How about now? You able to talk with the gun to your precious girlfriend's head?"

"P-please." Jimmy's lips trembled. His mind raced for what to say. "I-I didn't know they were going to shoot you."

"*Oh sure.* The ever-infallible Jimmy Hunter, who does nothing wrong." He twirled his hand in the air in a mock bow. "Let's not mention that you wounded my guard, beat up your friend, and stole my property. So, tell me…friend…if you weren't a part of sending those men to kill me, who was?" He dug the muzzle deeper into the skin on Elena's forehead, and she let out an involuntary sob.

"I-I—"

"They were operating on my orders." General Thurston stood up from his place, getting a rifle shoved into his back as a consequence. "These two young people had nothing to do with it."

Mr. Quinn's rage dissipated as fast as it came. His voice took on its customary control. He smiled. "Nothing a like a little calculated outburst to shake things up. It was a no brainer that the soldiers acted under your orders, General. I just needed confirmation that my friend here was not responsible for what your men did to me. Thank you for providing me what I needed. You're of no further use to me."

In a flash, Mr. Quinn pointed the pistol at General Thurston. The report of the bullet echoed in the large chamber and nearly burst Jimmy's eardrums.

Elena screamed.

"Dear God, no." Dr. Clay cried out.

General Thurston lay on his back, a large red stain soaking across the front of his military uniform. His body shook violently, his breaths coming in staccato shudders. A pool of crimson blood seeped out from under his body. With a gasp, his breath stopped, save for a slow final exhale. The general was dead.

Chapter Twenty-Nine

Mr. Quinn placed the pistol back in the holster of The Brotherhood soldier. He wiped his hand on his pants twice and grabbed another vegetable off the towers, this one a yellow bell pepper. He drove his thumbs into the pepper, pulling it apart. Ripping the seeds out with his fingers, he cast them aside and began to tear off pieces and eat them.

Jimmy trembled, his body flushed both hot and cold in a mix of rage and fear. Elena sobbed next to him. Dr. Clay muttered under his breath, possibly a prayer. Reaching up, Jimmy clutched the ring around his neck. His thoughts drifted to his parents. What would they do in this situation?

Mr. Quinn squatted again in front of Jimmy. "Not a bad acting job, if I do say so. Had you fooled, didn't I?" He slapped Jimmy on the shoulder. "It's good to know I can still consider you a potential friend, Jimmy. Just had to make sure. After all, that's what I want…people like yourself to join our cause. So, before I decide what to do with everyone else here, let me make good on the deal I offered. Would you like to join us, Jimmy Hunter? Of course, your lady friend here is welcome to join us, too."

Any fear inside Jimmy melted away into wrath at Mr. Quinn's offer. The level of insanity required to put on the display that he'd just seen sickened Jimmy. There was a terrible precision to Mr.

Quinn's delusion. The thought of joining such a man made him want to vomit. And as for Elena, he would do whatever necessary to keep her as far away as possible.

Jimmy met Mr. Quinn's eyes. "You can choke on your deal for all I care."

Mr. Quinn straightened with a sigh. He rested one hand on a hip while rubbing the bridge of his nose with the other. "I was concerned that would be your response. Believe me, this is one moment I wish my calculations had been wrong, but as per the usual, I've anticipated this moment. It's not without its merits for I get to finally put to rest another issue." He waved a hand at one of his soldiers. "Bring them in."

A minute later, he could hear footsteps approaching along with the muffled cries of a woman. The soldiers behind Mr. Quinn parted. Jimmy's heart raced as his mind attempted to catch up to what was happening. The first to enter was a soldier forcing a bound and gagged woman to step into view. Tears streaked her face as she pled through the gag with her captor. In his adrenaline-fueled state, it took Jimmy a second to put a name to the face—Cyndi Sheppard. This was followed by her children, also bound and gagged, which explained the frantic state of their mother.

The next group took his breath away. The bruised and battered face of Wyatt peered up at Jimmy through his one good eye, the other swollen shut. His hands were cuffed in front of him. Behind him was his captor—Nedra—who kept a firm grip on Wyatt's upper arm. Her face was stoic as she gazed down the bridge of her nose at Jimmy. He searched her face for any hint of support, but her expression remained flat and motionless.

"I see you recognize some of the faces that have joined us, my friend." Mr. Quinn motioned to Wyatt and Nedra with one hand. "Things have not been easy for your friend, Wyatt, since you departed our company. When I offered you a deal that competed directly with his, it was not a monumental leap to assume he'd do something rash to remove you from the picture. His foolishness gave you the opportunity to escape and told us everything we needed to know about his conflicting loyalties." With a hand, he lifted the chin of Wyatt, turning his head to the right and left. Mr. Quinn clucked his tongue in disappointment.

Mr. Quinn smiled as he approached Nedra, placing his hand on her shoulder. Her expression remained unchanged. "And this, of course, is the leader of my guard, but you knew that already. What you didn't know, my friend, is that I am fully aware of the conversations you two have been having."

Jimmy started at this news, involuntarily straightening.

Mr. Quinn grinned further at Jimmy's reaction. "Yes, Jimmy, I am fully in the know about the divisive exchanges shared between you and the captain of my guard. She has been telling you to keep the information of this underground oasis a secret from me and to do anything possible to prevent me from learning the information I needed off that tablet."

Jimmy's eyes flicked from Mr. Quinn to Nedra. She didn't move. *Why isn't she reacting? He knows what she did!*

"Furthermore," Mr. Quinn continued, "I am aware she delivered the tablet to you in person after your departure from The Brotherhood safe haven. She was waiting for you in your apartment I would guess. Assuming you would return home as your first stop was not a hard determination."

Any moment, Jimmy expected Mr. Quinn to retrieve the soldier's pistol again and threaten both Wyatt and Nedra. Was that what this was? Was he going to make Jimmy witness the death of his friend and the one person in The Brotherhood who'd truly helped him? As if on cue, Mr. Quinn held out a hand to the officer nearest him without even turning to look. The officer withdrew his pistol and laid it in Mr. Quinn's hand, who gazed at the weapon as he turned it over in his hand a couple times.

"Loyalty, Jimmy. That's all I ask for. It's not much. Not really. Just a promise." He peered up at Jimmy, face still turned down to the gun. "A promise to work together, to help each other. Is that so bad? Does that make me evil? I offer safety and order and provision in return." He paused. "I don't think it is too much to ask for a little bit of loyalty in return. And why do I explain all this like some villain monologuing in a badly written film? Because I need you to understand. I'm no unhinged monster. I am the purveyor of stability and peace."

Jimmy's breath quickened. He had no desire to witness another execution, and he had to swallow hard to keep his lurching stomach in check. He studied the room, looking for any possible exit from the situation. If not for Elena by his side, he'd simply take off running, but he had no way to communicate to her to join him. He turned to gaze at her. Her eyes, tear-streaked and red from earlier, now glared full of rage at Mr. Quinn. Her lips trembled, and he could tell she was restraining herself from hurling verbal abuse at Mr. Quinn. Wyatt was her friend, too, and her fury at his mistreatment was clear.

Mr. Quinn waited until Jimmy met his eyes again to continue. "Jimmy, I don't want you to miss this next part. You see, it's one of the better ideas I've had as of late. Things don't happen by accident under my watch. We've discussed the predictability of people before, so I am a little disappointed you didn't put it together." He stepped toward Jimmy and knelt in front of him. Jimmy couldn't help but glance at the gun in his hand. "My friend, did it ever occur to you, even a prickle at the back of your mind, that my captain would never betray me? Would you believe that her loyalty to me remains unquestioned?"

Jimmy's eyes shot to Nedra, who continued to stare down at him emotionless.

Mr. Quinn shook his head. "Really? I'm disappointed that you would think so little of my ability to lead predictable people that you would genuinely believe one of my trusted leaders was betraying me right under my nose." He stood again. "Insurance, Jimmy. Always have an insurance plan. I'd hoped to have you join our ranks and prove your loyalty to me by providing access to the tablet, but I knew you might be as stubborn as you appear, so I instructed my captain to win your favor. Should you refuse to help me, she could play the part of the subversive to get you to flee to this place with your lady friend and the tracker we placed on her. And as you can see—once again, I was right. Predictable. Obvious. Almost boring in its certainty, my friend."

Jimmy again glanced at Nedra. This time, she cocked an eyebrow slightly, almost imperceptibly. The corner of her mouth turned upward in the slightest grin. Jimmy's stomach turned at the revelation. She'd played him. They both had. Despite his efforts to work outside the bounds of Mr. Quinn's all-consuming control, he'd behaved exactly as intended. It was, as Mr. Quinn said, so obvious now as Jimmy considered the events of the last few weeks. Despair washed over him, and he doubled over wanting to vomit all over the floor.

"Good." Mr. Quinn let out a long, satisfied breath. "I'm glad you finally see the truth. I can't be fooled, Jimmy."

The concrete floor felt cool on Jimmy's forehead, keeping him conscious and aware. He couldn't run. He couldn't hide. He wouldn't plead. He was trapped in Mr. Quinn's calculated web.

"Don't worry, my friend. How you feel is understandable, but that is about to change. Let us discuss the loyalty of your friend, Wyatt. Or should I say former friend?"

That got Jimmy's attention, and he forced himself upright. With a nod from Mr. Quinn, Nedra produced a key and unlocked Wyatt's handcuffs. He rubbed at his wrists and glanced around the room, appearing unsure about what would happen next.

"Wyatt, as I predicted, you have been incapable of playing by the rules." Mr. Quinn sounded like a father lecturing his son. "Yet, despite the punishment you've received for your actions, you still insist that you want to be a full member of The Brotherhood. It's time to prove your loyalty to The Brotherhood—to me—once and for all." Mr. Quinn turned the pistol around in his hand and shoved the stock into Wyatt's palm.

Wyatt's hand gave way for a moment to the weight of the weapon. He gazed at the weapon as if he didn't understand what the object was. Mr. Quinn pointed at Jimmy.

"Wyatt, I want you to kill Jimmy Hunter."

Chapter Thirty

Jimmy's heart stopped. Elena gasped. Even the concussed Dr. Clay shot Jimmy a glance. Tension filled the room with suffocating thickness.

Wyatt stared at the firearm in his hands. He hefted the grip of the pistol a couple of times, testing its weight. He glanced up at Mr. Quinn before turning his gaze to Jimmy.

"That's right, Wyatt." Mr. Quinn resumed his instructive tone. "Want to show me you are loyal? Prove it by cutting ties with your former friend, permanently this time. No *helping him escape* to ease your conscience. No pulling the wool over the eyes of the young lady in hopes of maintaining her approval. Show you are loyal to me, and only me, by pulling the trigger. Only then will I be able to believe your promises to be part of my Brotherhood."

"You want me to…kill Jimmy?" Wyatt asked the question as if not hearing Mr. Quinn, but Jimmy knew better. Everyone in the room wore an expression that communicated they knew exactly what was happening.

"Are you deaf or stupid, boy?" Mr. Quinn shoved Wyatt toward Jimmy. "You want my trust? Earn it."

Wyatt gazed down at Jimmy. His face grew pale, making his purple bruises look all the starker against his skin. He pointed the muzzle at Jimmy's forehead. Surprisingly, Jimmy felt no fear. His hand found the ring around his neck again, and he reminded himself of his parents' example.

Greater love has no one than this…

"That he gives his life for a friend." Jimmy finished the statement in a whisper. Peace washed over him. If his death meant that Wyatt would no longer be abused…if it meant that Elena would escape unscathed…if it meant the end to the bloodshed, then it was worth it. Even if The Brotherhood took over the resources of the Lifeboat and eventually the city, at least his friends would live. In a world where sacrifice no longer felt relevant, he could save his friends at the cost of himself. He could die for that. He allowed himself to meet Wyatt's gaze.

A tremor that started at Wyatt's lip spread through his neck and down his arm until the muzzle of the pistol was visibly shaking. His lips parted like he wanted to speak…to apologize…to explain, but no sound came out.

Jimmy stared. He would not take his eyes off his friend.

Mr. Quinn let out a huff and approached Wyatt. He leaned into his ear. "Listen, you little wretch, I'm going to come out ahead one way or the other here. I wanted him,"—he jabbed a finger at Jimmy—"but I'll settle for you. But you have to prove yourself— to show me you have the stomach to follow, no matter what."

A tear escaped Wyatt's eye and ran down his cheek, dripping from his jawline to the floor.

"Wyatt, please." Elena's plea was soft and rich with compassion.

Wyatt swallowed hard. "I-I—"

"Don't you say you can't do it. Don't you say that you won't be loyal to me." Jimmy could see Mr. Quinn's spit hit Wyatt in the ear as he spoke. He walked over to Cyndi Sheppard, grabbing another pistol from a soldier on the way. "Like I said, always have an insurance policy. Boy, you pull that trigger now, or I pull the trigger on this family, starting with the mother." Vanessa and Matthias both cried out through their gags. "You know what it's like to see your parents die, don't you, Wyatt? Do you want to be the reason these children have to see that today? Why should the innocent die when it should be your betrayer? You trusted Jimmy, and he left you. Knocked you out cold and left you to face the consequences. Now you're going to let him live?" Mr. Quinn's voice grew more manic with each word.

"I can't." Wyatt whispered the words through tears. His good eye searched Jimmy's face. "I can't kill my friend." He lowered the pistol, allowing it to hang loosely at his side.

"You raise that gun, boy. Prove you are loyal or have the blood of this family on your hands."

Wyatt turned to Mr. Quinn, standing directly over Jimmy to place himself between his friend and the leader of The Brotherhood. His head hung in defeat. "Mr. Quinn, I-I can't do it." Lifting his head, he straightened. "I-I won't do it." With a trembling hand, he raised the pistol and pointed it at Mr. Quinn. "Let me and my friends go."

Mr. Quinn sighed as his gun hand dropped. With two fingers on his free hand, he rubbed at his temple as though quelling a headache. "So...predictable." Mr. Quinn's eyes glanced to a soldier across the room. He gave a slight nod.

Jimmy whipped his head in the direction of the glance to see the soldier's rifle pointed squarely at Wyatt.

"No!" Jimmy cried.

The muzzle flashed. The powerful blast of the rifle was deafening in the cavernous room. Jimmy's body hit the floor with enough force to expel the air from his lungs. For a second, he wondered if he'd been the one shot. He didn't know what the sensation of a bullet ripping through his body would feel like, but this didn't feel right. He lifted his hands to inspect his body, only to realize they were pinned. He tried again, and only now felt the weight of something heavy pressing him against the floor.

Wyatt's body lay motionless across his chest.

"Wyatt?" The name came from Jimmy's lips in a rasp as he was still straining for breath.

Elena cried out nearby. Glancing at her, Jimmy could see her shocked expression. Her hands covered her mouth, and she shook her head.

Wyatt grunted and rolled off of Jimmy, who reached to catch his slumping form. Wrapping his hands around Wyatt, his fingers felt wet as they gripped his shirt which was increasingly soaked in blood from where the bullet had entered.

Helping Wyatt to the floor, he gazed at his friend. Wyatt's skin paled, and his chin quivered. His eyes searched Jimmy's face.

"No. Wyatt, no." Jimmy whispered, hunching over his dying friend.

Elena scrambled over to them and brushed Wyatt's sweat-soaked hair aside. Her tears flowed. Wyatt's gaze shifted back and forth between the two of them, and tears escaped the corner of his eye. "I-I'm sorry."

"Wyatt, don't." Jimmy said.

"N-n-no. I'm really sorry. This is"—Wyatt strained as something inside of him shot pain through his body—"m-my fault." His trembling body grew still. His eyes stopped scanning and stared blankly at the ceiling. A long, final breath leaked from his mouth.

Wyatt was gone.

Jimmy shot upward and glowered at Mr. Quinn. A grin slowly spread across the murderer's face as he watched Jimmy reach for the pistol laying next to Wyatt. "Now, now, my friend." He waggled his pistol in the air, giving Jimmy pause. "See? Control. Despite your best attempts, I never lost it." He glanced down at Wyatt's form. "He was a liability anyway. I took a calculated risk with him, but I'm frankly glad to be rid of him."

Jimmy wanted to tear the man's face off. He didn't care if he got shot. His friend was dead, and this man was responsible. He readied himself to lunge when a hand found his, breaking into his bloodlust. He peered down to the tear-streaked face of Elena. She shook her head slightly as if reading his intentions.

Rage melted into despair. Grief overwhelmed Jimmy, and his heart sank inside his chest. He swallowed hard and forced himself to speak. "Let us go. You got what you came for. This place and everything in it is yours to control the entire city."

"Oh, that won't be happening. You're coming with me. I'm sure there is more I can learn from you, and your lady friend's safety will be the bargaining chip. And the doctor, here? I'm sure we have a use for him. I'm guessing he'll be interested in the safety of this family." He nodded at Cyndi Sheppard who was huddled with her children. "Men, prepare to transport these prisoners home."

Nothing. No movement.

"I said move." Mr. Quinn sounded annoyed.

"Uh, sir?" One of the soldiers dared to speak.

"What is—" Mr. Quinn's voice cut off as he turned.

Nedra stood a few feet away from Mr. Quinn. The muzzle of her pistol was pointed squarely between Mr. Quinn's eyes. She wore a satisfied smile. "Don't move if you value your life." Reaching forward, she grabbed the pistol in Mr. Quinn's hand, flipping the safety on with a finger and wrenching it from his grip.

Mr. Quinn cried out as his fingers were bent unnaturally, and he snapped his hand toward his gut protectively. Jimmy could see at least one finger was broken. The entire room froze with the only sound being the trickle of water from the plant towers.

Nedra tossed Mr. Quinn's gun out of reach. "I won't stand for the killing of innocents. You are a sick man." She scanned the room. "Everyone drop their weapons, or Quinn is dead where he stands."

Soldiers around the room glanced at each other. After a moment, one soldier placed his rifle on the floor. Another followed. Before long, the clatter of rifles being set down spread throughout the circle. Nedra waved Cyndi and her children away from the group.

"Good, now everyone take two giant steps backward from those rifles."

Everyone complied.

Mr. Quinn cradled his broken hand in his left arm. With a grunt, he straightened the broken finger. "I'm impressed, Captain. A double-cross? Or is this just impulsive? Either way, I didn't see this coming, for which I must commend you. Perhaps playing the betrayer has gone to your head."

"I was never one of yours."

"I'm not sure I believe that. I don't think you're strong enough to have planned all this out." Mr. Quinn studied her face. "I can see the sweat gathering on your forehead and your shifty eyes. You have no plan. You are searching for a way out."

"I'm more prepared than you realize." Nedra nodded at the surrounding soldiers. Six of them immediately picked up their rifles and moved to stand behind Nedra.

Mr. Quinn cocked an eyebrow. "So, this is not a singular betrayal…but a mutiny?" His face spread to a wide grin. "I have taught you well, my captain. Commanding the loyalty of others is an admirable trait. Still, I must wonder if you've thought beyond this point." Still cradling his broken hand, he straightened as if to expose his chest as a target. "You've stopped me. What now?"

Jimmy grimaced as he expected her to fire at any moment. Would she murder him in cold blood when she had him cornered? He extended his hand outward and prepared to intervene. The tension in the room was suffocating. Sweat dripped down Jimmy's forehead as he watched Nedra's trigger finger. Any moment, her finger could twitch, the boom of the muzzle fire assaulting their eardrums.

Nedra adjusted the grip on her pistol and gave the four men and two women who'd joined her a glance. With reassuring nods, they reminded her they were with her. Turning back to Mr. Quinn, she swallowed hard. "You are no longer in charge of The Brotherhood. Your manipulation and control are ended. We are going to rebuild and use the resources of The Brotherhood and now this bunker to rebuild our city…not to own it."

Mr. Quinn slowly nodded. "Admirable. Noble. Everything I've come to expect from you, Captain. When I brought you on and put you in charge of my guard, I did so because you have principles. You have rules that you live by. So have I. We share a kinship in that respect, you and me."

"I'm nothing like you."

"Oh?" Mr. Quinn's head cocked to the side. "You were a soldier in our former nation's military. You were trained to defend a set of ideals, for which you were willing when necessary to take lives. Am I wrong?"

Nedra said nothing, but Jimmy could see her eyes shift for a brief moment.

"I, too, have a set of ideals that I defend. And yes, there have been times when taking a life was necessary. I have never enjoyed it, but nonetheless, I am willing to do what is necessary. I think that makes us not so different."

Nedra's jaw flexed. "Maybe I'll pull this trigger and end this right here."

Mr. Quinn pursed his lips. "Maybe. But I think not. You still don't grasp the unoriginality of mankind. The likelihood that your character will change in the next moments is assuredly low. In the end, you know you have the upper hand. You don't *have* to kill me, so you won't. But…if the stakes were to change?" Mr. Quinn took a moment to assess the soldiers he had left with him. "In a moment, I'll order my men to pick up their rifles and shoot you. You will be forced to take action. You may get a shot off, but you won't live to see the end of this day."

Nedra's eyes shot a glance at the soldiers in the circle. It was all the moment Mr. Quinn needed. Reaching his good hand into his loosely fit right jacket sleeve, he produced a subcompact 9mm pistol from a hidden holster. He pointed and fired.

Chapter Thirty-One

The bullet ripped through Nedra's gut, throwing her to the floor, her pistol skittering away. The cavern erupted into a cacophony of screams and ear-splintering gunshots from both sides. As quickly as he'd fired, Mr. Quinn disappeared into the rows of garden towers. One of Nedra's men fell instantly along with two of Mr. Quinn's before each side began taking protective positions. Dr. Clay crawled to the corner where Cyndi Sheppard did her best to shield her children from any stray bullets.

Nedra lay doubled over on the floor, her hands clutching a wound on her stomach. She grimaced in pain as she attempted to roll over, causing her to fall to her back.

Elena cowered on the floor, her hands over her ears and her eyes squeezed shut. Her cries came in bursts betraying how overwhelmed her senses were by the chaos. Jimmy crawled to her. She jumped at his touch.

Two more of Mr. Quinn's men fell. Nedra had chosen her group well.

Jimmy motioned that they needed to get to safety and pointed to the door. Elena nodded. Cautiously, they got to their feet. Keeping in a low crouch, they scurried along the wall toward the exit. The soldiers, mostly focused on each other, did not fire at them.

They stopped at the corner of the room. The exit was only a few meters away, but it would require exposing themselves to the exchange of gunfire. Jimmy hand signaled that they would have to make a run for it. Elena's eyes grew wide, and she shook her head. He didn't blame her.

Searching the walls around him, he noticed the door to the kitchen they'd taken earlier. That way would take them deeper into the bunker, but it would have to do. He pointed to the door, and Elena nodded.

They turned to double back and stepped into one of the rows of towers. The plastic tower next to them shattered as a bullet struck it, spraying pieces in all directions. He pulled Elena back. Another explosion of tower material, and the structure of the tower gave way. Plastic sections, covered in vegetation, hurdled to the floor as water showered them from above.

"Jimmy Hunter! You don't think you're going to get away that easily, do you?" Mr. Quinn's voice shouted above the staccato gunfire from the soldiers.

Jimmy peered around the corner. Mr. Quinn stood farther up the row of towers, his pistol pointed in their direction. Seeing Jimmy, he adjusted his aim and fired.

He shoved Elena and fell on top of her as the bullet struck the tower they'd been hidden behind. With a groan, the tower began to lean in the direction of the gaping hole. The lean was slow before gaining momentum. A second later, the entire tower fell creating a domino effect with the two towers next to it. Water and plants plummeted to the floor, soaking their clothes. The two scrambled to all fours and ducked behind the next row.

The shots in the distance began to become fewer as one side was getting the upper hand. Crouching, Jimmy stared from the base of his tower and looked down the row. Mr. Quinn's feet took slow steps in his direction. Before long, he would be on top of them.

He waved that they should move. They crawled through puddles and spraying water to the next row, inching their way toward the kitchen door. A bullet struck the concrete wall beside them spraying them with bits of rock. Elena screamed and stood to run.

"No. Wait." Jimmy said in a harsh whisper.

Determined to flee, Elena ran for the kitchen door.

"Not so fast, missy," Mr. Quinn said.

Elena's footsteps halted, and she gave a whimper. Jimmy could hear Mr. Quinn take a few quick steps, bringing him close to Jimmy's position. "Stand right there, young lady. Jimmy? I have my sights set on your lady friend. She appears quite scared, and she should be. I'm going to shoot her where she stands if you don't come out of hiding."

Jimmy cursed under his breath.

"I'll give you to the count of three, my friend."

Chapter Thirty-Two

Jimmy stood, water dripping from his nose and chin. Slowly, he emerged from behind his tower with his hands raised. He glanced at Elena who stood shivering from the cold water. She offered an apologetic look. He mouthed, "It's okay" back to her.

Mr. Quinn redirected his aim at Jimmy. "The lovestruck are the easiest to predict. You could have made your way to the door, Jimmy. I don't think even the young lady would have been able to blame you. You could have been out the door and into the woods by now. Instead, you willingly surrender yourself to me."

Shots continued nearby, but only rarely. Through the rows, Jimmy caught sight of two members of Mr. Quinn's crew sneaking through the gardens. They were flanking Nedra's remaining soldiers. A moment later, three shots rang out. Then, the room was silent except for the never-ending spray of water.

Jimmy did his best to straighten despite the gun barrel being pointed at him. "Let her go, and I will go with you."

Mr. Quinn clucked his tongue and shook his head. "The time has passed for a deal. I broke my rule and offered you your deal a second time, which you declined. It's why I have the rule in the first place because you can see what it leads to." He waved a hand at the room around him. "Chaos. Pain. Uncertainty." He shook his head again. "No. No deal this time."

With a wag of the gun, he motioned that they should return to the open area where they'd been held earlier. Jimmy made certain to place himself between Mr. Quinn and Elena as they walked. Emerging from the rows of plants, they could see three men with their rifles aimed at Nedra, who still lay on the ground. A pool of blood had begun to emerge from under her body.

Nedra's men and women had done their damage, nearly taking out all of Mr. Quinn's soldiers before the flanking maneuver had finished the gunfight. Two of Mr. Quinn's men were dragging the bodies of the mutineers out into the open to ensure they were deceased.

Dr. Clay and the Sheppard's still huddled in the corner. Vanessa clung to her mom as Dr. Clay did his best to cover the three of them with his own body.

"Kneel with your backs against that wall. I want to handle my business in the order I received it. Besides, I plan to take my time with you, Jimmy Hunter." His tone unnerved Jimmy. Whatever, 'take my time' meant, it couldn't be good. They dropped to their knees with their feet and backs against the wall as instructed.

Mr. Quinn squatted over Nedra, who grunted with each movement as she tried to squirm away. He held his pistol loosely and motioned with it as though it were part of his hand.

"Nedra. Nedra. My once and former captain. What a waste." He glanced at the dead bodies laying around the room. "You cost me a great deal today. All for what? Some noble cause to help the city?"

Nedra glared up at him through pained eyes. A trickle of blood ran from her nose down her cheek. Her body spasmed from the mutilation the bullet had caused her insides, and she let out a cry.

Mr. Quinn frowned. "Now that hurts, doesn't it?" He slowly scanned the room. "Such a waste. You and I both know that control comes with power, and that power can change a person. It changed me from an anonymous professor of statistics into a leader and protector of my people. Should you have won the day, it would have changed you. All this"—he pointed to the towers of plants—"would have changed you. Your noble ideals would have flown out the window despite what you believe about yourself. No, in the end it would have been the same."

"I'm nothing like you." Nedra growled between sputtering coughs. "You're a heartless machine. People are nothing but calculations to you."

"There is beauty and order in calculations. Predictability is the only comfort this world has left." He smiled down at Nedra. "I'm glad at least we understand one another before you're gone."

Mr. Quinn stood and walked to Nedra's feet. "Men and women are replaceable. This bounty…" He took a moment to stare at the towers around him. "This bounty is going to change everything. It will launch The Brotherhood from the dominant power in this city to the only power. And you…helped me find it."

Nedra rolled over and spat bloody saliva at his feet.

Mr. Quinn turned to Jimmy. "You see, my friend. Predictable to the end." A smile spread across his lips as Nedra grimaced from a surge of pain. She clutched her wound with both hands, her body shaking from blood loss. Her breath sputtered. Her body grew still, and her arms fell to the floor.

"Farewell, my former captain." Mr. Quinn offered a mocking hand over his heart. With a sigh as though bored, he turned to Jimmy, his face growing dark when their eyes met. "Now, what do I do with you?"

Jimmy glared up at him, the fury at Mr. Quinn's nonchalance about Nedra's death sending a flash of heat to his face.

"I have to admit, Jimmy, you've proven to be quite the thorn in my side. Every chance you get, you run from me. Despite every deal I have offered you—every chance to join the winning side— you have chosen chaos." Mr. Quinn wiped water from his face with the back of his gun hand. He wagged the barrel at Jimmy. "You, my friend, are a loose end. An uncontrollable variable that must be eliminated from the equation."

"So…you're going to kill me." Jimmy swallowed hard.

"No. You've cost me too much." Mr. Quinn scanned the room at the fallen soldiers. He nodded at Elena. "I'm going to shoot her."

Jimmy directed a glance at Elena, who straightened with a muffled gasp. She searched his eyes for assurance, but he had none to offer.

"That's right, Jimmy. You're going to watch life drain from her body before you breathe your last. You will see the end that chaos leads to. First, the death of your friend." He glanced down at Wyatt's lifeless body. "Then, the death of your love. Even chaos is predictable, Jimmy. It always leads to loss."

"No!" Jimmy started to lunge at Mr. Quinn, but a kick to the stomach knocked him to his hands and knees.

"No heroics, Jimmy. This is the end. The doctor here will help me, I'm sure, with this family under threat, so you are of further use to me."

Jimmy's thoughts raced as Mr. Quinn raised the pistol to point it at Elena. Mr. Quinn had won. The bunker was his. The heirloom crops that could save the world belonged to the psychopath that ran the city. The worst of it all was that, except for a few seconds, he'd controlled the entire outcome. Mr. Quinn had predicted every move down to the motivations of the individuals.

There was nothing he could say to save himself or Elena. Mr. Quinn likely already knew every bargain he would attempt to make and every plea. Jimmy searched the room for something…anything…unexpected.

His attention fell to the corner of his vision. Above his head, recessed behind glass on the wall, was the failsafe button installed in the event the crops produced the virus and needed to be destroyed. He glanced at Dr. Clay, who shook his head slightly.

He whispered. "Elena, whatever happens. I love you."

She stared at the pistol, her voice trembling. "I love you, too, Jimmy."

Mr. Quinn's voice grated against their moment. "Jimmy, watch carefully. This is where trying to beat the odds gets you." His grip tightened on the pistol.

"Except that you forgot one of your most important rules, Mr. Quinn." Jimmy forced himself to sound confident.

Mr. Quinn's head snapped in Jimmy's direction, his finger pausing on the trigger. "And which rule would that be?"

"In any calculation, keep track of all the variables."

Jimmy shot to his feet and struck the glass with his elbow, striking the button inside a split second later.

Click.

Chapter Thirty-Three

Deafening alarms blared throughout the room. Lights flashing red and yellow swirled in Jimmy's vision. Mr. Quinn and his soldiers gaped at the room in confusion, unaware of what was about to happen.

"No, Jimmy! What have you done?" Dr. Clay cried out. He twisted to meet Jimmy's eyes with his hands gripping his hair.

"What is this?" Mr. Quinn demanded. When no one answered, he spun with his pistol outstretched at every person in the room, looking for answers. "Tell me, what is going on?"

"No. No. No. No." Dr. Clay sobbed with each word. "All those years of work—"

Mr. Quinn stepped over to Dr. Clay and placed the muzzle of his pistol against the scientist's head. "You seem to know something about this. Explain. Now." Dr. Clay clutched his stomach and rocked as his despair continued to overwhelm him. He didn't seem to notice or care about Mr. Quinn's weapon. A sneer spread across Mr. Quinn's face, and his finger began to curl around the trigger.

A ball of righteous rage formed in Jimmy's gut, rising until it found a home in his chest. "I'll tell you what is happening." Jimmy nearly had to shout because of the sirens. "Your precious prize is lost."

Mr. Quinn's attention snapped in Jimmy's direction, his trigger finger faltering. He straightened, pulling the gun away from the trembling body of Dr. Clay. Slowly, almost methodically, Mr. Quinn turned and took two steps in Jimmy's direction. He raised the miniature pistol and pointed it at Jimmy's head. His voice, though loud enough to be heard, was low and controlled. "Tell me, what have you done?"

As if on cue, nozzles in the ceiling began to emit a mist over the entire room. Caustic fumes wafted in all directions, and intermittent coughs came for everyone in the room as the failsafe chemicals began mildly burning their throat and eyes.

Jimmy let out a cough and straightened to meet Mr. Quinn. He stared at the hole in the end of the pistol. To his amazement, he felt peace. No fear of death overcame him. Mr. Quinn was willing to kill those he cared about for the resources in this room, and now there were none worth killing for.

"That's an ultra-concentrated, nonselective herbicide." Jimmy allowed himself a moment of amazement that he remembered the term. "The reason Dr. Clay is so upset is everything in here is now covered in it. These plants will die." Jimmy smiled, not a smug grin but a smile that knew that evil's plan had been thwarted. "And there's nothing you can do about it."

The rage on Mr. Quinn's face melted into a frown. Was that concern on his face? He reached over to the closest plant tower, which was now dripping in the herbicide. Running his fingers over a leaf, he brought the substance to his nose. He jerked away after sniffing. He hurriedly walked to another tower, repeating the procedure. A third. A fourth. With each tower, Mr. Quinn's steps quickened. His breathing came in short gasps. His eyes grew wide.

"It *cough* can't be! *cough*" he shouted. The burning rage in his face was gone. His wide eyes darted from tower to tower. "No. No. No. No! *cough cough*" He raced from tower to tower, grabbing vegetables and trying in vain to wipe the poisonous herbicide off with his shirt. "Men, grab what you can! Find something to stop this! Hurry!" The calculated voice that usually defined Mr. Quinn was missing, replaced by terror like a child who'd lost his mother in a supermarket.

Jimmy pulled Elena to her feet, meeting her eyes with an expression that asked, *You okay?*

She nodded and took his hand.

With a glance at Dr. Clay, who was gathering Cyndi Sheppard and her children, Jimmy and Elena made for the door, followed by the others. In the chaos of sirens and fumes, Mr. Quinn's few remaining soldiers were scrambling to help their powerless leader gather what food they could and completely ignored the fleeing prisoners.

Throwing an arm around Elena, who was still gimpy, they hobbled through the clean room and into the corridor. Doing their best to ignore the dead guards, they focused on the daylight at the end of the hall.

The six of them burst into the outdoors, the earthy smell of the forest a welcome change from the caustic air of the herbicide. Vacant Brotherhood vehicles still sat in a circle around the entry to the bunker. Jimmy only needed to check two before finding an old brown van with the keys still inside. Dr. Clay slammed the door as the last of the group jumped inside. Jimmy turned the keys and breathed a sigh of relief as the engine roared to life. Dirt flew from under the tires as he hit the gas.

Trees became a blur on either side of the vehicles as it lurched over the rough road that led out of the woods. With a bump, the van rocketed onto the paved roadway. It may have been his imagination, but he swore he could hear the cries of Mr. Quinn echoing from the gaping hole in the bunker as they drove away.

An evening breeze came over the hillside behind Dr. Clay's home carrying the scent of summer wildflowers that must be blooming nearby. Elena rested her head on Jimmy's shoulder, the previous night's tears still staining her face. They'd said little once they'd safely hidden the van away in a garage at a vacant home up the street. Dr. Clay had insisted they try to find some food before he'd left to help Cyndi Sheppard and her children return to their home. Neither of them was hungry.

It had only been hours since their escape, and the reality of what Wyatt had done for him was still settling in. His friend was gone. All the hurt and betrayal of their days since encountering The Brotherhood melted into oblivion, forgotten in the gaping hole of his grief.

Greater love has no one than this…than he lay his life down for his friend.

Wyatt had been a lot of things. He was immature, short-sighted, and hopelessly infatuated with a girl who did not reciprocate. He was selfish at times and struggled with giving in to his insecurity, trying to prove that he was better or more worthy in the group than he believed. Still, he'd survived with Jimmy and Elena for three years. Each day had been a struggle to survive as the world around them passed away. He'd risked his neck more than once to pull Jimmy out of a jam. He'd helped provide for the group. He'd stuck with them, even when times were lean. In the end, he'd refused to take Jimmy's life to save his own.

Jimmy didn't question who Wyatt had been. He was a friend.

He longed for the grief to burst from his body and release the growing void in his chest. The tears would not come. Somewhere inside, his soul would not grant him the relief of sorrow—only regret. He'd been responsible for his friends, and now one of them was gone. Guilt washed over him, and he gripped Elena tightly as if her light might spread into him.

He had no idea what had become of Mr. Quinn. Whether he was out searching the city for them or still crying in the remains of the bunker, Jimmy didn't care. They weren't sticking around long anyway. Despite their victory, if it could be called that, he felt nothing but loss.

Loss for Wyatt.

Loss for the hope that the Lifeboat represented.

Loss for the abundance of the greenhouse.

Loss of a future for the city.

Epilogue

Jimmy lay in a bed staring at the ceiling. It felt foreign to him to be sleeping on an actual bed instead of a thin mattress on the floor. The morning light streamed inside the window refracting off the dust floating in the air. The house creaked as wind buffeted the outside. He breathed in the musty, stale odor of the home, which had not been opened in years.

Sitting up, he turned and swung his feet over the edge of his bed. The activity of the last few days had left him with insatiable exhaustion. What sapped him most was the emptiness in his chest as the grief of Wyatt's death washed over him anew. The image of Wyatt's look of shock as the life drained out of him was burned in Jimmy's memory. He saw his friend every time he closed his eyes. He swallowed hard as a single sob threatened to unleash another torrent of tears.

Laughter rose up from somewhere else in the house. Elena. Despite his mourning, the sound of her laughter lifted him. She was his light and the reason he was able to keep going. He would not make the mistake of failing to care for his own again. He would watch over her at all costs, especially as they began their journey today.

Sliding out of bed, he threw on his clothes and tied his shoes. Taking a glance in the mirror, he did his best to manage his bedhead. Opening the door to his room, the quiet laughter from downstairs grew louder.

Dr. Clay's suburban home was modest. Before the pandemic, Jimmy would have thought the house needed desperate updating. The olive-green carpet in the hallway and exposed woodgrain trim made him feel like he was visiting his grandmother's home. He padded down the stairs listening to the soft tones of Elena's voice as she told Dr. Clay a story of their adventures over the last three years. Reminiscing was her way of grieving Wyatt, and Jimmy envied her ability to process that way. For him, the grief was a silent cancer eating him from the inside.

Dr. Clay's fascination with life outside the bunker was endless, and he never tired of hearing how they'd survived. He wanted to know everything and often reminded them how isolating the bunker had been.

"Then, as Jimmy crawled out of the attic"—Elena spoke between bits of laughter—"he beaned his head on the door and dropped the old radio on the floor. The thing broke into pieces, and the whole day was a loss. Wyatt busted a gut and actually fell to the floor he laughed so hard. You should have seen Jimmy's face. He was so mad at himself."

"That's a shame that you weren't able to retrieve the radio intact." Dr. Clay sounded concerned and a bit confused at Elena's chuckle.

"That's the best part of the whole thing. Jimmy was obsessed with exploring that attic, and he bragged how right he'd been when he found the radio. The only thing is, when we looked at the busted radio, we realized most of the insides had been removed. The thing was worthless. He'd gone to all that trouble *and* gotten a bump on the head for nothing." Elena let out another chuckle.

Jimmy's heart lightened hearing her joy. "Now that's not fair. Telling embarrassing stories without me present." Jimmy smiled as he rounded the corner into the kitchen. "At least make sure I'm here to defend myself. And that radio could have been repaired if I'd only had the chance." Elena gave him a doubtful look. "For real, I think I could have figured it out."

Elena bit her lips as her smile spread across her face, trying to contain the oncoming fit of laughter. She lost the battle as air escaped her lips in a raspberry before she fully succumbed to the guffaw. Even Dr. Clay, mild-mannered as he usually was, allowed himself a laugh at Jimmy's expense.

His moment of grief upstairs melted away as he joined the two of them in the hilarity. "Well, maybe you're right."

"I know I'm right. That thing was ancient. Even if you could have found the parts, you would have had no idea what to do, but I guess it's nice to have confidence in yourself." Elena gave him an amused smile. "Anyway, are you hungry? The doctor found some more stores in the house next door if you can believe it."

"Before I went to the Lifeboat, I encouraged my next-door neighbors to stock up on as much food as they could. I gave them what I had and helped them to hide it behind their basement furnace." Dr. Clay frowned. "When I went next door, I found their remains. They must have succumbed to the virus. Raiders had later looted their home, but they never found the cache in the basement."

Jimmy's stomach growled as they slid a bowl of granola toward him. There was no milk to go with it, and the granola was softer and staler than it should have been. He didn't care.

Across the kitchen counter, Jimmy could see the maps Dr. Clay had found in his home office, which they'd poured over for the last few days. Their journey was not going to be an easy one, and they'd opted to give themselves a few days to rest and recover from the bunker invasion. Dr. Clay's head injury had improved, and he was able to manage his headache with only a few painkillers each day. The plan was in place, and they were leaving today.

He nodded at the table. "We aren't missing anything, are we?"

Dr. Clay shook his head. "No. We should be able to make it to the air force base on the coast within seven days, less if we can find some good fuel for the van. There, our contact should be able to transport us by plane."

Elena frowned. "I can't believe that there are still planes in working order. How is that possible?"

"It's just like the power grid here in the city that keeps coming on and off. The military has tried to keep some services running. They've redirected the limited supplies of oil and fuel to their bases to maintain that effort."

"How do you know all that?" Jimmy asked.

"General Thurston." Dr. Clay choked as he spoke and took a moment to recover. "He made sure there was a plan B in place in the event the Lifeboat failed. I guess he was right."

"So you've been in contact with this person at the base?"

Dr. Clay took a deep breath. "Not exactly. But the general always swore that his contact was not the type to abandon his post."

"If he's still alive," Elena offered.

"I'm not sure we have a choice." Dr. Clay took a moment to gaze at both of them. "The pandemic is over, and the three of us are the only ones who know about the existence of the other Lifeboats. We must try to reach them. Opening even one could radically change the outcome of mankind."

Jimmy furrowed his brow. "Are you sure you don't want the help of the local military? They didn't believe us, but they might believe you. He could arrange transport or communication or even help us with the entire journey."

Dr. Clay shook his head. "The Lifeboats were a secret for a reason. We cannot risk word of their existence spreading and falling into the wrong hands. The captain you met probably means well, but the truth is we do not know the man or what he'd do."

"You don't exactly know us either."

"That is true, but your knowledge of the Lifeboats brings you into the inner circle. Besides, you've shown me what you'd do with that knowledge. You tried to inform us and get the restoration started. I have no reason to believe that isn't still your objective."

Elena smiled. "You're right. We want to help."

"Still, getting to Great Britian will be a challenge. We have no idea what we will find there." Jimmy frowned.

Dr. Clay let out a sigh. "That is true. But if we get there and find the Lifeboat has fallen, then we move on. There's one in Germany, which would be the next closest. We keep traveling until we can find one that is intact."

The task overwhelmed Jimmy. It felt larger than he was capable of, but he reminded himself of all that he'd been through in recent days. Surviving The Brotherhood encampment. Finding the Lifeboat. Outsmarting Mr. Quinn. He could do this, too.

Walking to the table, he carefully folded the maps and placed them in the waiting backpacks. Sliding one on his back, he helped Elena with the next one. Dr. Clay grabbed the third. The three of them readied themselves in silence as if the gravity of what they were about to undertake was finally hitting them.

They padded to the front door, which Dr. Clay opened. Morning sunlight poured in. Summer humidity wafted inside, blasting them with heat. They hesitated.

Dr. Clay turned to them. "We'll drive the van as far as it'll take us and then travel on foot. It'll take most of the day. If we get as far as I hope, I know a place we can camp. Let's not think about the whole journey. Let's focus instead on today's task. Make sense?"

Elena nodded. Jimmy did the same, though the idea of putting their whole journey out of mind seemed impossible.

With a smile and a nod, Dr. Clay stepped outside. Elena followed. Jimmy was the last to leave the house. For a moment, he regretted the thought of leaving the relative comfort it provided. Despite being looted, the house was intact, and it made for a comfortable place to live. He reminded himself of their mission and the limits of their rations. They could not survive here indefinitely. The human race couldn't either.

He let out a long slow breath as he shut the door to the home. The door clicked closed as if communicating the finality of their departure. He turned to the group. Dr. Clay was standing on the sidewalk next to the street, waiting eagerly for them.

Elena stood a few feet away. She extended her hand, which

he took as he approached. She studied his eyes for a long moment. "We will do this together."

Jimmy nodded. "Yeah."

"And we'll do this so what Wyatt did for us means something."

The words sunk deeply into his soul. It was what made his grief the most difficult to bear, the meaninglessness of Wyatt's sacrifice. Making it to the British Lifeboat would change that. Wyatt's death would be far more than a symptom of a murderous madman's rage. His death could mean the salvation of the human race. The idea filled Jimmy with resolve.

"Then, let's get about doing it," Jimmy said with a smile. He squeezed Elena's hand.

Wyatt had made this possible.

He'd given them a chance.

And for the first time since Wyatt's death, Jimmy felt hope.

Joining Dr. Clay, the three of them began walking down the street. The quiet of the morning disturbed only by their steady footsteps on the asphalt. Suburban homes, which might have had children playing in the yard or neighbors waving hello to each other, sat as silent sentinels to the loss the world had experienced. Not a soul was in sight.

It was hard to imagine they would be successful. That doubt melted away as they neared the hidden van to begin their journey.

For the sake of the human race…

For the sake of his future with Elena…

For the sake of Wyatt's sacrifice…

…they had to try.

Acknowledgements

Thank you to my Creator and Savior, Jesus Christ, who continues to give me stories to tell. Just when I think I am out of tales, He inspires my next book or series. I am so grateful to a creative God for allowing me the joy of creating worlds on the page.

To my wife Tirzah who celebrates with me with each win in my writing journey, thank you for encouraging me to keep on this path. It means the world to me to have you by my side cheering me on with the creation and launch of each book.

To my now adult children (when did that happen?), I love that you think it's cool I write and publish books. Yes, they are nerdy and not the genre you would pick to read, but you have never ceased to encourage your old man to keep it up. Thank you.

To the team at Mountain Brook Ink, you continue to give me the opportunity to put my words out in the world, and I cannot thank you enough. You're great to work with, and I have been so happy to have you as a publishing home.

As always, I have to mention my writing community at Realm Makers. What a bunch of nerds we are, but I love being one of you. Thank you for your endless encouragement, constructive feedback, and for understanding all my random movie references. May the force be with you.

Readers, you give me a reason to keep writing. Each review or email is food for my soul. Nothing makes me happier with my writing than seeing someone post that they read one of my books and loved it. I hope you enjoy every last one. Thank you.

Author's Note

Greater love has no one than this…

Friend, you need to hear this. You. Are. Loved. Whether you believe it or not, that doesn't make it any less true. The God of this universe loves you…yes, YOU…enough to sacrifice everything for your eternity. He did the same for me. We are not wandering aimlessly on a rock hurtling through space. We are a loved creation worth dying for in God's eyes. Friend, that gives you worth and dignity as a human being.

Yet, it is so easy to lose sight of that truth. I can take it for granted and find myself living each day for myself alone all too easily. On the flip side, I can spend far too much energy beating myself up because I don't think I'm worth very much. Neither are true…for either of us.

So what does that mean? If I am loved, then I have the capacity to love others. If I am seen, despite how invisible I feel, then I can notice those in the world around me. If I am valued as I am, then I can treat others with the worth they deserve as God's creation.

In short, God's sacrificial love is both the means and the reason why we can love others. I wish I was better at it. Yet, like Jimmy, I try to remind myself of those words above. When I remember what I was given, I find I am strengthened to do the same for others.

So, if you are finding yourself in a place where life feels like endless days of pointlessness stringing together, please see the greater picture and love those around you. If you are mired in the depths of self-worthlessness, please know you are the hand-crafted beautiful creation of God…and worth everything.

Friend, you are loved.

I would love to connect with you and hear what you thought of this first book in Jimmy's story. How do you think you would do surviving in a world where most everyone was gone? Who would be in your inner circle?

If you'd like to know more, the best thing you can do is visit my website and sign up for my newsletter. I send out occasional updates on what is happening with my books as well as the first glimpses of what is to come! In return, I give you a free novelette, *Kane: A Chase Runner Story*, which is a prequel to my debut trilogy.

Here's how to connect with me:
Website/Newsletter/Free Book: BradleyCaffee.com
Facebook: @bradleycaffeeauthor
Instagram: @bradleycaffeeauthor

Tag me in a picture of you with your copy of *Scavenger!*

MOST OF ALL, the best compliment you can give any author is to leave a positive review and pass on the word about *Scavenger*. Reviews are the lifeblood of authors like me, so if you loved *Scavenger*, please consider saying so on Amazon and Goodreads.

Until book two…thanks for reading.

www.ingramcontent.com/pod-product-compliance
Lightning Source LLC
Chambersburg PA
CBHW071220210726
48293CB00002B/506